I0609920

# Infinite Threat

## Travis Hurts
### Book 1

## Toby Neighbors

Infinite Threat: Travis Hurts #1

Copyright © 2023 by Toby Neighbors

ISBN:978-1-952260-64-3 ebook

978-1-952260-65-0 print

Mythic Adventure Publishing, LLC

Idaho USA

All rights reserved.

No part of this book may be reproduced in any form or by any electronic or mechanical means, including information storage and retrieval systems, without written permission from the author, except for the use of brief quotations in a book review.

# 1

He sensed the woman before she reached out and lightly touched his arm. It was just his way, always wary, even when he was sleeping.

"Sir," the woman said, giving his arm a little shake.

Travis Hurts lifted his hat off his eyes and looked at her. She was around his age, with red cheeks and bloodshot eyes. She worked for the transport company as the in-flight passenger experience specialist. That essentially meant she kept the serving droids doling out goodies to keep everyone occupied on hyperspace flights. They weren't supposed to drink on the job, but he could smell the liquor on her breath. And on the long flight from the Kingsbury System, her tight-fitting dress uniform had become wrinkled and bunched.

"Yes?" he replied, trying not to sound annoyed at being woken up, but failing.

Travis Hurts was a lot of things, but diplomatic wasn't one of them.

"There's a man, back in coach," the woman explained. "He's causing trouble."

"So, tell the air marshal," Travis said. "What's this got to do with me?"

"Nothing, except, the air marshal's hurt. The man's drunk. The service bots won't give him any more alcohol and he broke into their supplies. Everyone is scared. The air marshal said you could help."

"Me?" Travis said irritably. "It's not my problem."

He had paid through the nose for a first-class ticket from Kingsbury to the Putnum Interchange station, and if all went well it would be his last commercial flight. Travis Hurts was on his way to see a man about a ship. It had taken years of hard work and saving every credit he could, but he finally had enough for the down payment on his own ship. He didn't relish anything that might keep him from his appointment, and trouble with the Transit Authority was trouble he didn't need. But he had made enough flights in coach to know the people back there were packed into narrow seats, shoulder to shoulder, without much leg room. It was enough to drive anyone crazy. It was why he had paid through the nose for a first-class fare. For once he wanted the privilege of being able to close his eyes among civilized society, without fearing that some desperado might cut his throat.

"Please," the woman said. "He's hurting people."

"Look, lady, I don't know who this guy is, or why he's got a problem, but the spaceliners have the responsibility of keeping their flights safe."

"The air marshal said you were a lawman."

"People say a lot of things that aren't true."

"So you won't help?"

Travis sighed. "I get paid for my trouble," he growled.

"I've already spoken to the pilots. They'll authorize an immediate refund of your fare if you can get this animal under control."

Travis sat up a little straighter. A refund would fatten his expense account. The first-class ticket had taken him down into single digits, and he refused to touch the savings that he was planning to use as a down payment on his own ship. With a refund, he could provision his vessel with more than syntha-noodles and protein powder.

"All right," Travis said. "But it won't be pretty."

"Just get him under control," the woman said. "That's all anyone cares about."

Travis stood up and stretched. His weapons were all stowed safely in his hard case luggage where he couldn't get to them. Not that shooting firearms on a spaceship was ever a good idea. Travis rolled his head from side to side as he walked down the aisle toward the door that led through the servers' prep area and into the coach section of the spacecraft. He could hear the other passengers whispering about him. It was pretty common for a man in his profession. He was a hunter of men. It was an age-old profession that never really got the credit it was due. When he pulled into a city or colony town with a wanted outlaw in tow there were always whispers. It didn't matter that the prisoner was a killer, or that he had tried at every turn to hurt Travis. The onlookers, going about their lives in peace and tranquility because of the work he did bringing the guilty to justice, would whisper.

The commotion in the coach section was evident the moment the soundproof door that led to first-class opened. He could hear the slurred words of a drunk, highlighted with gasps of horror and muffled screams. When Travis pushed through the curtain and into the coach section of the spacecraft, he wasn't surprised. A big man, probably six foot six inches tall, was bending over a young woman whose male companion's nose had been broken. The air marshal was crammed into a corner like an old garment. He was unconscious and would probably need medical attention.

"How far are we from Putnum?" Travis asked.

"Forty-two minutes," the woman who woke him said.

Travis shook his head. Eleven and half hours in hyperspace was a long flight. People got restless. But it was almost over. The drunkard simply couldn't contain himself. Travis was right at six feet, with wide shoulders and narrow hips. He had traveled coach for a long time, and knew how uncomfortable it could get. The drunk was even bigger. He had pulled open his button up shirt. Travis could see the old military tattoos. It was a shame the man had caused trouble.

"Hey," Travis said in a low voice. "Leave that lady be and sit down, or I'll have to make the rest of this flight very uncomfortable."

"Who the hell are you?" the big man said, standing up.

He was sweating, his eyes dilated. Travis could tell he was on more than the watered-down booze the spaceliner served.

"Let's just say you don't want to know me, mister. Now sit down."

The big man barked a harsh laugh and started up the aisle toward Travis.

"You bow up on me, hoss and I'm gonna make you regret it," Travis said in a calm voice.

The big man hesitated just a second, his eyes narrowing suspiciously. Travis was wearing cargo pants and a tee-shirt under a long wool coat. Spaceflights could sometimes get cold, and Travis had planned to get as much sleep as possible. But he didn't look intimidating, or even authoritative. In his line of work, blending in was the way to be.

"I'm going to take that ugly hat off your pointy head and cram it down your throat, mister," the big man growled.

Travis just smiled. The die was cast. Like it not, trouble was in the making. And the truth was, Travis Hurts thrived on the

4

edge of danger. It's where he had grown up with an abusive father, who murdered his mother shortly after he was born. Leon Hurts had served ten years on a penal colony, and somehow got paroled. After returning to Traegen Major he kidnapped Travis, who spent the next seven years in alternate states of paralyzing terror and mortal struggle. His father ran with bad company, and Travis had to learn how to defend himself. When he was seventeen, a warrant was issued for his father. Travis saw his opportunity for freedom when Leon got falling down drunk and ordered Travis to take him home. His father passed out on the way, and Travis instead took him to the nearest law enforcement station. That had been on Rote Nine, a blue-collar lunar colony. Twenty years later, Travis was earning a living bringing outlaws to justice.

"Last chance," Travis said.

"Go scr—"

The big man was rearing back with a meaty fist, but Travis had already sized the big man up. He knew the larger man's weaknesses. In any confined space it was always best to strike fast and take his opponents down as swiftly as possible. All it took was one well-timed kick. The drunk was winding up to throw a powerful roundhouse punch, but never got the chance. The kick lifted his bulky body nearly six inches off the floor. Travis didn't play around in a fight. He had learned that lesson many times over, and never held back. People screamed as if they could feel the drunk's pain. Travis had never understood why some people reacted to violence the way they did. Some folks paid good money to see a fight, others acted as if it violated their wellbeing.

The man's legs gave out under him and he dropped to his knees. A punch would have been simple to land, but Travis didn't relish cracking his knuckles against the big man's thick skull. Instead, he grabbed the drunk by the hair on his head, jerking it forward, while at the same time driving his knee straight up into the big man's face.

The impact shattered the drunk's nose, and probably loosened his front teeth. Travis felt it in his knee, which he knew would likely swell up and get stiff. But the fight was taken completely out of the drunk. He was knocked unconscious by the knee strike. Travis stepped back and let the man flop onto the floor of the spacecraft's passenger cabin.

"He's down," Travis said.

His hands went to the seats on either side of the aisle. The passengers in those seats flinched as if he were going to hurt them. Instead, he pushed up on the seats to vault himself over the drunk. Then he folded one of the big man's legs across the back of the other knee. By pushing up on the lower leg, he could pin the larger man to the ground.

The drunk was coming around, but his nose was still bleeding, and his senses were slow to return. Travis took hold of the drunk's wrists and bent both of his arms behind his back.

"I didn't ..." the in-flight passenger experience specialist started to say. "Did you have to hurt him?"

"I told him to sit down," Travis said. "Everyone heard me."

"But you ...". She was still struggling to gain her bearings.

"I warned him," Travis said. "You needed him under control and that's what you've got. A pair of restraints would be useful if you've got them."

"Restraints? What? I don't have any ..."

"Check the air marshal's pockets. Maybe I'll get lucky and go back to my seat."

There was a doctor in first-class. After getting the air marshal's restraints, the only seat they could secure the bloody drunk to was Travis' first-class lounger. The doctor declared that the drunk had a concussion, a broken nose, and possibly a fractured orbital bone, in a loud voice that carried from first-class back into the economy section of the flight. When Travis sat down in the drunk's empty seat and discovered that he was tucked between a woman with a tiny dog in her travel case and a man with horrid breath, he decided he couldn't really blame the big man for wanting to get drunk.

# 2

As he had feared, Travis was detained after the flight. Transit Authority officers took the drunk into custody, then questioned many of passengers, before interviewing Travis.

"Don't you have half a dozen cameras on that ship?" Travis asked. "You have all the video evidence you need. The man was a menace, I was requested to help subdue him, and that's what I did."

The two officers in their silver uniforms watched him as if they were going to catch him lying about a grand conspiracy. It didn't matter to them that Travis had an appointment to get to.

"You can understand our point of view," one of the officers said. "The man you assaulted sustained serious injuries."

"I warned him," Travis said.

"You say you didn't know him, but maybe you bumped into each other on the flight," the other TA officer suggested. "Maybe he bumped your seat, or stayed in the bathroom too long."

"He was in coach, I was in first-class," Travis said. "I slept through most of the flight. I never saw the man before in my life."

"And yet you beat him within an inch of his."

"I did what was necessary. Just ask the air marshal."

They did in fact speak to the air marshal, who had sustained a broken jaw and a concussion from the drunk. After wasting nearly two hours of his time, they released Travis who, after ensuring that he did get his first-class space fare refunded, skipped the shower that he desperately needed, and went straight to the man who was selling his old freight hauler.

"You're late," the man said when Travis reached the gate that led to the docking arm.

"Putnum's a big place," Travis said. "And there was some trouble on my flight."

"Always is if you travel commercial."

"Is the ship still available?"

"It is," the older man said.

He was short, thick in the middle, with thinning hair slicked straight back over a glossy scalp. He stuck out a hand.

"Melvin Dresser," he said.

Travis shook the older man's hand. "Travis Hurts."

There was distrust in the older man's eyes. He didn't know Travis, and didn't trust him. That was okay. Travis was of the opinion that most people weren't trustworthy either. He certainly had his suspicions about the quality of the old ship.

"I've had the ship for over two decades," Melvin said. "Did all the maintenance myself."

"You have the logs?"

"Of course, I do," the man grumbled. "You sure you ain't a TA agent?"

"Positive," Travis said.

"What exactly do you want my ship for?"

Travis could have told the man it was none of his business. The vessel wasn't a space yacht. It was a fat, ugly, cargo ship, with quarters for a single occupant. It's not like Melvin was selling a rare and precious object. The galaxy was full of spaceships. There were vessels for sale in every port and planet, but Melvin's had the cargo space Travis needed, an up-to-date advanced autopilot, and most importantly, was the right price.

"I'm a man hunter," Travis said. "I need something that I can convert into half a dozen holding cells."

"Bounty hunter?"

"Some call me that," Travis said.

"Well ... I suppose you could convert the cargo space. It's set up for easy conversions. I always left it wide open and hauled freight."

"How's the engine?"

"She's not new, but she's in excellent condition."

"Can I see the ship?"

"You got proof of funds?"

Travis tapped his data slate and sent a copy of the loan approval to Melvin. The older man looked it over for a minute, then tapped a code into his own device. The door to the docking arm opened.

"She's at the end of pier," he said.

They walked down the docking arm to the very last airlock. A big window showed the old ship. Travis would have preferred to see it on a planet where he could walk around it, and get underneath it. In space dock he was limited to the inside of the vessel, but Travis had done his homework and knew what to look for.

It was tempting to go right to the cockpit or the living quarters. Travis was happy that Melvin instead took him to the engineering bay.

"Two Holstead FTL engines," Melvin said. "And I always

kept a full complement of spare parts. You buy her, and they're yours. It's foolish to leave the system without a way to fix your engines, that's just common sense."

"Agreed," Travis said. "They hard to work on?"

"No, they're built right. Everything is accessible and a standard set of tools is all you need. The parts aren't expensive either. You take care of these they'll last you twenty years, easy."

"What about atmospheric engines?"

"Quad repulser lift drives, and two Stanley jet engines. They're on foldouts. You can't get to them from inside the ship, but I put in computer diagnostics. A man on his own needs to have confidence in his equipment."

"That was smart," Travis said.

"Glad to see someone noticed."

They spent half an hour going over every system on board, from the engines to life support. The cargo ship had a tiny escape pod. The layout was simple -- a rectangular cargo bay, the engineering space, living quarters, and cockpit. She looked like a shoebox with wings that folded up along the side for flights in planetary gravity. The outside was covered with heat-deflecting tiles that could easily be replaced. Her tri-hull construction was sound. Not a spot of rust or a dent to be found on the inside.

The living quarters were spartan. There was room for a narrow bed, a comfortable chair, and tiny fold-down desk with a three-legged stool. The galley consisted of a sink and a microwave. By far the most spacious appliance was an upright freezer.

"You could change things, but I'm not much of a cook," Melvin said. "She's got hookups for a full kitchen, but I didn't need all that. Freezer meals were just fine by me."

"Can't say I disagree," Travis replied. "What about the head?"

"That's the one thing I did splurge on. A hundred-gallon

water tank with real charcoal filters. You can shower every single day. Instant hot water that will cook you if you aren't careful."

"That's pretty luxurious," Travis said.

"Cleanliness is next to Godliness," Melvin said. "You take care of your tools and they will take care of you. I spent half my life on this ship. I never shirked on her maintenance and I kept her clean."

Travis nodded. His diligent search for just the right ship appeared to have paid off. There were no surprises in the cockpit either. She had a flat front, transparent steel windshield. The cockpit was wide enough for two captain's chairs. The controls were simple, the navigation computer was up to date, and Melvin, true to his word, had installed sensors on every system and all around the hull.

"Sheila, show us all systems please," Melvin said.

"All systems are good," the automated voice said. "Maintenance is up to date, power is optimal."

The information showed up on a display screen flanked by individual instruments on a touch sensitive display running the length of the cockpit, as well as being projected holographically onto the transparent wall with only fifty percent opacity, so that a person could see right through it if needed.

"She's a one-man show," Melvin said. "I did mostly space runs, but she can handle atmo too, not a problem. An hour a week on maintenance, full service once a month, and she'll last longer than you or me."

"And the price?" Travis asked.

"Just what we talked about. I don't negotiate."

Travis stuck out his hand. "You have yourself a deal, sir."

"Best decision you ever made," the older man said. His voice sounded emotional, and he looked around the cockpit, obviously thinking of a lot of years spent there.

"I'll take good care of her," Travis said.

"You do that, son," the older man said. "I'll hold you to it."

# 3

Upgrades took two days. Travis hired a welder to install bars that turned the open cargo space into a set of three holding cells on either side, with a walkway right down the middle. He also added a set of Vanguard Deflector shields. And, like his predecessor had done, he installed computer sensors so that he could ensure they worked in case he needed them.

A new mattress on the metal bunk and a new easy chair in the sitting area were the only upgrades he made to the ship's living quarters. And he filled the freezer with simple foods; frozen biscuits, sausage, fried chicken and mashed potatoes were the staples. The ship was the first home that Travis had ever owned. Technically speaking the bank owned it, but as long as Travis made the regular payments it was his.

With his newly acquired ship customized to his liking, and his bank accounts nearly zeroed out, he prepared to leave the Putnum Interchange. The ship was ready for his first test flight. He had done a lot of simulation training to be ready, and the ship practically flew herself. All he needed was permission from flight control to decouple from the docking arm, and a clear flight lane out of the busy port area. It had been a busy week for Travis and he was anxious to get back to work. The biggest change had been the name on her registry: *Purgatory*. It seemed a fitting title to Travis, as the ship would be where wanted outlaws waited to be delivered to the judgment they were running from.

"Putnam Flight Control this is the *Purgatory*, ready for take-off. Please advise," Travis said. He didn't wear a headset. As the only person on the ship, he didn't need one. The cabin speakers were adequate for local comms.

"*Purgatory*, this is Flight Control. Release docking clamps and move ahead at impulse speed to heading three, eight, four. A clear flight trajectory has been sent to your computer. Please confirm delivery."

"Flight Control, I have full instructions. Releasing docking clamps now."

There was a thrum as the magnetic connection was cut. Travis didn't feel the ship moving, but he saw a slight movement away from the docking arm. He pressed his joystick forward, activating the simple thrusters to move the big shape around. The vessel moved as a point in space directly ahead of him was lit by an opaque dot on the forward view screen.

"Moving ahead at impulse speed to heading three, eight, four," Travis said.

There were ships docking and leaving. From where he looked it appeared that he was in a littered asteroid field, only instead of space rocks he was surrounded by starships. Some were huge, others were small. His own vessel was among the latter. He could walk from the cockpit straight through his quarters, the engineering space, and to the back of the cargo hold in less than thirty paces.

"Safe travels," the flight controller said over his ship's communication network. "Many happy returns."

"Thank you, Putnum Interchange," Travis said as he reached the space lane that lit up ahead of him. A golden line appeared through space. Travis pushed his engine throttles forward with his left hand, and used the joystick on his right to steer the boxy ship. The autopilot could have taken him out, but Travis wanted to get a feel for the vessel. She was new to him, and he was new to her. The ship's engines lit smoothly and propelled him forward. He was soon far enough from the space station that he brought up the rear video feed from the hull-mounted cameras.

"Sheila, can you put the rear vid feed on the screen for me?" Travis said.

"Activating the rear facing video camera feed, now," the computer voice intoned.

He was sitting in the left seat of the cockpit. The video from the rear camera was displayed in front of the right seat, leaving the area directly ahead of Travis clear so that he could see where he was going. Not that there was anything to see but the computer-generated navigation line. He looked over and saw the huge space station. It was like a beehive surrounded by hundreds of unique bees. Docking the ship, Travis thought, would be much more nerve-wracking than leaving had been.

"Dismiss vid feed," he ordered.

The computer removed the video instantly. The ship would only answer him when he used the name Sheila to address it. Otherwise, his voice had already been imprinted by the ship's security system, and would follow his verbal commands while he was in the cockpit.

There was something magical about being free and in open space. Perhaps it was the hint of danger, or maybe the freedom of striking out on his own, but he couldn't help but smile. There was nothing in sight but twinkling stars. Travis had always been a solitary person, but flying his own ship was an absolute dream come true. He wanted to savor it for a while.

"Sheila, activate the hyperspace navigation computer," Travis said. "Let's plot a course for Pergamum Prime."

"Navigation activated, but I must warn you, Captain, the Pergamum system is unregulated."

"I'm aware," he said. "This ship is no longer a cargo hauling freighter, Sheila. My job is catching people who are running from the law. We'll be going to some pretty dangerous places."

"I see, and will make the necessary adjustments," the computer voice said.

Travis pressed his finger to the touch screen that was labeled *Autopilot*. The real fun would be flying in atmosphere with gravity and cross winds and other aircraft. He stood up and went back into his quarters. There was coffee in a pot. Travis poured himself a cup, then returned to the cockpit and settled into what was quickly becoming *his* seat. He didn't need to be there. The ship was headed for a point in space far enough from the space station and surrounding traffic that igniting the hyperdrive wouldn't damage other vessels. Even without the autopilot, there was nothing to crash into. The trajectory was straight. There were no outside forces to act on his ship and push her off course. The jump itself needed precision handling that only computers could provide. The timing was down to the nanosecond, and the slightest mistake could spell disaster. But Travis wanted to see it. He wasn't crammed into a passenger cabin with two hundred other people with nothing to watch but the poor in-flight entertainment system built into the back of the seat directly in front of him. On his ship, he would watch the big show. A timer was counting down to the moment of the transition to hyperspace. It was projected low on the transparent window in front of him. Above the pedals that were used for atmospheric flight there was a brass rail. The former owner had kept it polished, and Travis put his boots up on the rail, sipped his coffee and watched as his ship took him to a system far, far away.

# 4

"Pergamum," Dice Jeater said. "Oh, that's beautiful."

"We got people there," Sid Ott exclaimed.

"Send them word," the boss of the Incendius crime organization said.

"Done," his top Captain said, already tapping out a message on the encrypted messaging system.

"I want them to be waiting when he lands."

"They can hit him the moment he steps off his ship," Lucius Griggs proposed.

"No, he'll be expecting it," Dice said. "We miss and he'll come after us."

"You saying we can't take down one guy, boss?" Sid Ott asked.

"You know how this works," Dice said. "All these guys are connected. You take out one, you've got twenty, thirty more breathing down your neck. The warrants on our people will suddenly be their top priority. We'll have trouble in a dozen systems. We don't need that kind of heat."

"I say we kill 'em all," Lucius Griggs said, earning himself a chuckle from the other tough guys around the table.

"That's because you're a fool," Iona Freeze said softly.

"She's right," Dice said. "Stop thinking like a hammer, Lucius. You think every problem is a nail."

"We need the law, and those who enforce it," Iona said. "We don't depend on them, or fear them, but if we're smart, we can use them."

"Manipulation is an art form," Dice said. "Now, tell our people to watch him. We need to know where he goes."

"P2 is a big planet," Sid pointed out.

"It used to be one of the big five," Harv Butler, one of Sid's lieutenants said. "Before the war."

"The aliens aren't our problem," Iona said. "Let the Alliance deal with them."

"Some of that planet's still hot," Lucius said. "Irradiated from all the nukes."

"Maybe Hurts will get lucky and die there," Dice said with a grin. He pressed a button on his control panel. He ran an intricate organization of thieves, tough guys, and drug pushers from his ship *Incendius*. The round table looked like it belonged in a casino, but it was custom built for the crime lord, and gave him access to all his top people at the touch of a button. One of those was an assassin. Morgan Black's face appeared in a hologram projected in front of the group, right over the center of the table, by a device hidden in the ceiling.

"You have need of my services?"

"I do," Dice told the man in black.

Morgan was protective of his identity. When he was on the job, he wore all black, including a face shield and dark hat. Even as a hologram the assassin was intimidating. For the right price it was said he could go anywhere, kill anyone. The way he looked in the hologram made the professional criminals believe it.

"If you have the time," Dice said.

"What world?"

"P2," Dice said. "You familiar?"

"I am," the assassin said.

"I'm putting a million in your account now," Dice said as he waved a hand at Iona, who began swiping on her data slate to send the funds. "The price is ten, plus expenses. And another five if it can't be tied to us."

"You'll have people there?"

"We do."

"I'll be expecting to hear from them once I'm in the system."

"They'll have all you need. I'm sending Iona to make sure of it."

Dice ignored the angry stare from his underboss.

"Very well."

The hologram vanished and Dice turned. He was a big man, with tattoos visible on his chest and neck. He wore a shirt that only buttoned halfway up his stomach, which was thicker than it had been as he fought his way up the ranks of the Incendius Organization.

Iona Freeze was a hard woman. She had symmetrical features, and could have been considered beautiful, but there was a hard edge to her. Perhaps it was the fact that she exercised constantly and had a very muscular physique that looked out of place on a woman. But Dice thought it was in her eyes. Iona was vicious, and there was no sympathy or emotion in her gaze. Cruelty was in her nature, and the truth was most people in Dice's orbit feared her as much if not more than him.

"Don't fight me on this one," he told her.

"P2, really?"

"I need my best," Dice said.

"It's a simple hit," she argued. "Any fool could do it."

"Maybe, maybe not. Hurts is good."

Iona leaned forward. She wore a leather vest. Her arms were long and veiny, the biceps and shoulders flexing. Her skin was so tight across them Dice could see the striations in the muscle tissue. When she tilted her head forward, her brow seemed to stick out over her eyes in a menacing fashion.

"You're wasting my talents," she said softly.

"It's my call," Dice said. "You want to take my seat, honey, roll the dice and take your chances. Otherwise, you do as you're told."

"You think I couldn't do it?"

"No doubt you could, darlin', but it sure as hell ain't guaranteed, now, is it?"

It was Dice's turn to turn in his seat, his shirt opening wider. There weren't just tattoos on his skin, there were scars too. A lot of them. The boss was a fighter and everyone in his organization knew it. Pain affected some people more than others. Dice Jeater just happened to be one of the few who could tolerate a substantial amount of pain and keep going. He had gained the top seat after a very bloody coup that he didn't start, but absolutely finished by stacking up over fifteen bodies. Everyone in the organization and many outside of it knew the story. Dice didn't furrow his brow, or glare like many people did when challenged. Instead, he smiled, almost welcoming the idea.

"Don't burn this place down while I'm gone," Iona snapped.

"Never dreamed of it," he replied. "We knuckleheads can get by a few weeks without you. Consider it a vacation."

"Good times on a junk world," Lucius said with a sadistic chuckle.

Iona was fast. Before anyone could react, she had her silver-coated Stinger out and pointed at Lucius' head. The Stinger was lethal at short range, if the shooter hit a vital organ. The cocky tough guy's grin faded and he raised his hands.

"Just a joke," he said. "No offense intended."

"Stand down, Iona. You got a beef with anyone, it's me," Dice said.

She slipped the pistol into a hidden pocket of her hip-hugging pants, and flashed the rest of the group a smile. There was no warmth or beauty in it. The woman was known as the ice queen, and not just because her last name was Freeze.

"Make sure it doesn't blow back on us," Dice said.

Iona nodded and walked away. There was nothing masculine about her. She walked with a hip-swaying grace that only women could do. From behind she seemed very attractive. But Dice knew that she was the epitome of a wolf in sheep's clothing. While she was smart and capable in the organization, he also knew it was only a matter of time before she tried to take the top seat. Her ambition was no mystery. And while Dice wasn't afraid of her, he recognized the danger she represented. If she didn't come back from P2, he thought, it wouldn't be such a bad thing.

# 5

It didn't take long for Travis to get bored staring at the streaks of odd colors that flashed by the ship in hyperspace. It reminded him of fireworks; once you saw a few go off, the show lost most of its appeal. Normally he tried to sleep on spaceflights. There was nothing that needed his attention. The autopilot would take care of anything that came up. His vessel, like most spaceships, had a litany of fail safes and safety protocols built in. Space was a deadly environment, and so vast that help couldn't be counted on from other travelers. Which was why spaceships were built to be repaired from the inside, and had a variety of systems to keep the occupants safe in almost any situation short of an attack.

But the coffee made sleeping nearly impossible, and the jump to the Pergamum System was only a little over three hours. Travis moved to his living quarters, but kept the cockpit's sliding door open. He settled into the lounge chair, reclining back and putting his feet up. The ship was small, but compared to commercial travel it was so luxurious Travis thought he might get too soft for his line of work. He pulled out his data slate and checked the open files. There were thousands of wanted criminals in the galaxy. Just about any system he could go to would have work. But Pergamum Prime, or P2 as it was often called, had become a haven for outlaws.

The history of the planet was widely known. It was one of the original colony worlds, a massive planet easily twice as big as most habitable worlds, and situated perfectly in the system's goldilocks zone. It had, as recently as a hundred and fifty years prior, been home to well over eighty billion people. It was tech hub, with a vast manufacturing sector. There were cities that rose over six kilometers into the sky. Pictures from those heady days showed ice and snow on the tallest buildings all round.

Then the invasion happened, not just on P2, but all the core worlds. None were hit as hard as P2. The Hash Gore species were merciless. War raged for decades, and eventually P2 became so infested with the insectile aliens that it was nuked from orbit. The vast, towering cities were destroyed. The planet fell into a nuclear winter which lasted nearly sixty years. Nearly ninety percent of the flora and fauna was lost. Of course, that didn't stop treasure hunters from going after the fortunes that had been hidden in the cities, which were devastated by the war. But that left fortunes to be made, if people were willing to risk the radiation and the dangerous conditions of the city. Nothing on the planet was stable, especially the ruins of the cities. Many people were lost digging under the rubble in hopes of striking a bank vault or a jewelry store. Every so often, some wretch whose hair had fallen out and who was covered with sores would appear with a haul of gemstones, or a lost painting that was worth billions of credits on the open market.

Most scientists agreed that a hundred years after the bombardment should leave the planet safely habitable again, but most people didn't want to take that chance. There were fortunes made by mining Dust, a very rare and valuable element called Dustincia on the expanded periodic table. It was found mixed into the topsoil from the nuclear impact sites. Still, reports of radiation sickness abounded, and few people were willing to do verified toxin testing on the war-torn world.

It was an open planet in an open system. That meant there was no customs service, and there were no identification requirements. People could come and go as they pleased, and on most of the world the only law was what you could enforce yourself. It was a place for bad people to do bad things. Nearly every criminal outfit in the galaxy had a presence there. No one was testing the air or soil yet, which meant it was the perfect place to cook up whatever mind-altering substance you wanted. From Dreamers to Zomlollipops, P2 was a drug manufacturing Mecca. It was also a place where criminals could move stolen items, then spend the proceeds on whatever vice they clung to. Most of the settlements were tent cities. There was plenty of building material in the rubble of the old towns, but that took work, and most of the people on P2 were either of the get rich quick variety, or people running from respectable values.

Travis cross-referenced the list of bounties against their last known locations to get a list of targets to search for. His new ship would hold six prisoners, and many of the people wanted on P2 would not only be profitable for him, but if he got lucky and captured the right people, he might be able to pay off his ship.

After getting his target list settled on his data slate, Travis fixed himself a sausage biscuit, then checked his weapons in the wide drawer built into the bulkhead under his bed. He was meticulous about his weaponry. They were the difference between living and dying. The people he tracked down were not inclined to face the consequences of their actions, and most would kill to keep from being captured. They often had little to lose in a fight to the death, which was exactly what awaited them for the crimes.

On most hunts he carried three firearms. His primary was a Slinger, a short barreled, lightweight laser pistol. They were the preferred weapon of most quick draw gunslingers. Made of an exceptionally light and strong hydrogen steel alloy, it was powered by a tiny power cell that would give the user five or six stun shots, but which added almost no weight. Travis kept the Slinger in a hip holster on his right side.

He also carried a short barreled, non-lethal rifle called a Kicker. It had twice the range of his Slinger, and could fire nearly a hundred times before needing a power reload. The Kicker worked using a different type of power frequency that disrupted a person's nervous system, leaving at least a quarter of their body completely numb for over an hour.

Travis was a hunter of men, but he was not an executioner. He only carried a single lethal weapon, a Ranger large bore tactical assault rifle. Most frequently used as a sniper weapon, the Ranger used a heavy Keystone Power Cell that cost nearly as much as the rifle itself. Deadly up to five kilometers, it had dual fold-out legs on the fore grip, and a high compression stock. When the rare bounty called for bringing in a prisoner dead, or when Travis was being pursued after a capture, the rifle was invaluable. He could, and had, shot a cup out of a person's hands at nearly four klicks. He could cut the reins on a horse, or blast a vehicle's power supply. If the bad guys were going lethal, Travis would too. It was the only way to survive in his line of work.

He kept the Kicker in a thigh holster on his left leg, and the Ranger hung on a swivel harness, hidden on his back underneath his wool duster. The rifle could wait until he was leaving his ship, but the Slinger and Kicker went on while he was still in hyperspace.

"Captain, we are approaching the Pergamum System," the computer announced.

"Thank you, Sheila, I'm on my way," Travis said.

He disposed of the wrapper his sausage biscuit had come in, and rinsed out his coffee mug before returning to the cockpit. The ship dropped out of hyperspace just ten minutes from orbit around P2. The world was a swirl of color and already the size of a beach ball through the transparent view screen. In the distance the system star looked tiny, the size of a green pea. How something so far away could warm a planet the size of P2 was beyond Travis' ability to understand. The planet had been on a warming trend since the nuclear winter ended forty years earlier. It was a haven of villainy the likes of which couldn't be found anywhere else in the galaxy. The worst of the worst were down there, and any one of them could be looking to kill Travis Hurts. He had no illusions of safety, just a grim determination to do what he did best.

"Sheila, plot a course down to a safe place outside Camp Sherman. Walking distance is fine, nothing too close. I want a lot of open space around the landing zone."

"Calculating," the computer voice said. "Would you like a plot line, Captain?"

"This time around," he told her. "It's my first atmospheric flight and landing."

"Here it is, Captain," the computerized voice said.

There was no flight control to get permission from. His new ship had a navigation computer capable of calculating an entry vector that would get him where he wanted on the planet with as little friction as possible. The line curled around the edge of the world. Travis settled into the pilot's seat and took the controls.

"End autopilot," he ordered.

"Autopilot disengaged."

"Check the hydraulics. I don't want any surprises."

"Hydraulic fluid is warming; all atmospheric flight systems are green."

"Good," Travis said. "That's good."

The golden flight line dipped down toward the planet. Travis pulled his safety straps down. They crossed his chest and hooked into the bottom of his chair. He cinched them down tight.

"There we go," he said. "All right. Shut off the artificial gravity generator."

"Artificial gravity is offline," the computer explained.

After his stomach flipped inside him, and his hat floated off his head, Travis put his feet on the pedals that operated the repulser lifts, and flipped the joystick's activation switch from thrusters to the ship's extendable rudder. He pressed his toes down on the right pedal and kept his heel down on the left. The ship rotated over along its horizontal axis, so that it was coming down to the planet upside down.

The planet's gravity took hold and pulled the ship down. Suddenly it felt to Travis like all the blood in his body was rushing to his head. His stomach felt a little queasy too, and a bead of sweat halfway down the side of his head reversed course and slid back up where it came from.

"No problem," he said to himself.

Travis didn't get nervous in a fight, even if he could foresee taking some painful damage. And he didn't get nervous facing down a wanted killer. In those instances, his adrenaline flooded through his body and he felt more alive than ever. The danger was exciting in those instances, but flying his new ship made him extremely nervous. There was no insurance for starships. If he crashed her, and didn't die the process, he would still be on the hook to the bank. And if he failed to pay, they could issue a bond warrant for him until he could work off the balance he owed in a Debtor's Sweat Shop.

But the flight went smoothly. The ship, although she was all hard angles, glided through the atmosphere with relative ease.

"Extend the wings," Travis ordered the computer.

"Atmospheric flight peripherals fully extended.

"Spin up the jet engines."

The entire ship hummed as the engines engaged. Travis gave the throttle levers just a slight push, enough to engage the jet engines but still letting gravity do most of the work. A time or two the ship seemed to drop suddenly, and it shook as it bumped into warm air. Travis kept one eye on the hull's heat gage, but it never got above the halfway point on the temperature status bar.

Below him, he could see the ruins of a huge city. Beyond that were tiny little squares of dull white assembled in a grid pattern. Further out, the land was multiple shades of gray and brown. Most of P2 resembled desert, although it wasn't as hot or as dry as most desert biomes. In places the flora was coming back, but it was a slow process. The *Purgatory* glided over the ruins, then circled wide around the tent city that had sprung up on the outskirts of what had once been the metropolis of Keystone.

They flew out a full ten kilometers past Camp Sherman, as the tent city was called, and landed on a hill with a clear view on every side. It was an arid-looking wilderness, all dirt and rocks, none much bigger than a child's ball. The landscape was hilly to the north, and what had once been a wide plain where the city of Keystone was built was now covered by suburbs, providing accommodation as the population grew.

"Shut down the engines," Travis said. "And Sheila, thanks."

"Excellent landing, Captain. I think you're a natural."

Travis knew the computer didn't *think* or have opinions. What it had were preset responses to almost anything a person might ask of it. Including compliments and quirky sayings. Some people paid top dollar for ship computers that were lifelike to a strong degree. Travis was happy with one that did what he asked and didn't complain about it.

"Activate the security protocols," Travis said.

The ship would only respond to him. His voice, facial

features, retina map, palm prints, and DNA had all been registered to the ship's computer. It wouldn't open, or power up any systems, unless he was there telling it to. A good hacker could break in and reset the security system, but that was a lot of work for an old freighter.

"Time to take a walk around and see what you really look like," Travis said as he gathered his wallet and slung his rifle. He had to pick his cowboy hat up off the deck and pushed it down on his head. Only then was he ready to go to work.

# 6

"Who the hell are you?"

"I have many names, Johnny," Morgan Black said.

They were in a dark room in an exclusive high rise on the banks of Wonder River of Kingsbury Three. It wasn't a penthouse; Johnny Grissom couldn't afford more than a studio in the upscale building. Kingsbury was one of the most expensive planets to live in the entire galaxy. The small world was one enormous city, home to the rich and famous. The Wonder River was one of the more exclusive areas on the planet. Johnny Grissom had conned his way in. The man was a genius, constantly shuffling accounts and moving money so that it seemed like he had more than he did.

"Your final bill has come due," Morgan said.

"I don't know who you are, or who sent you, but I don't want any trouble," Johnny said.

Many people who met Morgan Black in person were so terrified they could hardly speak. He was grim figure, all in black, a wide-brimmed Spanish-style hat that sat low over his mask, so that only his eyes were visible. He wore a cape that covered his left shoulder and left his long-barreled Widow Maker laser pistol visible in the holster he wore low on his hip. His gloved hand rested easy on the pistol's grip.

Johnny was different. He was afraid, of that there was no doubt. But instead of stammering or just staring in terror, he was talking. A smooth-talking con man, he could usually talk his way out of any situation. But he wouldn't talk his way past Morgan Black.

"I'm not fluid at this very moment," Johnny said. "But I can get you whatever you want."

"I'm here for blood, Johnny," Morgan said.

"Well, now, hang on," he said.

Morgan was near the big windows. The only light inside the studio apartment was from the city. It left them in shadows. Johnny was against the door, his face fixed in a smile that was meant to disarm.

"I've got money. Better yet, I've got some things right here that are worth millions. You probably already know that. I'd ask how you got in, but it doesn't matter. Who do you work for?"

"I'm an independent contractor, Johnny," Morgan said.

"That's good, that's really good for you. See, I can pay you more than whoever sent you to do something stupid, I promise you that. They're just trying to make you the scapegoat. You and I can work out an arrangement."

"They want you gone," Black said.

"All right, fine. That's fine, I can disappear. You don't have to hurt me. I'll slip away in the night and no one will ever hear from me again."

"Indeed," Black said as he slowly pulled the gun from its holster.

"Hang on, hang on now, let's talk it through. I'm sure we can reach an understanding that's good for the both of us. Look, I've got hard credits, half a million in gold medallions. You can have them. And that painting over the bed, it's a Claude Vander Hausen. It's worth half a billion. That's billion with a capital B my friend. I'll sign the certificate of authenticity over to you. I was planning to auction it myself, but you can do it. St. Sebastian's over on the coast has been trying to get it in their fine art collection for a long time. You take that, and just tell whoever sent you that I never came home. I'll grab a few things and disappear my friend. We all get what we want here."

"Show me the money," Morgan Black said.

He was an assassin, and no fool. He knew what was coming, but shooting a helpless man was no fun. His employer wanted blood, all six liters from Johnny Grissom in fact. As Johnny shuffled toward his bed, which easily took up half the space in the cramped apartment. Morgan knew that for the amount spent on the tiny space Johnny could have lived in a sprawling mansion on a colony world. But people didn't live on Kingsbury because they were tight with their money, or looking for a bargain. It was a world full of people who were all show. It was about keeping up appearances, and for a con man like Johnny the apartment on the richest planet, with a view of the Wonder River, was a sign that he had made it in life. He clawed his way out of poverty and obscurity, rising to the very highest of heights. Well, pretty close at any rate. The view from the studio was excellent. The Silver Falls was visible, as well as the neon strip. Morgan had studied it as he waited for Johnny to return.

Of course, he knew there was a stack of gold coins and some fine jewelry in a drawer by the bed. Morgan knew the painting over the bed was a fake, a very well-done forgery, but still worthless. Morgan had seen the sewing kit that Johnny used to put bootleg designer labels on his imitation clothing. And of course, the go-bag, a small satchel full of the essentials that Johnny might need if he was forced to start over somewhere else. There was money inside that bag too, not gold, which was too flashy, but a roll of paper credits, along with different sets of identification, a kit to modify his facial features, and a universal, one-way ticket that was good to get him wherever he deemed it necessary to run to.

Morgan opened the drawer where the gold was stacked. It wasn't much, maybe a hundred thousand credits worth of round coins. The contract on Johnny's life was ten million credits, half of which had already been paid. The money held little interest to Morgan, but there was also a Slinger in the drawer with a Fusamani battery in the grip with enough power for two, maybe three kill shots. Morgan guessed it was Johnny's emergency weapon, perhaps for self-defense, or maybe, with that heavy battery inside, he meant to use it on himself eventually. Johnny wasn't smart enough to get into politics where a con man could really make a name for himself. He knew his time had to be running out. Debts didn't go away even when the debtor changed their name, or moved to a different world. The kind of debts that Johnny had taken on would only grow more demanding, until they could be repaid many times over or until they cost the borrower their life.

Morgan could have slid the power dial on the Slinger to stun just in case the con man was fast and lucky. But Morgan was fast, and he didn't need luck. Nor did he want to hedge his bets; what was the fun in that? He lived for moments like this, when his heart rate sped up, and skin tingled with the possibility of pain and death. It was one of the reasons his clothing was puncture resistant, but had no heat-reflecting plates. Morgan was smart enough to prepare for the eventual knife in his back, but he refused to wear armor for a showdown.

"Go ahead," Morgan said. "Pick it up. We can do this the right way."

In that moment Johnny made the first good decision he had

made in years, perhaps decades. He left the pistol in the drawer and picked up the stack of coins.

"Here it is," he said, holding out the stack, which caught the light from the window and flared a little the way only pure gold can do. It was one of the reasons gold had retained its value as a currency through the millennia.

"I don't want your money, Johnny," Morgan said. "Pick up the gun."

"What?" he asked, his voice shaking for the first time. "Why?"

"I'm not a cold-blooded murderer," Morgan said, his smile hidden by the smooth, black mask that covered his nose and mouth. "We'll make this a fair contest. Man to man, face to face, you're armed, and I'm armed, that's only fair."

"No," he said. "I won't. You can't make me."

"Pick it up, Johnny. Groveling is beneath you."

"Take the money," he said, holding out the gold coins in a trembling hand.

"Money won't buy your way out of this, Johnny. You've only got one chance of seeing the sun rise. Who knows, maybe you'll pull it off. The odds are in my favor, but there's a chance, right? A better chance than those fools who spend their hard-earned credits on lottery tickets every week, or blow their paycheck betting for the losers in a sporting event. Pick it up Johnny, and face me like a man."

Of course, Johnny Grissom wasn't a man -- he was a sniveling, conniving coward who had long ago deviated from the path that led into manhood, opting instead to merely pretend. He didn't want a fair fight, not Johnny, who felt that life was a rigged game to begin with. That's why he only bet when he could ensure the outcome, and why he felt no remorse in stealing from people, or ruining someone if it got him what he wanted. Johnny Grissom had left a trail of destruction in his wake.

He reached for the gun, but just as his right hand hovered over the drawer where the weapon lay, he flung the gold coins at Morgan. They were heavy, and while they wouldn't hurt him, they would have created enough of a distraction, had they hit their target, to give Johnny the edge he felt he needed, perhaps he even believed that he deserved, to beat Morgan.

But this wasn't the man in black's first gunfight with a coward. He had anticipated the duplicitous action, and even prepared for it. There was just enough room behind Morgan for him to drop backward. He hit the marble tile on his backside, tucked his legs up, and rolled over his shoulder. The gold coins hit the thick safety glass, not Morgan, who was bringing his long-barreled laser pistol to bear. As Johnny whirled back with his pistol in hand, time seemed to slow down for Morgan. He saw the con man's eyes widen when Morgan wasn't where he expected him to be. The assassin pulled the trigger on his Widow Maker. The studio flashed red. It was so fast Morgan didn't think anyone who happened to notice the flash outside the apartment would even be able to say where it came from. The focused light hit Johnny low in his stomach, and angled up through his guts and out through his spine. He crumpled to the floor, his Slinger bouncing across the marble tile floor.

Morgan rose slowly. Johnny was gasping for breath, struggling to cope with the intense pain. The hole in his belly was cauterized, but still oozed a clear liquid onto his silk shirt. The area around the wound was charred and blackened. Morgan enjoyed a low shot that left his victim alive, their body cavity filling with blood and the filth from their digestive tract. The spine, once severed, usually caused a paralytic effect. If he hit his target too high, the shock would cause them to pass out, or the evisceration of a vital organ could cause immediate death. Morgan didn't want his victims to die peacefully, what was the fun in that?

Morgan walked over and used a boot to flip Johnny Grissom onto his back. The dying man held his stomach. His face was twisted with pain, but his eyes were wide open and alert. Morgan felt a thrill and squatted down by Johnny.

"Hurts, doesn't it?" Morgan said. "My guess is you've got maybe half an hour left. I suppose you could try to make peace with God, if you're a believer. But somehow, I don't think you are, Johnny."

"Why ... why?" he managed to croak.

"Artists paint not because they want to, but because they have to, Johnny. I don't do this for the money. I don't do it out of loyalty or because, like you, I'm in debt to another person. I do what I do, because I simply love doing it."

"You ... you're a ... monster."

"Yes, that's right. I'm the monster who comes in the dark and makes all your nightmares come true."

Morgan stood up. "Sometimes I like to stay and watch, but I'm afraid I'm wanted elsewhere. It seems my skills are in great demand."

"Help me," Johnny begged. "Please."

"Oh, there's no one who can help you now, Johnny. The laser burned through your digestive system, and it's inevitable that your gut is leaking. The filth has poisoned the blood supply, and even if you could be saved you would never be able to walk again, Johnny. You would be forced to wear a bag to collect your excrement. Other people would have to dress you and clean you. That's no way to live."

"Hurts," Johnny said, tears running down the sides of his upturned face.

"Yes, that's the point, isn't it?" Morgan said, standing up. "Have a good death, Johnny Grissom. Say hello to the devil for me."

# 7

The *Purgatory* was a clean ship. Travis had gone around her three times. The previous owner had taken good care of the vessel. There were no dents or dings. She wasn't sleek, or sporty. In fact, the refitted cargo ship was plain, utilitarian, and obviously made for space travel. There were no aerodynamics other than the wings, which had folded up into the slots along the hull, leaving the ship looking more like a cargo container than a spaceship. But Travis wasn't a vain man, and didn't need a flashy ship. What he wanted was something reliable that wouldn't attract attention. If anything, the *Purgatory* was too clean. She certainly wasn't new, but she looked well-maintained.

After the inspection Travis checked his coat pockets. He kept a variety of different trade goods for worlds like P2. He could use hard currency there, but it was rare to do business with it. In his experience, goods from off world were worth more than money to people on planets where certain things were hard to come by. On P2 he guessed that iodine pills, which helped protect and treat persons exposed to radiation would be worth their weight in gold. He had a few hundred in a couple of bottles inside his coat. He also carried small containers of simple spices; salt, garlic, cumin, pepper. In his experience, people would do a lot for something that made whatever gruel they were living on a little palatable.

The walk to Camp Sherman took nearly two hours, but Travis didn't mind. After being in space where room was at a premium, he enjoyed being outside on a real planet. The rugged landscape had a certain kind of beauty to it, and the bright blue sky with puffy white clouds was worth the energy spent walking. He was a little surprised that there wasn't more air traffic as he approached the camp.

None of the communities on P2 were large. Most of the people were used to packing up and moving frequently. Camp Sherman was one of the few more permanent villages. Water had to be pumped up from the aquifer, but Camp Sherman had a good well, and the water was clean. Between the local treasure hunters and the nearby Dust mines, there were enough people to keep merchants around.

He smelled the village before he could see it. Trash, human waste, animals, he decided, sniffing the wind the way some people smelled fine wine. Animals were a surprise, but not entirely uncommon. A goat would eat nearly anything, including trash, and could produce milk. Pigs could feed a lot of people at one time. And horses were more reliable than vehicles on a world without access to mechanical parts. Eventually, the galaxy would come back around to P2. Real colonies would once more be established, and goods shipped in, but until then, horses were easier to maintain than machines.

There were large vats near the edge of the tent city. Distillers and brewers were busy taking advantage of the clean water supply. Signs for the various merchants, set up in a row along either side of a wide, dusty road through the middle of the village, were painted on bits of odd junk. One of the first that Travis saw was a stable. There actually was no stable, just a corral made of metal beams and rocks. Inside the corral were a few horses, and nearly a dozen mules. A small tent was set up beside them, and an old man with a limp was carrying a plastic bucket of water from the well in the center of the town back for the animals.

"These yours?" Travis asked, resting his weight on the corral fence.

"They're for sale," the older man said.

"Any of those horses rideable?"

"All of 'em, if you know how."

Travis could ride. He didn't enjoy it very much. But riding horseback, or even on a mule was preferable to walking long distances, especially on arid worlds like P2.

"You have tack?"

"Saddle, blanket, bit, and reins is two hundred hard cred," the old man said, pouring the water into a trough, which brought the animals slowly meandering over. "Horses are one fifty, mules one hundred."

"You take trade?"

"Might, what're you offering?"

"I've got iodine pills," Travis said. "Say fifty for a horse, a mule, and riding tack."

The old man barked a harsh laugh. "I look like a miner to you, mister?"

"You look like a businessman," Travis lied.

"Bah!" he said waving a hand as if to shoo Travis away. "Leave me alone."

He had an old laser rifle with a crescent moon stock, and a dented barrel sheath. He picked it up, and held it in his arms as he sat down on the same bucket he had been carrying water in.

"Tell me what you need, old timer," Travis said.

The old man cleared his throat and spit. "They cut me off over at the Dry Camel. You clear my tab and you can take the animals. Tack too."

Travis could have just paid for the animals. He had a few thousand credits in hard currency, mostly bills, carefully folded in his pants pocket. He had a couple of gold coins too. And Travis had no doubt that the man's bar tab was more than the four hundred and fifty credits it would take to buy the animals and tack outright. Still, if he could trade something that only cost him a few dozen credits, for something worth hundreds of credits, he was better off in the long run.

"I'll see what I can do," Travis said, touching the brim of hat.

The old man just leaned over and spit again. The tent city was mostly an entertainment hub, although there were a couple of merchants dealing in goods for mining or treasure hunting. They sold everything from shovels, to power jacks, to Geiger counters. There were saloons, some with sporting girls, others with gambling tables. The biggest tent in the town belonged to a Dust merchant. Most of the miners didn't get more than an ounce or two at any one time. If they had to leave P2 and go to another system to sell their meager ore, all their profits would be spent on travel. Plus, they ran the risk of someone else laying claim to their mining pit. So, they sold their Dust to the merchant, who paid them half of what it was worth, and that money then went to a binge of liquor, drugs, girls, and gambling. After a few days of hedonistic pleasure in the tent city, the hungover, broke miners would crawl back to their holes and start digging again.

It wasn't much different for the treasure hunters. Whatever sellable goods they found were rarely the type to change a person's fortune. But Travis wasn't there to buy Dust, or some long forgotten objects dug out of the rubble of the city. He was there for a different kind of quarry, the type that didn't want to be found.

The Dry Camel was a tent with old whiskey barrels and two long pieces of metal that had been sanded down to form a bar. The proprietor was refilling old bottles with clear liquid that Travis had no doubt would be put to better use cleaning engine parts. But he didn't judge people for what they drank, or how they made a living. What he did judge was an opportunity when he saw one.

There were no tables in the Dry Camel, and the handful of patrons stood leaning on the bar, nursing their drinks. A few looked Travis over as he approached, but most had the sad, vacant stares of drunkards who were busy forgetting whatever drove them to the bottle.

"Help you?" the proprietor asked as Travis put his hands on the smooth, metal bar.

"I'm looking to trade," Travis said.

"You looking for a quart? A pint? Something bigger?"

"What's the stableman's tab up to?"

The barman smirked. "It's more than his animals are worth."

Travis reached into his coat and pulled out a small glass vial. It was filled with cinnamon.

"You distill that liquor yourself?" Travis asked.

"I do," the barman said. "You mind?"

Travis held out the bottle. It was purchased for less than ten credits on Putnum Interchange space station. It was sealed with a clear plastic wrapper, and the label said **Ground Cinnamon**.

"I don't have to tell you that a pinch of that in a bottle of your spirits and you'll get twice as much for it."

The barman shook his head, as if he were getting robbed. And in a way, he was. Writing off a large tab just to get something that cost less than a single bottle of cheap whiskey on a civilized world, but on P2 supply and demand were different. Something like cinnamon was much harder to get than money, and liquor that didn't taste like the metal container it was distilled in was rarer still.

"In exchange for Tubby's bar tab?" the proprietor asked.

"The stable man," Travis said.

"That's Tubby. You got a deal, mister." The barman extended his hand to Travis, who shook it.

"I'll write him a note, send it over with a quart. You want a drink while you wait?"

"Just a shot," Travis said.

Getting drunk was a good way of getting mugged, robbed, maybe even killed on a world like P2. Travis had too much to lose, but he wanted to get a feel for what the locals were ingesting. The bartender splashed some of the clear liquid from a half-filled bottle into a tiny shot glass, the kind that was more glass than container. Travis guessed his drink would fill a thimble, or just slightly more. It was a regular swallow of liquid, not a gulp like many shot glasses. But Travis didn't mind, he didn't really want a lot of the moonshine. There was no regulation of the distillers on P2, and no telling what might actually be in the drink. He turned the little glass up, let it roll across his tongue just long enough to taste what seemed like engine grease. It was cool in temperature, yet it left his tongue numb, and then scorched his throat. The fumes from the single swallow rose up into his sinuses and made his eyes water. Heat rolled out from the center of his body, almost like he was slipping down into a hot tub of water.

"Thank you," Travis said in a husky voice.

The barman handed him a quart bottle. On it he had written with a grease pencil the name Tubby and zero with a line slashed through it.

"Tell him he's welcome back, but his tab limit is a hard hundred," the barman said.

"I can do that," Travis said.

He turned around and found two men near the door of the tent. They were hard looking men, both dirty, with crudely patched clothing. More to the point, they were both heeled with what Travis called Franken-pistols that were made from various parts. One had his tucked into the waist band of his pants, the other had a metal ring on his belt that he was using as a holster.

Travis put the quart of whiskey back on the bar without turning around. He knew trouble when he saw it. More importantly, he recognized one of the men. It was a welcome surprise.

# 8

Iona Frost left the luxury transport she had chartered for the flight to Pergamum Prime. She was not an overly frivolous woman; she didn't spend money on designer handbags or insist on lavish vacations. In fact, she didn't enjoy traveling, which was why when she was forced to do it, she spent extra to make it as swift as possible.

P2 had no spaceport. The transport she hired came down in Incendius territory, near the shanty town called Dusty Springs. A smaller, two-person atmospheric vessel was waiting for her nearby. A man in a wide-brimmed hat with thick sideburns and scar across his chin was waiting. She could see the sweat stains on his ugly shirt.

"You Orvil?"

"Orvil Potter, yes ma'am."

"Do I look like a ma'am to you?" Iona snarled. "You call me Freeze, got it?"

"Yes. Yes I do," he replied.

She could see his paunch. He was a made man, who earned his bones in a spat over the old laboratory that had somehow survived the war. All the buildings around it had collapsed, but it was Orvil who found the place, and managed to get a wind turbine that would power an old generator, which in turn kept the lights on and the ventilation system running. It was the perfect place to cook Dreamers, the most desirable narcotic in the galaxy. A rival OC had tried to take it from them, but Orvil had stood firm, fighting off the rival gang, and securing the lab for the Incendius organization. For that alone, Dice had put his stamp of approval on Orvil Potter and made him head of operations on P2.

Like every other OC on the planet, they ran an exchange to move Dust and other valuable goods pulled out of the rubble. Their primary settlement was Dusty Springs, but they also had several other settlements in their territory, which required that Orvil be mobile. While most people used horses or mules to travel on P2, Orvil had one of the few well-maintained airships on the planet. His was a standard hovercraft, with all-terrain repulsers and a flex frame chassis. It wasn't really comfortable, but it was fast.

"This us?" Iona asked, pointing to the hovercraft.

"Yes," Orvil said. "We can leave whenever you're ready."

"I'm ready now," she said.

"Oh, all right then," Orvil said.

They climbed into the vehicle. It had two racing seats, a soft top, no windows, and no safety belts. Iona didn't understand why men liked dangerous vehicles, but she wasn't there to criticize Potter, or evaluate their operation. Orvil pressed the ignition button, and the repulsers fired up with a puff of dust. He was smart enough not to sling his boss around, and was careful with the throttle. The hovercraft made a slow turn, then sped on across the wilderness.

Iona was not impressed with the slowly rebounding world. It was hot, dusty, and looked barren, although she had been told that much of the wildlife was nocturnal, and they did occasionally see low, gnarled trees and dense shrubs.

"Do you have eyes on the mark?" she asked as they sped along.

"Yeah, I've got my best guys on him," Orvil said. "He's in Camp Sherman, that's Mojito Territory, and I've already made sure their people know we're doing some work in their camp."

"Is that really necessary?" Iona asked, thinking that she was high enough in the Incendius organization to be an attractive target. They could kidnap her for ransom, or just kill her to weaken the Incendies, but Orvil dissuaded her of that notion.

"The Mojitos are a local group. They run interference for us occasionally. Usually sub out the Dust they acquire. Think of them more as subcontractors. I didn't need their permission, as much as I was warning them that VIPs were headed their way."

"How long has the mark been on world?"

"Came down a few hours back. Plenty of time for my people to get into place. I've eyes on his ship, and eyes in town. Word just bounced down that he's in Camp Sherman, probably looking to outfit for a hunt."

"Damn bounty hunters," Iona snarled as she leaned forward and drew out a short-handled, slender-barreled laser pistol from her boot. She checked the charge, which she knew would be full. Still, it paid to be prepared.

"We ain't taking this one down, are we?" Orvil heard. "My orders were to keep eyes on him only. And to keep our distance."

"That's right," Iona said. "The boss doesn't want us attached to this hit in any way."

"We bringing in a shooter?"

"The name Morgan Black mean anything to you?" Iona asked.

She knew Orvil would have heard of the assassin. There were few in the underworld who hadn't. And she wasn't personally impressed with his reputation. A gun fighter was a gun fighter to her, just a trigger puller whose life wasn't worth worrying about. Not like a made man who had proven their worth. Earners were hard to come by, trigger men were a dime a dozen.

"The Specter? Are you serious? He's coming here?"

"He's just a man," Iona insisted.

"Not according to the stories I've heard."

"They are stories, nothing more."

"I wouldn't want to find him waiting for me," Orvil declared.

Iona wasn't so sure. She had yet to meet a man who couldn't be distracted by a flirtatious smile, or a glimpse of cleavage. Iona was not ashamed of being a woman, nor did she see herself as the weaker gender. Women didn't have the muscle mass or bone density that men possessed, but nor did she have their weaknesses. Her body was her slave, and she was meticulous about honing her physical abilities. But she had a clear understanding of what men considered attractive. That had led her to augment certain areas of her body to ensure that despite having the utmost physical fitness, she also had what she considered to be an attractive body.

"You aren't fast with that skull crusher?" she asked.

Orvil carried a military issue laser pistol. It wasn't made for quick draws, or even precision shooting. The pistol was made from strong, hardened steel that was too heavy for most shootists. It was, however, a favorite of law enforcement, who could use the heavy barrel like a club, hence the nickname *skull crusher*.

"Never had the need for speed," Orvil replied. "Slow is smooth, and smooth is fast, that's what my daddy always said."

"Was he a gunslinger?"

"No, he was a treasure hunter," Orvil said. "One of the first on P2."

"Were you born here?"

"Nah, my mother was from Larada Station, in the Mendius system. He came out here when I was just a pup."

"And you followed him, just like a puppy?"

"I suppose so," Orvil said. "Wasn't much for digging through the heaps though. Claustrophobic I suppose."

Everyone had a story, and Iona didn't really care enough to ask more. They rose in silence, the hovercraft skimming over the landscape. The wind blowing through the aircraft was hot and sometimes stung her skin with tiny bits of grit. She couldn't help but resent Dice for sending her on a mission to clean out the garbage. At least that's how she saw it. Travis Hurts was nothing to her, just a lawman, of which there were thousands in the galaxy. She knew he had a reputation, and could be relentless, but she didn't understand why Dice would shell out a significant sum to have the bounty hunter put in the ground. Sooner or later his luck would run out -- why pay a premium just to speed it along?

If not for Iona, Dice and his cronies would have ruined the entire organization. They were short sighted, and impulsive to a fault. They cared about respect, and their precious reputations, but they took unnecessary risks and believed the hype around people like Morgan Black. He was, in her opinion, just another assassin. He might wear a black cape, but that did not make him any deadlier, or any more frightening. It was his brand, she supposed, and he was good at creating the story of his brand. But it didn't take much strength to pull a two-pound trigger. In her opinion, killing people was as simple as pointing and shooting.

# 9

"Hey there mister. You leavin'?" the man with the gun in his pants asked. Travis didn't recognize him, but that didn't mean he wasn't a killer.

"Man like you, flashing your high-end goods," the other man said, "wouldn't mind buying us a round or two."

Travis recognized the second man. His name was Bill Teagan, wanted for murder on Lakish Grand. He had a long record, two stints on two different penal colonies. He had facial augmentation, either surgical or topical. It was difficult to tell. He looked like a cave man, with patchy facial hair, and a heavy, protruding brow. But try as he might, he couldn't hide the scar that ran from his forehead down to his jaw, and the blood-red eye that was a result of the cut.

"You boys don't come in here looking for trouble!" the bartender barked from behind Travis, who still hadn't said a word.

"Ain't lookin' for trouble, we's looking to have a good time," the first man said.

"Ain't no law against it," Bill Teagan said.

"What'a ya say, mister? You buyin'?"

"No," Travis said coolly. "I was just on my way out."

"How 'bout you hand over that bottle then?" Bill Teagan said. "That'll get us started."

"This?" Travis asked, picking up the quart of whiskey. "It tastes like the grease of a hundred-year-old engine. If you want it, come and get it."

"I said out!" the bartender thundered.

But neither of the men moved toward the door. Bill Teagan began to tap on the grip of his Franken-pistol.

"That piece of garbage even shoot?" Travis asked.

A man looking to avoid trouble could have left the bottle of whiskey and just moved aside. The two outlaws could then get drunk while swearing that they scared Travis off. But Travis had other plans, and he was looking for a good excuse to use his Slinger. Most bounty hunters preferred to watch their quarry from a distance, make contact at an opportune moment when their quarry was alone and either unarmed, or completely unprepared for a fight. Travis knew some that shot first and didn't even bother to confront the outlaws.

Travis did things differently. It wasn't because he had a code of honor, or wanted to give his opponent a fighting chance. The truth was, he just liked being the fastest guy around. He liked the challenge. He was a good hunter, but he was a great shootist. He put his life on the line every time he drew down on an outlaw, but he had yet to miss.

"You callin' me out, Mister?" the man with the gun in his pants said.

"What's your name?"

"I'm Adam, he's Bill."

"Oh, I know who he is. Wanted on Lakish Grand, for murder I think."

"What are you, a bounty hunter or something?" Bill Teagan snarled.

"That's about right," Travis said with a smile.

"You better walk off right now, Mister," Adam said. "There's two of us, and only one of you."

"If you draw on me, either one of you, I'll put you both down," Travis said. "Teagan can surrender and put his hands on his head."

"The hell I will," Teagan said, his hand flexing over the handle of his pistol.

"You been shot before, Adam?" Travis asked, keeping his eyes on Teagan. "It hurts, for days. Worse than any hangover you've ever had."

"Don't listen to him," Bill Teagan snapped.

"As close to one another as we are, you'll have a burn too. I aim right for the center of your chest, and I seen guys get their sternum cracked from a close shot like this."

"We ain't shooting stun pistols," Bill Teagan said. "You come here lookin' for me, then you know what I'm capable of."

"Shooting a man in the back while you rob him?" Travis said. "That sounds about right. But I ain't gonna turn around, Billy. You want to kill me you've got to do it while you look me in the eyes, and you gotta be fast about it too. This isn't my first shootout. I don't do this for a living because I make a lot of money. I do it because this is what I'm best at."

"Wh-who you gonna take us to?" Adam said. "Ain't no law here on the Perg."

"That's okay," Travis said. "I'm like the mail, I deliver."

"You run your mouth," Bill Teagan said.

"Don't talk the talk 'less you can walk the walk, something like that, Billy? You want to see if you're fast enough? Jerk that pistol and let's go to work then."

"Like you said Adam, he can't take us both," Bill Teagan said.

"Looks to me like I can put you down Billy, before the kid gets his pistol pulled out of his pants," Travis said. "A cobbled-up shooter like that can get hung on your waistband real easy. And even if he gets it free it might not shoot."

"It shoots all right," Bill said, but he didn't sound very confident, and Adam looked afraid.

"Last chance," Travis told them.

And then Bill Teagan's jaw flexed. It might not have been visible without the augmentation that was meant to throw off the facial recognition computers. But Travis saw it, and knew what it meant. Bill went for his gun, got his hand on the grip and pulled it free of the metal ring holster. But Travis had a Slinger that was light and fast. His holster was stiff synthaleather with a glaze of gun oil. The pistol cleared the holster and Travis fired before Bill could get his Franken-shooter level. The stun blast was bright orange and hit the outlaw in the chest, knocking him backward out of the tent's main flap. Adam reacted to Travis, but he barely had his hand on the grip of his ugly pistol when Travis shot him. The angle was just slightly off. He hit Adam on the left side of his chest, just below the shoulder. It spun the man around before his legs gave out and he dropped in a heap.

Travis looked around, but there weren't any other threats inside the tent. He put the Slinger back in his hip holster and pulled out his Kicker from the thigh holster on the opposite thigh.

"Sorry for the disturbance," Travis told the bar tender as he picked up the quarter of whiskey and stuck it in his back pocket.

"You taking them out of here?"

"Taking Bill Teagan for certain, I can't say yet about his friend."

"All right then, enough gawkin' and more drinkin'!" the bartender barked at the other patrons.

Travis went over to Adam, who lay on his side. He had to bend over with his data slate and get a facial check on the man. It came up empty, which probably meant he too had some sort of augmentation. Most people were in the system, and a no hit didn't mean a person was innocent. In most cases it meant they were hiding from someone. Travis had to holster his Kicker to pull open Adam's eyelid. The eyeball was protruding, which was one of the effects of laser stunning, and made getting a scan of his retina easy.

"Bingo," Travis said. "Adam Turney, wanted for robbery on Cintiq Six, and for questioning in a missing persons case on Datzun Superior."

He couldn't help but frown at the bounty. Just the minimum twenty thousand for the robbery charge. If he was found guilty in the missing person case the bounty would be higher, but the authorities on Datzun Superior were still trying to understand what happened. A young woman had gone missing. She was only nineteen years old. It was a tragedy, and Travis knew he would forego the bounty and deliver Adam Turney to the authorities on Datzun Superior.

"Drag him out of here," the bartender shouted. "And away from my saloon."

Travis thought the tent was a sad place, but he understood how the proprietor felt. It was his business, and he didn't want it besmirched by bad men -- of which many people considered Travis to be one. Bounty hunting was a vital but unsavory business to most law-abiding citizens on civilized worlds.

Travis could have pulled the men down the dusty street to the stables, but instead he removed their pistols, checked them for any other weapons, and left them outside the Dry Camel face down in the dirt. They looked like a couple of drunks who had had too much to drink. And they weren't the only ones sleeping it off on the street, or even outside the Dry Camel.

After returning to the stable the old man looked him up and down. "Well?"

Travis tossed him the bottle. "Paid in full, Tubby. I want that dappled horse, and a good mule. Don't try to cheat me now. I've got a long memory."

Tubby pulled the cork on his bottle and took a long, gurgling pull. Then he smacked his lips. "What'd you do to those two goons back at the saloon?"

"Them? They did me a favor."

"How you figure that?" Tubby said, getting to his feet and holding onto the corral fence for a moment while a wave of dizziness passed. Then he trudged toward the gate.

"They're wanted men. And they saved me the trouble of tracking them down."

"You're a damn bounty hunter, huh?"

Travis thought maybe they had discussed it before, and it really didn't matter to him. He just nodded. "I'll take the mule first."

The mules already had bridles but no bit or reins. Tubby pushed one out of the way, took hold of another and led it out. He tied a nylon rope to the ring on the side of the bridle and handed the end to Travis. "I'll have the horse saddled up when you get back."

"Much obliged. You have extra rope?"

"What do I look like, the general store?"

"Do you have one in this town?"

"Far end of the street," Tubby said, with a wave of his hand.

Travis could feel that people were watching him. It wasn't unusual. He led the mule back down the street. The effects of the stun gun would last around an hour, depending on the target's metabolism. Both Adam Turney and Bill Teagan were thin. They had the look of rough living about them. Drugs were the most obvious culprit, but on a world like P2 it was very possible they were simply malnourished.

The two men weren't all that heavy. Travis got them laid across the back of the mule. He used thick plastic restraints on their hands, binding them behind their backs. Then he led the mule down the street. He passed a cafe and was struck by the smell of fried onions. It made his stomach growl, but there was not time for a meal. He found a dark gray tent with the words **General Merchandise** stitched into the fabric above the tied-open flaps. The general store took only hard currency, but the prices weren't outrageous. He bought two bundles of half inch, 48 strand nylon rope that promised to be strong enough to pull seven thousand pounds. Travis had traditional leg irons in the *Purgatory*, the kind with feet, and weight chains, and another set of shackles that connected their hands to the feet. He hadn't brought any along because he hadn't expected to find any of his quarry so quickly. But he wasn't going to complain about it either. He used the rope and tied the two men to the mule so that they wouldn't fall off. Once they were awake, they could walk. They wouldn't like it, but it would be better than hanging on the back of the mule with the blood filling their heads. He hadn't been lying when he warned Adam about the aftereffects of getting stunned. The men would be feeling the soreness and trauma for days.

In the store, Travis also purchased two large bags of oats for the horse and the mule. There wasn't a lot of vegetation for the animals to eat on P2. He had seen some on the walk from his ship, but not enough to keep the animals healthy. He also bought a sack of rice and another of red beans. He kept protein at the ship, and drink powders, including coffee; enough to supply him if he had to be gone on a long hunt in the wilderness. But the beans and rice were priced well enough that they were worth picking up and would be useful.

"That all you need?" the shopkeeper asked, after taking the money for the goods Travis bought.

"Actually, I'll be looking to hire someone to keep an eye on my ship, feed the prisoners, that sort of thing."

"I don't sell people," the shopkeeper said.

"Slavery is illegal," Travis told him. "I'm a licensed bounty hunter. I want to hire someone, not buy someone."

"Lots of things are illegal," the shopkeeper said. "Doesn't mean it don't happen."

"I'm just looking for someone honest that needs work."

"Not much of that around here," he said. "But it just might be that I know someone. It's a woman, if that matters. She's pregnant. Came out here with her husband and he got himself killed."

"She's looking for work?"

"She's looking for a way off this planet," the shop keeper said. "And God knows there's precious little opportunity of that here. I've helped her out a little, but this isn't a charity I'm running."

"What's her name?"

"Ava Lynn Baxter."

# 10

He didn't get far outside of town before the two captives woke up. They groaned as he threw them off the mule, but the animal didn't seem to mind. Travis didn't mistreat his prisoners, but he didn't baby them either. And he knew what was coming. The aftereffects of being stunned were universal. Both men began to retch. Neither had much in their stomach to vomit up, but they gagged and spit, getting to their knees and bending low as their belly's spasmed.

"Untie us!" Bill Teagan demanded. "We're sick."

"You can be sick with your hands behind your back," Travis said calmly.

His years as a fugitive recovery specialist had taught him a lot about dealing with prisoners. His first rule was to never believe them. And he had learned to ignore them too. Oftentimes when in leg irons and behind bars, all they could do was to verbally try to manipulate their captor. It was wise to be able to tune it out, otherwise they could drive a person to the point of cold-blooded murder.

He retrieved the rope he had bought. He was pretty good at tying knots. And he wasn't worried about the two men escaping. He just needed a way to keep them moving. He tied each of them with a separate rope, using a simple slip knot that tightened as they resisted. The opposite ends of the ropes were tied around the mule's neck, with only about six feet of length behind the animal.

Once the prisoners were done being sick Travis got them on their feet and explained their situation.

"We've got a solid two hour walk to reach my ship," he said.

"You couldn't land closer?" Adam Turney complained.

"I wasn't focused on your comfort," Travis told him. "You'll walk. If you resist both ends of the rope tighten. You may not mind a little pinch, but he will."

Travis pointed at the mule, who was looking at them with dull, disinterested eyes.

"Who the hell cares about your stupid animal?" Bill Teagan snapped.

"You will, because if he feels a pinch he's probably going to start kicking. Have you ever been kicked by a mule? I don't recommend it."

"You can't do this to us," Adam Turney complained. "It ain't humane."

"Was it humane what you did to that woman on Datzun Supreme?" Travis fired back.

The look of shame in Adam's eyes told him everything he needed to know. Adam Turney wasn't the first person to lose his temper with a woman and fly into a fit of rage that ended with murder. Travis was a professional who chose fugitives that had the highest bounty whenever possible. But there were times when taking an outlaw to justice was a reward in itself. He wouldn't make any money with Adam Turney, who was taking up his time, and a valuable spot in the *Purgatory,* but that was okay with Travis. Justice for the missing woman's family would be served, he was certain of that. Adam wouldn't hold up under questioning, and the truth would come to light.

"That thing kicks me I'll kill it," Bill Teagan said.

"Again, I wouldn't recommend that," Travis said. "Especially with both hands tied behind your back. I guarantee you that mule kicks harder than you can."

He climbed back into the saddle. Riding a horse was not Travis' preferred method of travel, he had no illusions about that. But there was something that struck a chord when he climbed into the saddle. Deep down in the depths of his core it felt manly to sit astride a horse and ride through wide open spaces. He would feel it later, but if he spent much time on P2 his body would adjust. And it was better than walking, by far.

The horse was mature and well accustomed to having a rider on its back. It was patient and calm, not jittery or clumsy, which Travis was grateful for. He stroked the horse's neck and made a kissing sound. There was no need to goad or kick the animal. She understood his intent and made her way forward at a steady pace.

Travis held the mule's lead, and it too moved easily. Mules could be stubborn, but both of the animals seemed pleased to be out of the little corral, perhaps away from the smelly tent city. Travis knew he was, even though he also knew he was going to turn around and go right back.

They reached the spaceship without incident. The two prisoners were exhausted, and too sick from being stunned to do anything other than complain. He took them into the ship one at a time. Neither balked at the sight of the metal containment cells. The floor of the cargo hold was metal plate. Travis gave the two men water in a big bottle, and cooked up some biscuits in his small kitchen. They were both half-starved and hungry, but Travis didn't want to give them anything they might not keep down. The only comfort they got was a plain synthetic wool blanket. The life support kept the cargo hold at a reasonable temperature, and there was enough space in each of the six cells for a person to lay full length, plus the open bars made it so they could see and talk to one another.

"I'll be gone a while," Travis said, after moving their restraints to the front of their bodies so the two men wouldn't be uncomfortable. "There's cameras in here, so I'll know it if you cause trouble and when I get back, I'll chain you up. I don't want to do that, but I won't have a choice if you're too stupid to know what's good for you."

"What's to stop us breaking out of these cages and just stealing your ship," Bill Teagan said, supposing it was a threat.

"If you can break through two-inch tungsten steel bars, be my guest," Travis said with a chuckle. "Maybe chew your way free. That would be something to see."

Adam didn't complain. He had already wrapped his blanket around his shoulders and slumped against the wall. Travis set the ship's security system, then saw to the mule and horse. A small scoop of oats and plenty of water cemented the bond between the three of them.

"I think I'll call you Macy," he said, patting the horse's neck. She neighed in response. "You like that, huh?" He turned toward the mule. "How about Tuck, that sounds like a good name for a mule."

Once the animals had finished their meal, they set out back across the desert landscape. Travis was thankful it wasn't as hot as a real desert. The sun was setting by the time Camp Sherman came into view. Electric lanterns were hung up inside the tents and a few outside too. Travis would have business in the saloons, getting a feel for the place and making some connections. He could trade his iodine and spices for information about the fugitives on his list. But first he wanted to find Ava Lynn Baxter.

Outside the main street, between the ruins of the old city and the new shanty town, there were shelters. Most were made out of the debris from the city that had been destroyed during the war. There were some tents too, mostly camping-style quick set up tents with flexible supports. Fires were kindled and the smoke from whatever was burning wasn't pleasant, but not much about Camp Sherman was. He got off his horse and led the animal through the rows of tents and crudely constructed junk shelters. He saw women and children, most looked half-starved and desperate. Life was hard on P2, there was no doubt about that. He could hear music and laughter from the saloon tents nearby. He caught sight of more than one injured person being nursed back to health, or more likely, comforted as they passed away. There was no law in the shanty town, and no doctor either. Even a simple cut could lead to an infection that could poison a person's blood if they weren't careful. Life was cheap on a world like Pergamum Prime.

"You know where I can find Ava Lynn Baxter?" Travis asked an older woman who stood like a sentry in front of her tent. She had a fire going with a pot bubbling over the coals.

"Far end of town," the woman replied.

"Thanks," Travis replied.

He dismounted and led his animals through the residential part of the camp town. There were no neat rows or straight paths through the mass of humanity. It seemed odd to Travis that there could be so many people crammed together outside of a tiny row of shops. He once more caught a whiff of food cooking. Somewhere nearby, not on the waste fires outside the tents, meat was grilling. Travis could smell the fat cooking, a rich, savory aroma that was the complete opposite of the base odors that sat like a pall of smog among the tents.

After asking about Ava Lynn Baxter a few more times, he came to a tidy camp. It was a two-person dome tent, a camp stool, fire, and collection of usable junk from the ruins of the nearby city. Someone had stretched a tarp across some metal poles that were half buried in the ground. Ava was busy, half bent over an old wash tub, scrubbing clothes. There were wet garments hung around the edges of the canopy. Travis saw the swell of the working woman's belly. She wasn't as big as she would get with the baby in her womb, but she was clearly showing.

Travis looked at her for a moment. Ava Lynn Baxter was not a petite woman. She was tall, almost as tall as Travis himself, and big boned. She had the curviness that pregnancy brought on, of course, but she looked strong besides that. Her hair was in a messy bun, and she wore a tattered apron over a sweatshirt, and a long skirt that was made from scraps of other things.

"Help you?" she said without looking up. "You need washing?"

"No," Travis said. "But I'm looking to hire someone. I was told you might be the person for the job."

Ava Lynn looked up, really seeing Travis for the first time. He thought she might be pretty, if not for the grief and exhaustion that were visible on her face.

"You're the bounty hunter," she said.

"Fugitive Recovery Specialist," he corrected her, trying to sound a little more legitimate. In some circles any law enforcement was seen as being the lowest of the lowly professions a person could possibly have. As if the people sworn to protect and serve were somehow traitors to the human race.

"You killed two men today," she pointed out.

"I didn't kill anyone," he said. "I don't kill people unless I have to."

"What kind of work are you offering?"

"I've got a ship a couple hours from here," Travis said. "Like I said, I took two men captive today. Hopefully I'll have more soon, up to six. I need someone to keep an eye on them for me while I'm out doing other things."

"You think a pregnant woman would make a good prison guard?"

"My ship's no prison," Travis said. "And they won't be a threat unless you were to open up the cage door."

"People in cages don't seem right, somehow," she replied, drying her hands on the tattered apron.

"You can read what they done and then decide if keeping them locked up is right or wrong."

"What's this job pay?" she asked.

"It's based on commission," he said. "Ten percent of what I bring in after turning the prisoners over for their rewards."

"How much will that be?"

"More than you're making washing clothes," Travis said. "Plus, there's food on my ship. I probably got some vitamins for that tyke you're growing. You can stay in my quarters, sleep on a real bed. There's even a hot shower you can use as often as you like."

"I ain't no whore," she said. "I don't sell my body."

"That's not what I'm after," Travis said, thankful that it was gloomy enough in the twilight that she didn't see him blushing. "You mind if we sit down and talk?"

She waved at her little camp. There was a coffee pot on the coals of what was probably a fire made from dried animal dung. It had been a small fire to begin with, and Travis saw no food.

"Tell me why a woman like yourself is here on this world

alone?" Travis asked as he squatted by the fire, leaving the lone camp chair for the pregnant woman to sit in.

She settled onto the chair, squirming to find a comfortable position, and clearly tired. She smoothed her skirt over her legs. Travis saw that her boots were held together with tape that wouldn't hold up much longer.

"My husband was a miner," she said. "He was a genius really, and built a machine that would separate Dustincia from other elements."

"And he came here to test it out."

Ava nodded. "It worked too, after some adjustments. We tried to keep it secret, but that sort of thing doesn't stay hidden in a place like this long."

"How big was it?"

Ava held her hand about four feet off the ground. "You put the dirt in the top. It spewed the worthless stuff out one side and collected the valuable ore in the other."

"And word got around?"

She nodded. "It didn't make mining any easier. It certainly didn't give you any more Dustincia than what was already in the ground. But Ray had a nose for finding the stuff." She shook her head, and the tears came whether she wanted them or not. "But he wasn't a fighter."

"So they took it from him," Travis said. Ava nodded. "You know who?"

"They came at night," she explained. "If he had just let them take it …"

"It was his invention. And he had proof that it worked. That's not something a man can just walk away from very easily."

"They killed him for it," she said quietly between sobs.

"And you don't know who they were?"

She shook her head, and wiped her nose with a rag she pulled from the pocket on the front of the apron.

"Would you recognize them if you saw them again?" Travis asked.

She nodded. He couldn't make promises he wasn't able to keep. There was no guarantee that Travis could find the men responsible for stealing her husband's invention, or for murdering him for it. But the chances were pretty good that they might already be wanted for something else. And Travis had no qualms about letting her look through the postings of wanted men and women that he kept on his data slate.

"Did your husband know he was going to be a father?" Travis asked.

Ava shook her head. "I was pretty sure, but I was waiting to know for certain."

"Why didn't you just leave once he proved the device worked?"

"We were making plans," she said. "But there isn't regular shuttle service off world. Ray thought that if he could get enough Dustincia that it would be enough to start manufacturing the devices ..."

She looked away, staring out into the darkness. Travis understood her pain. Regret was always the same. A person just didn't know when things would take a turn for the worse, and Travis didn't blame Ava's husband for wanting to take advantage of being on a world with known Dustincia deposits. It all made perfect sense, and yet it had turned out to be a grave mistake. Travis felt like he had found someone who could help him, and in turn, he could help her.

"I can't let the prisoners starve. I need someone I can trust to feed 'em, give 'em water too. Occasionally there might be a need to nurse a wound if they're injured. But that's all, Miss Baxter.

For that you can stay on my ship, which has a full security suite. It's a lot safer than you are here. You'll have all the food you can eat, indoor plumbing, even a washing machine. Once I'm through here, we'll take the prisoners to the systems where they're wanted, and you'll get ten percent of whatever bounties I earn. Plus," he knew this was the real remuneration that would seal the deal for her, "you can stay on any planet or system we go to."

Ava Lynn Baxter couldn't hide the surprise on her face, or the hope in her eyes.

"How long will it take you to get a full ship?"

Travis shrugged. "Maybe a couple of weeks, to a month at most," he told her. "You could be on a civilized world with real birthing centers and midwives to help when the baby comes."

"I'll do it," she said. "I'll take the job."

"Good," Travis said. "You know how to pack a mule?"

He left Ava Lynn to pack her meager belongings onto Tuck, while he went to check things out on Camp Sherman's main street. Unlike the camps, the street was well lit, and there were men everywhere. Travis saw that most were armed. Not that he expected anything less, but drunk, armed men, on a world with no law enforcement, were dangerous.

He pulled his Slinger, popped out the little six shot power cell, and replaced it with a fresh one. He gave the pistol a twirl on his finger, then slipped it easily into his hip holster. Travis was no showoff, and he was hidden in deep shadow, well away from the busy street. Twirling his weapon was purely habit. He was familiar with his weapons, and well versed in handling them. At times he even played with them. Spinning a properly weighted firearm was easy and if he was being honest, it was satisfying as well. There was nothing quite like having one's weapons at hand, especially when you were good with them. And Travis was better than good.

The nearest tent was labeled with paint on a broken piece of wood that had once been part of a picnic table. The blocky letters spelled out **Al's Lounge.** It was pretty obvious from the stench of the smoke wafting from the tent that it was a drug den. Travis knew he wouldn't get the information he needed there. Across the street was a tent with a banner hung over the flaps that read **Madame McCall's**. It didn't take any imagination to wonder what went on inside, as there were three scantily clad women trying to entice anyone passing by to take a taste of their charms. Travis was reminded of the ancient story of Ulysses tying himself to the mast of his sailing ship as he passed by the island where the sirens called to him. He hadn't trusted himself to resist, but still wanted to hear their song. Travis had learned a long time ago that entertaining such base ideas often led to trouble. Besides, he could hear what was taking place in Madame McCall's tent, there was no mystery to be solved there. No help on his task either.

Instead, he ambled down to the cafe, tied his horse up to the pole that had both the sign and a lantern hung near the top. He went inside, and found over a dozen customers at two makeshift tables. The back of the tent was tied up, and he could see a big man cooking slabs of meat on a gas grill. There were vats with rehydrated potatoes, and pans full of dried mushrooms and onions being sautéed in a brown sauce. Travis knew there wasn't a lot of food growing naturally on P2; most everything was brought in from off world. He sat down and a teenager with a dirty apron and shaggy hair brought him a mug filled with foamy beer.

"Dinner is twenty credits," he said. "Gratuity not included."

"What's on the menu?" Travis asked.

"Beef steak, potatoes, mushroom gravy with onions," the kid repeated. He had said it all a thousand times and was bored. Travis couldn't blame him for that. It wasn't his business; he was probably working for his family with no wages other than tips.

"Fresh butchered, frozen—"

"Vat grown," the kid said. "Beer is two credits extra."

Travis didn't dare eat vat grown foods very often. They were never quite the right texture, and loaded with preservatives, but every once in a while, he didn't mind. It was all a person ever got on the long, interstellar flights. And there were enough other people eating the food that Travis was fairly certain he wouldn't get sick from it.

"Tell you what," Travis told the kid, pulling two twenty credit notes from his pocket. "I'll take a meal, plus some information."

The money was gone the moment it hit the table. The kid swiped it up and stuffed it into his dirty apron.

"I'll get your dinner," he said, almost as if he was angry about doing his job.

Travis pulled out his data slate, unlocked it, and opened the file of wanted men and women he was hoping to find. When the kid came back, he had a plate of food, a fork, and knife. He set the food in front of Travis. The smell of grilled meat and onions made his mouth water, even if he didn't care to know where it came from or exactly how it was grown. Travis handed over his slate.

The kid took a look at the pictures.

"These two are the only ones I recognize," he said, pointing at a man with a fancy, waxed mustache, and a woman who was attractive but had hate in her eyes.

Travis took the slate back and slipped it into one of the cargo pockets on his pants. Then he picked up the knife and fork, one in each hand.

"How often?" Travis asked.

"The man only once, a few weeks back. The woman, she's always around."

"Whereabouts?"

"Comes in early most mornings. Gets some biscuits, rides out on a pretty little appaloosa pony."

"Thanks kid, that helps," Travis said, cutting into the steak with the serrated knife.

"You're the bounty hunter everyone's talking about, aren't you?" the kid asked.

"Maybe," Travis replied, taking his first bite.

The meat was strange, almost spongy, but it had a meat flavor to it. The gravy had an earthy flavor, and not much salt. He could have taken his seasonings out and enhanced the food, but he didn't. Like everyone else in the cafe, he just ate fast. It was hot and filling, which was all most people were looking for.

"If you ever need help," the kid said, leaning closer. "I know how to handle a gun."

"That a fact?"

"Yeah, and I'm pretty fast too. I don't take up much room, and I know how to cook."

"Stick with the Cafe," Travis told him. "It's safer."

The beer was foamy and cool, but not as cold as Travis would have liked it. It was just a tad on the sour side, and a little bit watery. Still, it went down pretty well with the meal, and was better than Travis had hoped.

"I don't want safe, man, I want action. I'm dying here. They don't even pay me."

"You get the tips though," Travis said.

"I have to split them with my sister."

Travis saw a girl in the back plunging plates and cups into soapy water. There was no sense in trying to convince the kid of anything. Travis had felt the same way at that age, only he understood all too well what danger really was. His father had used fists, his friends were worse. More than one died from alcohol poisoning or from getting beaten. Travis had seen them, seen their bodies, he had a healthy respect for his own mortality from a very young age.

"Sorry, kid, I don't need any help," Travis told him.

"Whatever," the kid snapped. "Your loss, old man."

The kid stormed off and Travis couldn't help but chuckle. He finished his meal, wiped his mouth on a neatly folded handkerchief he kept in a pocket, and drained the rest of his cup of beer. He had meant to buy a meal for Ava, but he didn't think the vat grown meat and highly processed gravy would be good for the baby.

When he stepped outside the cafe tent, he found Ava approaching with Tuck in tow. The mule was loaded with a several neatly bound bundles.

"Perfect timing," he said.

"Tell me the food on your ship is better than the slop they serve here," Ava said.

"Beggars can't be choosers," he replied.

"I won't feed my baby that garbage."

"I wouldn't either," Travis said. "Everything I've got is real, unprocessed, but frozen, other than the rice and beans I bought here earlier today."

"Frozen I can live with," Ava said. "But mystery meat is not acceptable."

He took the mule's lead rope, and pointed to his horse. "Ava Lynn, meet Macy the horse. You ride?"

"I never have," she admitted.

"You climb up there, and hold onto the saddle horn," Travis told her. "I'll lead the animals."

"Shouldn't you ride? It's your horse after all."

"I think I'll be sore enough as it is," he confessed. "Riding will save your legs, but take a toll on your backside."

He helped her climb up into the saddle. She had tights on under the skirt, and a quilted coat on over the sweatshirt. The temperature had been moderate in the day, and was growing cooler with the sun down. Travis was grateful for the warm food in his stomach. His duster was warm enough to get him through a cold night, but the hot meal helped too.

"How far to your ship?" Ava asked.

"A couple of hours. I'll get you settled, and show you the security settings. Then I need to come back."

"You don't need to sleep?"

"I can sleep when the cells are full and we're off this planet," he said. "Until then, I plan to keep one eye open at all times."

# 11

"That's him, leading the horse," a skinny man in a dirty black overcoat told them.

Iona Freeze and Orvil had reached Camp Sherman just before nightfall. Orvil called one of his crew and the man in the coat had pointed Travis out. Iona would have recognized him herself once he got closer. But in the gloom and shadows of the street at night he wasn't easy to recognize. Everyone had a coat of some kind. She would have to get one herself before long. And everyone was armed, she saw. The rowdy main street of Camp Sherman was exactly the kind of place she expected on an open planet with no law. Every form of vice was available at all times. Iona wasn't a stickler for morals herself, but she detested the way so many men were ruled by their base instincts.

"Who's that with him?" Orvil asked.

"I just found out," his crew member replied. "It's a widow woman. She's pregnant."

"A pregnant fugitive?" Iona asked.

"No boss," the man in the dirty black coat said. "She ain't no outlaw."

"They kin?" Orvil asked.

"Not that I know of," the man said.

"This is Reg, by the way," Orvil explained to Iona. "He's one of my best."

"It's a pleasure, Ms. Freeze," Reg said.

"Tell me everything," she ordered, never taking her eyes off Travis at the far end of the street. "What has happened since he's been here?"

"Showed up in town about midday," Reg explained. "Zony is out there watching the ship. It's about two hours walk from here."

"What did he do?" Iona said, enunciating each word to show her frustration.

"Oh, yeah, well, he did some horse trading. Wiped out old man Tubby's bar tab at the Dry Camel in exchange for a bottle of ground cinnamon, if you can believe that."

"Why would he?" Iona pressed the crewman.

"Oh, yeah, he cleared Tubby's tab in exchange for a horse, riding tack, and a mule."

"All that for a bottle of cinnamon," Orvil said in surprise.

"He's clever," Iona Freeze said. "Don't underestimate him."

"We taking him down, boss?" Reg asked.

"No, we're just the eyes on this one," Orvil replied.

"And we don't get too close," Iona said. "I'm here to make sure of it. We don't want any blowback once the hit goes down."

"He's a lone man operation from what I can tell," Reg said. "Not counting that widow woman of course."

Iona let Orvil explain how things worked to his henchman. Reg didn't seem stupid, but he was ignorant of how the galaxy worked. She wasn't surprised to see that Orvil's crew was made up of native-born men. There weren't many opportunities on P2, and joining the Incendius crew was probably the best anyone on the barren rock could hope for.

"So he bought a horse and mule," Iona said. "Then what?"

"Then he took down a couple of guys that had been hanging around Sergio's crew for the past few weeks?"

"Prospects?" Orvil asked.

"Nah, nothing serious," Reg explained. "They weren't tough guys. Runners, by the looks of 'em. Probably wanted somewhere else. Sergio talked to Faulkner over at the Dry Camel. That's how I know about the trade situation. Anyway, he said those two gun thugs didn't know who our man was. They just saw someone with money and tried to shake him down."

"So he killed them," Iona said appreciatively. She often wished she could be as exacting to the people who bothered her.

"No, he didn't kill 'em, just stunned 'em. I saw one come flying out of the Dry Camel. I thought he was dead, but your man trussed 'em up. Sergio said Faulkner heard him tell those two losers he was gonna stun 'em. Said he was a real quick draw artist. Took 'em both down before either of 'em could get a shot off."

"He was faster than both of them?" Orvil asked.

Reg nodded, just as Travis passed them on the busy street. Iona, Orvil, and Reg were holding mugs of beer and standing between two tents, in the shadows. Travis may have noticed them, but Iona stayed in the darkness, out of his sight. He didn't have any kind of night vision glasses, or even a lantern. His face was uncovered. He wasn't handsome enough to stand out in a crowd. His face was round, his beard trimmed, but showing touches of gray. He wore a gray, wide-brimmed hat, and had a bandana tied around his neck, probably to keep the dust out when the wind kicked up. His duster, like everything else, was plain, a very light brown color. She saw glimpses of his Slinger. The Kicker strapped to his left thigh, butt out for a cross draw, stood out. She despised non-lethal weapons, and couldn't understand the point of them. Why shoot someone if you didn't want them dead, she thought. And while she couldn't be certain, she thought that Travis Hurts had another weapon, probably a rifle, slung across his back from one hip to the opposite shoulder. It was an old military trick, and easy to do with a body harness. He could swing it around into action easy enough, even with his long coat on.

"Doesn't look like much," Reg said.

"Just another tough guy," Orvil said. "The galaxy is full of 'em."

"Not like Travis Hurts," Iona warned them as they watched him lead the animals, and the pregnant woman out of town. "He is not just another thug with a gun."

"He's a lawman, right?" Reg said. "He's got rules he has to follow."

"He's a bounty hunter, not a TA officer, or a beat cop. He hunts killers to make a living. Think about it," Iona said. "He took out two guys, gunned both down before they could even get a shot off. He's dangerous."

"So, we hit him from a distance," Orvil said. "I know a guy who can hit a rat from three kilometers out."

She shook her head. Men were so stubborn. She couldn't understand why they refused to face the reality that some people were tougher, meaner, faster, deadlier than they were. Maybe, she mused, watching the bounty hunter ride off into the darkness, they just needed to talk about it like they were hard men, true killers, not the kind that slinked around in the dark waiting to stick a knife in your back.

"You ever hear of the Coleman Gang?" Iona asked.

Reg just had a blank look.

"Four brothers, got their tickets punched on Nuvo Jumo in the Los Munos system," Orvil said.

"That was Travis Hurts," Iona told them with a grim smile. "Let's get a decent drink and I'll tell you how it happened."

# 12

"The Coleman gang were wanted for robbery," Iona said. They were seated around a small table in one of the few establishments that had any. "Two point eight billion in hard currency, taken while the cash was being moved from the casinos on the floating islands of Cameroon in the Caeruleum system to Kingsbury Three. They stole an interdictor ship from the Transit Authority. Some people believe they had an inside man on that job, but it was never proven. With the interdictor, they ripped the armored carrier out of hyperspace."

"That's not possible," Orvil said. "It's just an urban legend."

"And yet somehow they pulled it off," Iona went on. "They killed the guards on board. Every last one of them. Then moved all the gold in zero-G to their own ship. It was never seen again."

"What's the good of stealing gold if you can't spend it?" Reg asked.

"They had to melt it down, move it through the right channels," Iona said. "Some people say most of the gold is still hidden somewhere. The reward for the four brothers totaled one million credits. Back then, Travis Hurts was a junior agent at the Rosenthal Detective Group. He was tracking an escapee on Nuvo Jumo, and came across the brothers in a cantina in the old city.

"It was completely by accident. No one knew the Coleman Gang was there. The TA was hunting for them in a different arm of the galaxy. But Travis Hurts recognizes the brothers. The story I heard was that Hurts called in and told his superiors what he had found. They told him to walk, leave it to his betters who would be along in a few days. Travis knows the brothers will be long gone by then. Some versions have him ignoring their orders, but the story I heard says he quit on the spot. Either way, he decides to take them in by himself."

"One guy, against four?" Reg asked.

"That's insane," Orvil added. "The Coleman gang was known for cruelty. They're already wanted across the galaxy. Things won't get any hotter for them because they killed a junior agent from a PI firm."

"But that's exactly what he does," Iona said. "Only he doesn't go in guns blazing. He's too smart for that. The brothers are expecting trouble. Instead, he starts drinking at the bar. After downing a few shots, he gets loud and boisterous. The brothers are in the VIP section, bottle service only as the girls working at the cantina hurry back and forth to the bar for them. Travis Hurts intercepts one of the girls. He's got her by the arm and he's being rude. Razzo Coleman goes to teach Travis a lesson, make sure he realizes who his betters are. They start arguing, and then Travis hits Razzo in the shoulder. Some people say he had on a stun glove or a stinger hidden in his sleeve. Either way, Razzo's gun arm goes numb. Meanwhile, Travis is challenging him to a duel. 'Let's take this outside!' he keeps saying. Malachi, the youngest overhears the challenge and steps in.

"That's when things get nuts. The bar clears. Both men are staring each other down. Groucho and Torrance are in the process of angling around to get the jump on Travis. No one ever accused them of being honorable. But Travis Hurts goes for his gun before they can get set up. Both men fire, but Malachi misses. He goes down, Razzo leaps on Travis Hurts, who is so fast he reholsters his Slinger before the second Coleman brother wrestles him to the ground."

"Shoulda shot him too," Reg says.

"He shoots Razzo and the other two brothers would have slaughtered him," Orvil points out.

"Exactly," Iona said. "Groucho and Torrance can't shoot because he's on the ground, fighting Razzo, who still only has one good arm."

"Wouldn't be much of a fight," Reg said.

Iona nods, "Except that our man Travis is taking his lumps just to get into position. Once he's able to get back on his feet, with one black eye already swelling and a broken nose for his trouble, Travis draws again. For just a second Razzo, seeing the pistol, freezes. But Travis doesn't shoot him. Instead, he takes out Groucho. And Torrance doesn't have a shot because Razzo's in the way."

"That's two Colemans down," Orvil said.

"By that point the cantina, it must have been some really busy place on Nuvo Jumo, is chaotic. People are running out screaming. Razzo throws caution to the winds and charges Travis, who lunges down, slamming his left shoulder into Razzo's bread box. The useless fool folds over Travis, who comes up shooting with his right hand. He takes down Torrance who still won't shoot because his brother's in the way.

"Damn, that's crazy," Reg said. "He took out all three."

"All four," Iona says, "but not before Razzo sticks a stiletto in his back. It cost Travis a kidney, at least that's what I heard. He dropped Razzo on his head. The last Coleman brother collapses in a heap in front of the cantina bar. Travis Hurts pulls the knife out of his back and looks around. He's just taken down the most wanted men in the galaxy all by himself. The sirens from local law enforcement are already audible, but before Travis can reach the door of the cantina, he collapses."

"What happened?" Reg said. "Did he get the reward?"

Iona shakes her head. "The locals collect," she explains. "Travis wakes up in the hospital with no money, no job, and charges against him for bounty hunting without a license."

"And they say crime don't pay," Orvil said.

"No good deed goes unpunished," Iona continued. "But it just goes to show that we can't ever, ever underestimate Travis Hurts. He's creative and fast. That's why Dice called in the best."

"Who?" Reg asked.

"The Wraith," Orvil said.

"Who?"

"You've never heard of the man in black?" Iona asked.

"Hey, I look pretty good in black," Reg said, dusting the sleeve of his overcoat.

Iona thought it would take more than a dusting. She could smell the man from across the table, and his coat looked like he had worn it through a sandstorm.

"Don't joke," Orvil said. "We're talking about one scary hombre."

"I thought you weren't afraid of no man?" Reg challenged.

"They say Morgan Black isn't a man," Orvil replied.

"He's just a hired gun," Iona said. "But he's fast, maybe the fastest there is."

"Good enough to take down Travis Hurts," Reg said.

"The big boss thinks so," Iona said. "And he's paying handsomely for the job."

"He don't have no confidence in us?" Reg asked.

"The point is to avoid any blowback on the organization," Iona said. "Hurts works alone, but if it gets out that we put the hit on him, every lawman and bounty hunter in the galaxy will go after our people. They get up in arms when we cross that line."

Iona pulled a hundred credit note from her vest and dropped it on the table.

"Ain't no need for that," Orvil said. "Sergio's people won't take our money."

"Sure they will," she said. "That covers our tab and then some. When I'm in someone else's backyard, I make sure they know it's appreciated. Where are we staying tonight?"

"Not in this dump, I can assure you of that," Orvil called.

"This place ain't so bad," Reg said, his eyes already on one of the sporting women near the bar.

"Not with my money," she warned him. "Screw around on your own dime."

"He knows better," Orvil said.

"Of course," Reg said, but he looked like a kid who was told he couldn't have a cookie. "I would never."

"Damn right you wouldn't," Orvil said. "You're on the clock here."

"What for? Hurts is gone."

"But he might come back," Iona said. She put her hand on the man's shoulder and squeezed hard enough that he squirmed. "Didn't you just hear the story I told you? He's unpredictable. You can't underestimate him."

"You stay here and keep your eyes open," Orvil said. "He comes back, you call us."

"Yeah, yeah, I can do it," he said, his voice strained from the pain in his shoulder.

"You better," Orvil said after Iona released him. She started for the exit of the tent, but Orvil leaned close to Reg. "Freeze ain't no slouch. She's the toughest broad in the outfit, right under the big boss. You get me?"

"Yeah," Reg said, rubbing his bruised shoulder. "I got it, I got it."

"No second chances, Reggie. You mess this up, she might just kill you."

The younger man looked up, frightened, but trying to hide it.

Orvil left and hurried after his superior, hoping that if she got in the killing mood, she didn't target him too.

# 13

I t was a relief when they reached the ship. Travis was tired and he knew that Ava was too. Not that it was so late, but two hours on horseback was a long time. He helped her down and she stretched.

"You were right," she said. "I'm going to be sore tomorrow."

"Who knows, a hot shower might fix you right up."

"You really have running water?"

Travis nodded. "It was one of the bells and whistles I went looking for in a ship," he told her.

He opened the rear hatch and Travis went in first, his Kicker held ready. But both prisoners were asleep. Not that he could blame them. There was a relief to being captured. When a person knew there was nothing else they could do, the weight of their worries fell away. They would, of course, return with a vengeance as they approached the systems where the men were wanted. They would face judges who had little mercy for outlaws who ran from justice.

"This way," Travis told Ava. "Until we leave P2, this is your new home."

"Can they get out of there?" she asked.

"No, they cannot," he assured his temporary partner. "Those are inch and half tungsten steel bars, welded in place by pipefitters on the Putnum Interchange station."

"But I have to give them food," she said. "They could grab me."

"They could, but all you have to do in that case is throw your weight to the side." Travis made a popping sound. "That's how easy a bone breaks against cold hard steel."

She shivered, and pulled her quilted coat tighter around her body. Travis showed her the living quarters. The kitchen first, and the food supplies. There was enough on the ship to last Travis and six prisoners for a full month. He hoped that would be enough, but if not, he could always buy more food.

"And here is the bathroom," he said. "It's kinda small, but the water is hot."

"Can't wait," Ava Lynn Baxter said. "I haven't had a hot shower since we got to Pergamum Prime."

"Feel free to take as many as you want. There's plenty of water. It's a recycled system. You'll never run out."

"It cleans the water too?"

"Yes, filters everything and recycles automatically. Here's the clothes machine, it washes and dries. You can throw the bedsheets in there if you like. Won't hurt my feelings."

"I haven't had clean sheets in ages. Not to mention a real chair," she said, looking longingly at the reclining lounger.

"That's the grand tour," he said. "If you're up to it, I can record your voice for the ship's computer system. You'll have secondary controls, which means you can do everything but fly the ship, and remove me as the primary user."

"Why are you trusting me with all this?" she asked. "Don't get me wrong, I'm thrilled that you did. But why me?"

"I asked around," Travis said. "And ultimately, you need what I have to offer."

She looked at him suspiciously. "What's that mean?"

"A way off this planet," he said. "Worlds like this don't have many options."

"Especially for a woman?"

Travis shrugged. "I suppose that's true."

"Well, you won't regret bringing me on. I'll take care of the ship when you're away."

"Good," he told her. "Let's get you set up."

Once the computer recorded her voice and had Ava installed as the secondary user, she could order up the video displays. Travis had threatened Adam and Bill, saying he could keep an eye on them with his data slate, but that was a lie. The ship's cameras, both external and internal, were part of the security system. It was impossible for an outside computer to access them. But Ava could leave the wall displays on with views from the ship's external cameras, as well as the cargo bay cameras. She also had access to the ship's library of entertainment features. It was enough to keep her from getting bored while Travis filled up the remaining four holding cells.

"I'm going back to Camp Sherman," he said. "But before I go, I want to show you the list of wanted fugitives I work from."

"So I can help?"

"Actually, I thought there might be a possibility that the men who killed your husband might be on it."

The relief on her face from the amenities on the *Purgatory* was suddenly gone. In its place was the grief and horror of having the lost the man she loved.

"You think that's really possible?"

"Yeah, I do," he told her. "I'm going back for this woman, Sandra Mayfield."

"Who is she?"

"A murderess. She murdered three different husbands on three different worlds. I can't say what name she's going by, but she's in the area. The kid at the cafe said she stops by there most mornings."

"Is she dangerous?"

"Everyone I go after is dangerous. And that's something to keep in mind. No matter how friendly any of the people on this ship seem, they cannot be trusted."

"Does that go for you too?" she asked.

He wasn't sure if she was joking or serious, but he nodded. "You won't go wrong keeping a little distance from everyone you meet here."

"Okay," she said.

He showed her how to scroll down the list and how to read what each individual was wanted for. The most wanted list showed bounties, last known residences, last seen records, and their full criminal records. The list was for law enforcement personnel only, but Travis had hired Ava Lynn, and even though she wasn't a registered LEA, she was close enough.

"If you want to go outside, feel free," he told her. "The ship has radar. She'll pick up any approaching vessels. I would do a full visual scan before opening up, and then take the spare computer slate out with you. That way you can see all around the ship at a glance. One of the reasons I put down this far out was so I could see for a long way off. There's no reason anyone should be out here but you and me. Anyone else is suspect. You go inside, activate security protocols, and wait for them to leave."

"What if they don't leave," she said. "What if they break open the rear hatch, or the airlock?"

"In that case you lock yourself in the living quarters and press that tab."

The tab was just a little medallion on the wall. It was so well worn that it was hard to make out what it said.

"Should I?" Ava asked.

"Go ahead," Travis told her.

She pressed the tab and the panel swung open. Inside was an old-fashioned scatter gun.

"You ever shoot one before?" Travis asked. Ava shook her head. He pulled the gun out. It had a tactical length barrel, and a full stock with recoil absorbing material. Along the stock was a row of extra shells in little loops. "It's got a lot of kick, so hold it tight. The shells are filled with rubber pellets. They won't kill, but they might draw blood, and they will break bones. It's a short-range weapon. If someone gets through that door, you let 'em have it."

"Do I have to cock it or something?" she asked.

"No, just slide the safety forward, point and shoot. Easy. There's eight shots in the rifle, and eight more on the sleeve. If you don't stop the bad guys with the first eight, fall back to the cockpit, lock that door and reload."

"All right," she said.

He put the rifle back in the mount and closed the panel.

"But you're not going to need that. This is all just precautions."

"I know this is a dangerous world," she told him. "I won't take chances."

"Good. Hopefully, if all goes well, we'll be out of here in a few days."

"That sounds too good to be true," she replied. "Thank you again, Mr. Hurts."

"Call me Travis. You need anything else?"

"No," she said with a shake of her head.

"Those prisoners won't need anything till morning. Get some rest. You deserve it. I'll lock up and set the security system as I go out."

She smiled, and he thought again that she could be pretty.

Maybe when the fear was gone, and the fatigue had faded from her features, she wouldn't look so wary and defensive. Maybe when she had reason to smile again, she would look pretty, maybe even beautiful. It was a shame that she had lost so much and endured such hardship, but he would get her off world, with at least a little bit of a stake to get her started on a new path. It wouldn't make up for losing her husband, but it might just be what she needed to find happiness again.

# 14

Morgan Black's ship popped into the Pergamum System after coming out of hyperspace. It was a sleek, one-man vessel with a fighter style cockpit, and simple living quarters built between the two big engines. There were deflector shields of course, not to mention fore and aft guns that were hidden from sight until they were needed. The ship carried more power than the engines or life support needed, a lot more. Morgan Black wasn't the type to hide out on his ship, but he was a man who preferred the privacy and safety of his own vessel.

For a while he sat looking across open space. Pergamum Prime was before him, a swirling ball of white clouds, brown landmasses, and blue-green oceans. It was a massive planet, with twelve habitable continents, at least before the nuclear attacks had destroyed all the major cities and poisoned the atmosphere for a century.

Morgan was familiar with P2. It was a haven for people trying to avoid the law. Morgan rarely had trouble with the law, and when he did, he often found that a generous sum of money in the right hands could cause those officials who had taken too close a notice of him to look the other way. And when that didn't work ... well, he had his methods. Fortunately, he had only been forced to utilize them on an unsuspecting law enforcement official once, and that had been years ago. He was wanted in that system, but not by name or even with a picture. He was officially just "gunman" wanted for murder of a police officer, but no one knew who he was.

His ship was registered in Kingsbury as a personal transport owned by Andrew Gunderson Senior. And Morgan had four sets of identification stashed in hidden compartments on his ship. If it became necessary to run, he could swap out the transponders so that this ship wouldn't be stopped by TA officers, or orbital patrols. His hyperspace FTL drive could take him to the other side of the galaxy without the need to refuel or charge the ship's internal batteries. But in the worst-case scenario everything could be powered electrically, and the ship had a massive solar sail that it could eject and unfurl to recharge his power system.

Then there were the homes. Most were off grid, but a few were in major towns. He had no fewer than eight homes, listed under various aliases, that he could run to for protection should the need arise. What else was he going to spend his fortune on other than contingency plans? He wasn't a thief, and had no need to hide his money. He was officially an employee of Ares Consulting, a shell company that was owned by seven other companies, each headquartered on a different world with strict privacy laws, and no extradition treaties. His fees came in through those disparate business entities, and funneled down to Ares. It was all above board and legal -- not the work he did, but the way he was paid was completely legitimate. He even paid taxes, not because he wanted to, but because it pleased him to circumvent the legal system in such a direct manner.

His ship, the *Dymetr*, glided toward the planet. His autopilot would slide the sleek vessel into a high orbit and let him take his time with the atmospheric entry. It didn't take long for his computer to ding with instructions that were waiting in system for his specific vessel. His name wasn't attached to it, and being in Pergamum there was little chance it would be noticed by civil authorities. Everyone knew that P2 was a haven for outlaws, and they just didn't care. Eventually someone would propose that P2 be recolonized. They would come with equipment to clean up the planet, recycling the materials left after the orbital bombing attacks, and laws to get rid of the riffraff. But that initiative had not even been discussed in committee yet, and P2 was still a dangerous world full of people who didn't want to be found.

It seemed a bit ironic to Morgan that he was going hunting for a man known for tracking down, catching, and bringing other men to justice. Morgan had done his homework. Travis Hurts had a reputation as a capable Fugitive Recovery Specialist and a skip tracer for hire. As an independent contractor, Travis Hurts often sought out the more dangerous elements wanted by law enforcement. FRS was better known as bounty hunting, and while that activity had a bad reputation, Travis Hurts was respected by most judicial agencies. He was fair to his prisoners, rarely bringing them in with injuries. He was also a reliable witness when called upon, showing up on time, and giving beneficial testimony to the prosecutors working to convict outlaws, although most of his targets had already been found guilty. The right of the accused to face their accusers was not a high priority for most outlaws. If the chance opened up before them, most would run. Morgan found that to be cowardly, and he even had a sense of respect for what Travis did bringing the cowards to justice. But it seemed a waste to Morgan, who preferred to kill rather than capture.

He ran a search for news on Kingsbury Three. It wasn't difficult to find the writeup about a con man found dead in his highrise luxury apartment. The police had discovered multiple identities for the victim, and evidence of several crimes. The story all but said the murderer had done the people of Kingsbury Three a favor. Morgan knew they wouldn't try to solve the crime with any real urgency. It was just another notch on his Widow Maker's handle, and another deposit into his many accounts.

It was time to turn his attention away from his last kill, and onto the mark that awaited him on the planet below. The *Dymetr* was descending to a low orbit. The navigation computer had already selected a trajectory that would take him into the planet's atmosphere, and down to a landing in the right geographic area. Morgan enjoyed immersing himself in the environment where he would discover his quarry. It was necessary to keep from standing out too much, and avoiding the attention of the authorities on planets where law enforcement had a strong presence. But Morgan also liked to feel as though he were fully part of the environment. To him, a job was like a fine dining experience. One didn't rush in and gobble down a gourmet meal. The idea was to slow down, to excite the senses by what he could see and feel. He wanted to experience what life was really like on P2 before he snatched away the life of his target.

Pergamum Prime wasn't a planet with a lot to offer by way of sophistication. He had spent time in the tent cities before. It took a bit of adjusting to let down one's natural sense of privacy. There were things a person could do in P2 that couldn't be done anywhere else in the galaxy. Life was cheap. For a price, anything and everything was available. But one had to adjust to the fact that one's vices would be practiced in a tent, with nothing between you and the rest of the world but a flimsy sheet of canvas. For an intensely private person like Morgan, that was the biggest adjustment. He was a naturally solitary person, which was just one of the personality traits that made him a good assassin. Even on highly populated worlds he preferred to keep himself to himself, as the saying went.

The ship passed through the upper atmosphere with ease, then glided down to a landing just outside Vicksburg, a boom town near a large impact crater where a lode of Dust had recently been discovered. The tent city was a hundred miles north of the location where his contacts reported that Travis Hurts was currently plying his trade. Morgan had both respect and contempt for bounty hunters. They were brave or foolish, depending on one's point of view. Tracking down killers and attempting to return them to justice was a daunting task, and not for the weak willed. Travis Hurts had a reputation among that ilk of being fair. He didn't hide in the shadows and stun outlaws in the back. Morgan could respect that, but he also couldn't help but feel that bounty hunting was barely a step above slave trading. A bounty hunter trafficked in human lives, and that seemed an unsavory way to make a living. Perhaps Morgan's own chosen profession was only slightly better, but in his mind, death was better than slavery, be it servitude or penal sentencing, they were the same in his mind.

Perhaps, he pondered as he changed out of his customary black clothing into something that would draw less attention, he would one day face the ultimate test of his convictions. He was an outlaw, and a notorious one at that. If he were caught and brought to justice, would he choose death over enslavement? He honestly couldn't say. In his mind he always imagined himself dying with his boots on and his pistol in hand, not bested but at the very least going down in a blaze of glory. They didn't tell stories of insurance salesmen who died of old age in hospice care. No, they told stories about people who lived adventurously and died dramatically.

As he dressed, Morgan thought about the stories that sometimes ended with bold adventurers who met their end in an unsavory fashion. There was nothing worse in his mind than a gunslinger who was shot in the back by a coward unwilling to put their abilities to the test. Or the foolish rogue who got drunk and had his throat cut in a dark alley when he was too compromised to defend himself. Morgan took certain precautions against such a fate. He had a varied wardrobe, each garment carefully designed to allow him to fit in on almost any planet. For P2 that meant hardscrabble, well-worn clothing, not threadbare, but not new and not neat. He pulled on a pair of workman's pants that appeared to be made of similar material to the tents that were so popular on the planet. His shirt would be a loose-fitting button up with a leather vest. All his clothing, and his variety of hats, while looking normal, had filaments within the woven fabric that were meant to weaken a laser blast. It wouldn't deflect a laser, but it might save his life if someone shot him in the back.

He added a cap to his head, and a desert scarf which he tied around his neck. Looking at himself in the mirror he realized how plain he appeared. Cosmetic surgery had hidden most of the scars that covered his face. No hair grew on his chin or cheeks. His teeth were fake. The reconstructive surgeries on his tongue and lips, along with speech therapy, had allowed him to communicate without anyone knowing about the horrors he had lived through. He was just another miner or treasure hunter once he walked off his ship. The only sign of his true identity was the long-barreled Widow Maker pistol, which he carried in a low hanging holster on his right side. It had the benefit of being deadly, without looking like a shootist's quick draw weapon. The fact that Morgan could draw the large pistol and gun down anyone who got in his way was a secret that he guarded closely, even sometimes feigning clumsiness with the weapon when he was in disguise.

Certain that he looked the part, he put a roll of gold coins in one pocket, a fold of paper money in the other, and set the security systems on the *Dymetr* before setting foot on P2. Armed with money, a sure disguise, and his reliable firearm, Morgan began another adventure in the life of a paid killer.

# 15

Travis spent most of the ride back to Camp Sherman thinking about Ava Lynn Baxter. Yes, there was something about the woman that he admired, but he was more focused on her plight. He wondered what it must be like to feel that she was trapped on a world with no hope of escape, and no prospects for safety or prosperity. The best a woman in her condition, meaning a widow with a child on the way, could hope for was to blend in. Had she simply been a widow she might have had more options. There were plenty of hardworking, decent men on P2 who could have married her, and provided some kind of life for her. Not that a woman needed a man to have security or prosperity, but without the protection of law and order, a woman on her own was extremely vulnerable on a planet where desperate men had no incentives to resist their base urges. Yet a woman clearly with child made her less desirable to many men. Taking on a wife who could cook, clean, and provide a certain amount of comfort to a man's life was one thing. But taking on the responsibilities of fatherhood was a much heavier burden, and one without a return on the investment for at least a decade.

His thoughts about Ava were also related to his focus on his next fugitive, Sandra Mayfield. Like most criminals she had a pattern, or modus operandi, that she followed. On the three civilized worlds she had lived on, she took a wealthy husband and slowly poisoned him. As her unsuspecting spouse grew sick, becoming weaker and less astute, she would steal his money, which she used to reinvent herself on a new world, all the while living in a luxurious style that her ill-gotten gains afforded her. After three murders on three different planets her secret was out, which forced her to disappear, at least for a while. P2 was the perfect place for such a disappearing act. It wasn't luxurious, but it was a lawless world where no one would care that she had poisoned at least three innocent people and stolen their money in the process. That money should have gone to children, or charities, but instead it was moved from one account to another through a variety of banks and financial institutions, until it was safely hoarded where only Sandra Mayfield could find it. Returning her to the authorities to answer for her crimes wouldn't repay those she had robbed, but it would keep her from robbing and killing anyone else. And her victims could take solace knowing that she would spend the rest of her life on a penal colony, the likes of which they would prefer not to contemplate.

A woman alone, who had developed a routine of visiting the cafe in Camp Sherman on an almost daily basis, would stand out among the desperate, hard-worked locals. She couldn't hope to blend in and disappear the way that Ava Lynn had tried to do. Perhaps both were avoiding the unwanted attention of the local men, but Sandra Mayfield wouldn't be able to hide from Travis. That begged the question of whether he would find her desperate or deadly. He couldn't help but believe she was probably the latter, with ways to protect herself that might not be visible at first glance.

He reached the camp an hour before dawn. It was quiet. Macy and Tuck ate some oats from feed bags outside of Tubby's corral, and drank water. The old man was passed out inside the little tent, and snoring so loudly that there was no doubt he was asleep. People in the camp were already up, preparing for a day of work. The saloons were dark and quiet, the brothels too, but the trade posts, the general store, and the cafe were busy. Just as the sun began to turn the horizon a beautiful shade of red, a woman on horseback rode into town. She went straight to the cafe. Travis was watching and led his own horses behind her, eventually tying Macy to the same light pole as the sleek, black animal the woman had been riding.

They weren't the only people stopping in the cafe. Biscuits were sold with thin sliced meat, probably left over from the night before. Men dropped in, purchased half a dozen biscuits and left out on their return journey to their mines, or the tunnels leading deep into the mounds of debris that had once been the booming metropolis of Keystone. Travis imagined the meal, probably stretched out over the day, as the last remnants of the hard-working locals' wild times in the city. A mouthful of memories, he imagined sadly. It seemed a poor way to live one's life.

He stepped to the side of the tent, patiently waiting his turn to place an order. A bleary-eyed teenager was in the back opening hot biscuits and inserting the mystery meat. For those not taking food to go, there was gravy, thick and creamy, but probably from a powder. Still, it went well over the dry biscuits and chewy meat. The woman was eating slowly in the corner, her hair wrapped in a long scarf. She was older than Travis expected, and didn't look up from her food often. He tried to study her from a distance out of the corner of his eye, while he ate.

When the initial rush died down, the teenager delivered a sack of biscuits to the woman. She looked up at him and flashed a dazzling smile. Travis had to admit that she was attractive, although he guessed her to be in her late forties, and he saw that she wasn't wearing any sort of cosmetics or facial augmentation. There was also no doubt that she was Sandra Mayfield. The teen glanced his way, then leaned down and whispered something in the woman's ear.

If she hadn't clocked his presence by that point he would have been surprised, but she certainly knew who he was and what he wanted after the surly teen told her. The boy was looking for an escape to the hard work his parents expected of him. And it was a shame that it seemed like he was willing do anything to get free. After finishing her meal, Sandra Mayfield stood up. She wore a dark dress, and moved across the cafe so smoothly it seemed more like she was gliding than walking.

"Is this seat taken?" she asked, indicating the bench across from where Travis sat.

"Be my guest," he said without standing up.

"Thank you," she said, sitting with her legs outside the table, and twisting her upper body so that she leaned on one elbow. Travis made sure he could see both of her hands. "I know why you are here."

"Is that a fact?"

She nodded. Every move she made was graceful, as if she were performing a dance rather than confronting a Fugitive Recovery Specialist.

"You want me," she said with an alluring smile.

"I think you're mistaken," Travis said, his food forgotten.

"Oh, come now, you misunderstand me, sir. You're here to arrest me, are you not?"

"Why would I do that?" Travis asked.

"For the reward money, I should think. My late husband

Arnold's son didn't care for me. He was a spoiled, self-important, brat, but he had connections in government. He was never slow to remind me of that fact. I can only wonder how he is getting along without daddy's fortune."

"Fascinating story Miss," Travis said.

"Oh, please," she said suddenly, "do I look like a grieving widow? Call me Sandra."

Travis smiled. He couldn't help but be amused by the woman. She had charm, and a disarming smile. But Travis knew what she was truly capable of. He also guessed that somewhere in the folds of her fancy dress was more than one weapon.

"I guess word travels fast," Travis said. "I apprehended a couple of miscreants yesterday, but that was more their doing than mine. They made the mistake of trying to shake me down."

"I can't imagine anyone underestimating you."

"It happens," Travis said. "More often than you might think."

"So, you aren't after me?"

Travis shook his head. Across the tent the teenager, back to making biscuits, watched them with undisguised jealousy.

"And if I got up and walked out of here, you wouldn't shoot me in the back?"

"That would be a crime," he told her.

"There's no law on P2, present company excluded."

"I'm not a back shooter, Sandra. My name is Travis Hurts, and if I come for you, you'll see me."

"A man of honor," she said, smiling again.

Travis didn't deny the tingles he felt at her smile. He wasn't sure if it was attraction or fear. Some women simply had a way of being irresistible. Travis wouldn't say that Sandra was still a Siren, but to an unsuspecting man looking down the barrel of sixty years of age, she might seem like an angel sent from heaven.

She stood up and smoothed her dress.

"I'll be seeing you around, Travis Hurts," she said.

"I look forward to it," he told her.

She walked out of the tent. Travis saw the look of surprise on the teenager's face in the back of the cafe tent. It only took her a moment to retrieve her horse and ride away. The hooves clip-clopping at a steady trot that Travis guessed was faster than she normally rode.

"You just let her leave?"

Travis looked up and saw the teenager standing in front of him.

"Sure," he replied calmly, pushing his half-eaten breakfast away and standing up.

"But why? You had her dead to rights?"

"Why'd you tell her who I was?"

The teen's face turned red, and he stammered. "I ... I didn't."

"Okay," Travis said calmly.

"She'll get away."

"I hope so," Travis said.

"I don't understand," the boy said.

"I don't expect you to. But that's okay. I know what I'm doing, kid."

Travis sighed and walked out of the cafe. It was turning out to be a beautiful day on P2. Travis wondered what other surprises lay in store for him on a such a fine morning.

# 16

Travis didn't check his saddle for the tracking device. It was the only logical place for it. He didn't have saddle bags, or a bedroll tied up neat behind the saddle. Tuck, the mule, had no gear other than the bridle and the two coils of rope. Travis spent the morning talking to the various shop keepers, showing them the mug shots of the wanted outlaws he was hoping to find. Most weren't interested in helping. He even paid two sporting women for their time and information, but the only other person on the list of outlaws with rewards for their capture that any had seen was Walt Zineman, a thief who had passed through Camp Sherman a month prior. The second woman that Travis questioned, a woman calling herself Red Ember, remembered that Zineman had talked about moving north.

"There's a boom camp north of here," she said. "More people, more money."

"Why don't you go there?" Travis asked her.

They were outside the Silver Lode Saloon and Gentlemen's Club. It was smoke-stained tent that looked like it had once been part of a circus. Red Ember wore a bright red, tight fitting party dress that looked like it had seen better days. She was sitting outside the tent washing clothes in a tub of brown water, and looked up frequently as if she feared the proprietor of the saloon might see her talking to him.

"You think I can just up and leave?" she said quietly. "We ain't got no choices. If I was to leave, Bruno would hunt me down and leave me bleeding somewhere."

"I'm sorry to hear it."

"Yeah, not as sorry as I am that it's true. Besides, Vicksburg is like a hundred miles north. Can't get there without a transport. It would take you four or five days on horseback, if you weren't bushwhacked and killed along the way. I'll take my chances right here, thank you very much."

"You think Zineman was headed to Vicksburg?"

"He didn't share his plans with me," she pointed out. "That ain't the kind of company he was paying me for. But to my knowledge ain't nothing else up that way. It's colder too. But that's where the action is."

Travis fished a gold coin from his pocket. It was worth a lot more than the information he was getting from the woman, but he couldn't help but feel sorry for her.

"You got some place you can hang on to that?" he said, handing it to her. "Some place Bruno won't find it?"

"He won't," she said, slipping it into a little pocket on the side of her dress. "You want to come around back and—"

"No," he said with a smile. "I want you to use it to get off this crummy world when the chance comes along."

"That's pretty rare, Mister."

"But a woman with means, and an eye for it can find opportunities," Travis said. "We both know what happens to women who stay in your line of work too long."

Her eyes were suddenly brimming with tears. "Why would you ... Never mind."

Travis walked away, knowing that the odds were against her. If Bruno caught her holding out on him, he might kill her. And if she ran and he found her, he would certainly kill her. She was living a dangerous life, probably because she had no choice, but in his mind, it was better to die trying than simply give up.

Slavery, especially sex slaves, had been around long before P2, and it would always exist in the shady parts of cities and towns on every world where people were living. It was evil, and Travis knew it sprang from more than just perverted outlaws. It ran much deeper than that, and was more nefarious too. Travis had taken down outlaws who were no longer just people. He had seen prisoners break the chains that bound them, heard them curse the world and the God who made it. He had even seen some things that just couldn't be explained, like the case of Luka DePalma, a murderer, rapist, and cult leader on Caspian C. Travis had tracked the man down to a squalid building on the outskirts of Golden Hills. The outlaw was wanted for a dozen crimes, some he had committed, and others he had manipulated his followers into doing, before he took the money and ran. Travis knew all too well that most crimes boiled down to the money. People did terrible things for it, and despite all his talk of spirituality, DePalma was just another con artist, or so Travis had believed.

He found Luka DePalma squatting in the basement of an abandoned building. The fugitive spent days, maybe weeks scribbling on the walls and floor of that building. There were occult symbols and words that made no sense. When Travis found him, he was completely naked, filthy, his body covered with shallow cuts in strange patterns. His hair and beard were wild, and he was hunched over in the corner, mumbling to himself. Travis had started to simply stun the man and drag him out of the basement. It would have been the easiest way to get the fugitive into custody. But it wasn't Travis' way. Instead, he called out to the man, ordering him to surrender.

Luka DePalma stood up and screamed as if someone was tearing his guts out. It made the hair on the back of Travis' neck stand out, and he sometimes still heard that scream. It didn't seem human. Then the laugh turned into maniacal laughter that was somehow worse than the screams. His eyes glowed as he looked at Travis, which could have been a trick of the light, or some type of implants. There were even simple contact lenses that could glow, he had learned, but he didn't think that was what happened. Something else had control of Luka DePalma, something that wasn't human. The fugitive reached out for Travis, who was safely thirty feet away, and rushed toward him. When Travis fired at the man his shot missed because Luka DePalma disappeared.

Travis spent hours searching the basement. There was no trap door, no mirror or projection device. Even a stun beam traveled at the speed of light, and no one, no matter how fast, could dodge it, much less run out of a building in less time than it would take to blink. The basement had been like a cave, just a simple storage room. There wasn't even a drain in the floor, just concrete walls, floor, and roof. The one door in or out had been behind Travis. Stranger still, the trail for the fugitive went cold. Most civilized worlds, including Caspian C, had a myriad of ways they could identify people: facial recognition, DNA scanning, gait tracking, voice recognition, the list went on and on. What happened to Luka DePalma simply made no sense, and could not in any way be explained without involving the supernatural. And whatever was in Luka was not something good. It was evil.

After getting what information he could, Travis mounted up and headed out of town. Camp Sherman was no longer a productive place to be. And he knew it wouldn't be long until

Sandra Mayfield caught up to him. The odds were good that she wouldn't be alone. He was fine with that, and stayed alert despite the fatigue that was clinging to him by that point, threatening to pull him down into an exhausted stupor that could get him killed. He kept a bottle of smelling salts in his coat pocket. He pulled it out, unfastened the cap, and breathed in the ammonia.

The smell was a bit like breathing fire. His entire body reacted, his head turning, his arm extending to get away from the fumes. But his breathing sped up, and his eyes opened a little wider. The fatigue fell away and his mind sharpened. He cleared his mouth and spit, as his sinuses began to drain. He found a boulder nearly as big as Tuck the mule. He stopped there, got off his horse, and paced for a bit, waiting.

He wasn't disappointed. In the wide-open landscape Sandra Mayfield couldn't get the jump on him. Maybe if she had ridden far ahead and found a good ambush point, but she hadn't known where he was going or where he might stop. So, she followed, and she wasn't alone.

"This should be interesting," Travis said as he leaned against the boulder and watched the murderess approaching.

She wasn't alone, and Travis hadn't expected her to be. Sandra Mayfield had long ago learned to turn her appeal to men into an unhealthy dynamic. The pattern was nothing new. She was clearly a world class manipulator, and probably had no fewer than three people vying for her affections when she wasn't hiding out on P2. The man coming with her rode an old horse that looked as if it weren't used to having a rider on its back, while Sandra rode a young stallion that could have run laps around the older animal. And Travis guessed that the man with her was probably the same way, a pleaser willing to do anything to gain her affection, even kill.

Travis found the tracker just under the edge of his saddle's rear flare. It was a thin device, normally used for keeping up with small, personal items that people were prone to misplace. It was not a sophisticated device. Travis guessed that Sandra was off her game. A woman couldn't successfully poison three different men without being careful and knowing how to cover her tracks. He guessed that his appearance at the cafe had caught her off guard. Having a routine, even on a lawless world, was also careless. She had let herself slip into lazy habits, and he guessed that she would be looking to clean up her act, starting with him.

He brought the little device to the boulder. He wanted to make sure when the shooting started that no errant shots hurt the animals. As the couple approached, Travis' keen eyes took the measure of the man with her. He was about her age, balding, with a round belly and hunched shoulders. Maybe it was the horse, but the man just didn't look comfortable riding. He was, however, wearing a holster with what appeared to be a Settler 1880 laser pistol, the bulky home defense model. They were common enough, but rarely used by shootists for speed draws, or by criminals, who liked a little more style in their weapons. He wore the pistol right on his belt, high on his hips, the bottom flapping a little as he rode.

"Fancy meeting you again," Sandra called out when they were close enough to be heard. "We were just out for a ride."

"Who's your friend?" Travis asked.

"Blake," the man said, his voice high and soft. "My name is Blake Evans."

"Mind if we join you, Mister Hurts?" Sandra asked.

"I'd be offended if you didn't," he told her, holding up the tracking device. "I mean, you did slap this onto my saddle after all."

"What?" Sandra asked. "I have no idea what you're talking about."

He had to hand it to her. She wasn't just committed to her

lie; she was completely convincing. Travis had known his fair share of deceptive people, but few had the personal charisma to really sell their version of reality. Sandra was in a league of her own.

"I told Blake we should take a ride. It's such a beautiful day. Do you know what I love about this planet, Mr. Hurts? It's never as hot as it seems. I find the temperatures to be pleasant, don't you, Blake?"

"Yes, I do," he replied, eager to please.

Travis thought Sandra could have asked if he liked eating dog food and he would have agreed if there was a chance of making her happy. She was conniving, but some men were easier targets than others. Blake obviously was a lonely man who didn't have a lot of self-confidence. Life could be cruel to people like that, and Sandra Mayfield was an expert at turning their weaknesses against them. He was infatuated with her, and she was probably just flirtatious enough to keep him close, believing he actually had a chance for a love affair with the beautiful woman. Of course, she would never consummate his desires. That was reserved for the wealthy men she targeted for their money, and besides, if she gave him too much of herself, he might gain enough self-confidence to see through her manipulation.

"Why don't you step down from your horse, Blake?" Sandra said. "Stretch your legs a little."

"I think I will," he said, as if the idea had been his own.

"Perhaps officer Hurts needs a hand," Sandra said.

"I'm fine, thank you," Travis said.

"Oh, don't be so modest, sir. You put your life on the line to protect us. Thank you for your service."

Travis was not a flashy man. He simply pulled the edge of his duster back and hooked it behind the holster on his right hip, then put his hand on the pistol's grip.

"Mr. Evans, I have no quarrel with you," Travis said. "But I will be taking Miss Mayfield in for the murder of her husbands."

"Wait, what?" Blake Evans asked.

"Now, Blake!" Sandra cried out.

It was all a diversion and Travis was no fool. He pushed himself away from the boulder as Blake fumbled for his pistol. But it wasn't the potbellied, balding man who was a threat. A small laser pistol appeared in Sandra's hand. She expected that Travis would be concerned with stopping Blake, and in doing so give her time to shoot him down. The woman had little if any concern for her companion. She was using him for whatever he could provide, and if he was gunned down, she would simply take whatever she wanted from his meager possessions and move on to someone else.

But Travis knew that Blake was no gun hand. He might eventually get around to pointing his bulky pistol in the right direction, but not before Travis shot Sandra. He pulled his Slinger and fired just a hair after she did. But Sandra Mayfield was not a good shot. She preferred poison, the better to manipulate her victims and draw out the exquisite agony of their demise. Evil came in many forms, and with Sandra Mayfield while the package was pleasing to look at, the insides were just as cold, dark, and wicked as they came. She missed, her shot going wide. Travis hit her in the shoulder. While her laser had almost certainly been a high-power beam meant to kill, his Slinger was dialed to stun. She was knocked backward off her horse and fell into a pile, as the spirited animal trotted forward toward the boulder where Travis' animals lingered.

"No!" Blake cried out.

He lifted his pistol in a shaking hand. Shooting him was the only option that Travis had, yet he felt a twinge of regret as he pulled the trigger. The beam hit Blake in the stomach, folding him in half as it drove him backward. His horse didn't move as he collapsed by its feet.

Looking around, Travis was a little surprised. The attack had been predictable and it ended quickly. His emotions didn't know that, though, and he had to walk off the feeling that he was missing something. Could there be a sniper out in the distance somewhere, training his scope on him at that very moment? His instincts told him to be wary, but there was no elevated hill to shoot from. And Travis had only seen two horses, which had been visible from a long way out. Blake's poor mount certainly wasn't carrying two men. And Travis doubted that Sandra would let anyone close enough to ride behind her. They would have to wrap at least one arm around her, and she didn't strike him as the kind of person who was willing to let someone take hold of her if she could help it.

He found her pistol. It was small, a one-shot blaster, the power cell spent. Weapons like that weren't very useful in Travis' opinion, but they were easy to hide and in close quarters did what they were designed to do. Sandra should have known better than to shoot at him with it until he was closer. With just enough power for one killing blast, the user couldn't afford to miss. He kicked the little blaster away from her and set about searching her for other weapons. She had several blades of various types tucked into the folds of her fancy dress, and even a sharp hair pin with a blade long enough to reach a man's heart through his ribs if necessary. He removed all the weapons and secured her hands behind her back. She didn't look as vivacious lying unconscious in the dirt. Instead, she looked weary and worn, still attractive, but her flaws were more visible. Travis saw the tiny suture scars from more than one face lift just inside her hairline. There had been neck work too, with skin tightening therapy, and rejuvenation treatments. It made him wonder just how old she really was.

Blake had no other weapons. He had a sturdy set of saddle bags, though. Travis scanned his DNA and retina just to make sure he wasn't wanted for any crimes. The man wasn't in the system. He might have left Blake in the shade of the boulder where he had left his horses, but the man might wake up desperate for revenge. It was better to bring him along, and prove to him that Sandra wasn't who she claimed to be. He could then take her horse and his own nag, and return to whatever life he had left.

Once more, Tuck proved to be of value. Travis slung Sandra and Blake across the mule's strong back, and secured them with a rope. With the other he made a lead line for the stallion and the older horse, then mounted up to finish his trip back to the *Purgatory*.

# 17

At the ship, Travis was met by Ava Lynn Baxter. She seemed relieved when he opened the rear compartment.

"You're back," she said.

"Yeah, I need some water for the horses."

"I can fetch that for you," she volunteered. "You have more prisoners?"

"One," he told her. "She's unconscious on Tuck."

Bill Teagan and Adam Turney were awake and watching from their cells. Both had plates of half-eaten food beside them. While Ava filled a bucket with water for the animals, Travis carried Sandra Mayfield into a cell. He put her in one closest to the engineering section. There was no doubt in his mind she would have the other prisoners eating out of the palm of her hand in no time at all. It was best, he figured, to keep them apart as long as possible.

"A woman outlaw?" Ava said, as if the idea that a woman could break the law was a novel concept to her.

"Indeed," Travis said. "She poisoned three different

husbands on various worlds that we know about. My guess is that's just the tip of the iceberg for her, but we'll probably never know. Lying is her native language. She'll try to con you into helping her escape if you're not careful."

"What's the reward for her?" Ava asked.

"Seventy-five thousand credits," Travis said.

"Don't worry, I won't listen to a thing she tells me," Ava assured him.

They left Blake outside in the shade of the ship. After Travis had untied him, he made sure that the poor man wouldn't be any worse for wear when he woke up. He was sick of course, and felt miserable. He was too weak to be a threat. Travis and Ava stayed with him while he came to after Travis waved his smelling salts under the bald man's nose.

"You shot me," Blake complained.

"You were planning to shoot me," Travis told him.

"Yeah, I was," he grumbled. "You're too damn fast."

"Have to be in my line of work," Travis said. "Blake, this is Miss Ava Lynn Baxter."

"Knew your husband," Blake said as he slowly sat up. "Shame what happened to him."

"Thank you," Ava said.

"What now?" Blake asked. "You taking me to jail?"

"Nah," Travis said. "I think you've suffered enough. Besides, there's no money in it."

"I've got money," Blake said. "Nearly five hundred in gold, and some Dust too. You can have it, every bit, if you'll just ..."

He didn't finish as Travis shook his head.

"The reward for Sandra is seventy-five thousand credits," Travis said. "And my guess is your money isn't where you think it is. She's a thief."

"No, she's a wonderful person," Blake argued. "She's just down on her luck's all."

Travis pulled out his data slate and brought up Sandra Mayfield's arrest records. She had been picked up a few times for theft. In each case she either talked her way out of jail time, or fled the jurisdiction. There were multiple warrants for her arrest on nearly a dozen worlds. But she was wanted for murder in three, and she was known to have at least eight aliases.

"This might change your mind," Travis said, handing over the slate.

Tears filled Blake's eyes as he read it. Ava left him and went to check on Sandra in the ship. Travis knew she couldn't stand to see the man weeping. It was a sad sight as the truth became undeniable. He had to face the fact that she didn't love him. He had convinced himself she did, that all the things he had come to believe about himself weren't true. And it was a difficult discovery to make. Nor did the prospect of returning to his solitary life seem like any sort of consolation.

"Might have known," he said, swiping at his nose and handing the slate back to Travis.

"She's a master at manipulating people," Travis said. "The best thing you can do is put her behind you. There's no shame in caring about someone, Blake. It's not your fault she wasn't worth your affection."

"It's gonna be difficult going back home now," he said.

"I put your pistol and hers in the saddle bag of your horse," Travis told him. "It might not be easy, but you should take the horses the two of you came on and go back home. Search her things and I'm guessing you'll find what's left of your savings."

"All right," he said. "You think maybe I could say goodbye to her?"

"She's still unconscious," Travis said.

"You didn't hurt her?"

"She'll be sore, but she's still alive and well. I don't mistreat my prisoners. But even if she was awake, Blake, I wouldn't let you see her. She doesn't just poison the body; she'll poison your mind too."

Blake nodded, got to his feet and shuffled away. He didn't bother trying to ride his horse. The old animal seemed to feel his pain. She neighed and walked close behind him. The stallion's reins were tied to the older horse's saddle. It followed, almost prancing as it went, oblivious to the fact its master was a killer.

"Sad," Ava said, as she watched Blake leave on the ship's cameras.

"At least he has a chance to get over it," Travis said. "Most of her victims don't live long enough."

"So what now?" she asked. "There's three more empty cells."

"We go north," Travis said.

"Vicksburg?" Ava asked with trepidation in her voice.

"That's right. What have you heard about it?"

"There's a Dust boom up there," she said. "Fortunes are being made. But ..."

"But what?" he pressed her.

"There's a version of news you hear on the street," she explained. "And a version you hear from the women who come around the camp from other places. Vicksburg is a bad place, Travis. It's run by the Volinski Syndicate. They're terribly cruel by reputation, and violent. Nothing is beneath them. I've heard they traffic children. It's all just rumors I suppose, but the looks on the faces of the people who came from there were awful, just awful."

"Bad men are who I came here for, Ava. That's how I make a living."

"You won't be able to just stroll into Vicksburg and start taking prisoners," she warned him. "It's not like Camp Sherman. The Volinski people hate the law, and despise anyone associated with it."

"They sound like cheerful folk."

"It's not a joke," she said solemnly. "If you're going up there, you better teach me to fly this ship first. I don't expect you'll make it back."

"I might surprise you."

"I don't like surprises," she said, and there was weight in her words. "Not anymore."

"All right," he said, softening a little in response to what he knew was real grief in her voice. "But I have to go up there, Ava. It won't be the first rough camp I've been in. I know how to take care of myself. Still, if you're really interested, I'll set up the flight training simulator for you. The autopilot does most of the work, but it won't hurt for you to learn."

She was eager to do anything that might move them along. Travis thought she might complain when he brought Macy and Tuck into the cargo hold and secured them between the cages so they could make the flight north. They waited until sundown, with Travis napping in the lounge chair after taking a long shower.

When night fell, they lifted off. The ship might not have looked sleek and powerful, but she rose up smoothly, and made the eighty-mile trip north in under half an hour. Once more Travis put the ship down in the open, although the terrain had changed slightly. Instead of arid, desert landscape, they found several wide fields covered with coarse grass. It was just the beginning of the planet's recovery, and only the hardiest flora was growing naturally. Still, they landed, and put the animals out. Travis hobbled the horse and mule, but put them on a long rope tied to the back of the shuttle, and allowed them to graze on the native grass.

"You have a plan, don't you?" Ava asked, as they shared dinner together. It was just frozen fare, individually packaged meals, but the living quarters had a little table with two chairs. And Travis thought it was nice to have someone to talk to.

"I'll go in tomorrow," he said. "Just hang around, get the lay of the land. See if I can identify the outlaws I'm looking for."

"And if you can?"

"I'll mark 'em, watch for a day or two and get a read on their habits."

"Still, if you start arresting people the Syndicate could turn on you."

"True," he said. "Normally, I just go after one fugitive at a time. The *Purgatory* allows me to do more in less time."

"But that isn't really safe," she pointed out.

"True, but they don't give ships away," he said with a chuckle. "Fuel, provisions, it all costs money. I need to make the most of this trip, and that means filling all the cells."

"You could take one outlaw, and then we could go somewhere else," she pointed out.

"We'll see," he told her. "It really depends on what I find in town."

She didn't come across as a nervous person, but he could tell she was frightened. And who could blame her? She might not care about him, but he was her way off P2, her only way. Travis knew she had let herself believe it was possible. She had thought about it, about the possibility of getting back to a civilized place, of raising her baby on a world where she had options and the child would have a future. On P2 the only future was a dangerous search for treasure, or joining an organized crime outfit. Neither option was safe, or respectable. Travis didn't know it, but she still had her husband's blueprint for making the Dustincia ore-separating machine. It wouldn't be as valuable as it might have been, but she still hoped that she could find a way to sell it. Perhaps even get enough credits for her child, their baby, to get an education. She could work, she didn't mind it. On a civilized world she could earn enough to get a little place for the two of them, especially if Travis made good on his promise of sharing the bounties with her. But all that really mattered was getting off P2. And she needed to make sure it happened whether Travis came back or not.

The night passed quickly. The compartments on the ship were all soundproof. They didn't hear Bill Teagan and Adam Turney shouting and acting foolish in their cells. They kept the security system active, and used the ship's cameras to keep tabs on their prisoners and the surrounding countryside. They were still six miles from Vicksburg, which was set up near what had once been a small community called Shepherd. It had sprung up as a flight-testing site, first with just enough housing for the workers of Aerotech Unlimited, but growing as a few more businesses in complementary fields built offices there. When the Hash Gore invaded, the airfield was converted to a military base, and had been overrun by aliens. Eventually, the site was hit with a high yield nuclear warhead that vaporized the town and left a massive crater.

At dawn Travis was up. He brushed down Macy and Tuck, gave them some oats to supplement the tough grass they were munching on, and watered them both. The animals had fouled the cargo area the day before, and Ava used a power washer to flush it out, along with the vomit where Sandra Mayfield had been sick upon waking after being stunned.

It didn't take long for the cargo hold to air out, and by noon Travis had the ship locked up with his prisoners on board, and Ava watching over everything. He had switched her user authorization to secondary. It gave her flight controls. She couldn't add users, or change the security settings, but she could fly the ship away. It was a risk he was willing to take after spending some time with her. Maybe he was just as much of a fool as Blake Evans, but he didn't think that Ava Lynn Baxter was the duplicitous type. She was smart, but not manipulative. In his opinion, a strong worth ethic said a lot about a person. Ava didn't shirk her tasks or try to get Travis to do them. She didn't have to be told what to do either. She saw to the prisoners, and even cleaned up after Travis in the ship's living quarters, all of her own initiative. When he rode out, she was busy working her way through the training simulation. Still, he had put an active tracker inside the ship, and one on the outside, just in case she took off before he came back.

Vicksburg was another tent city, only much larger than Camp Sherman. There was actually a group of aircraft parked at one end, and many of the residents rode motorized vehicles, from ATVs to hoverbikes and open cab skiffs. There were rows of shelters made from prefab materials, and even a working industrial 3D printer. But most of the structures were tents, some big, others small. Most were shabby, but a few had tassels and embroidering. There was an open-air kitchen, with only a tarp stretched tight over the cooking pits and sitting area.

Travis rode in on his horse, Macy, feeling a bit like a rube. Not that he was the only rider, but a large painted sign at the edge of town said: **Horses and Livestock not allowed beyond this point.** There was a corral nearby for mounts. Travis paid the five credits to keep his horse inside the corral, but not the extra cash for care. He took Macy's saddle off himself, and made sure that she had a serving of oats and fresh water before he left her with the corral keeper, who was only fourteen or fifteen years old.

Making his way down the main street, Travis took in the feel of the place. There were all the usual types of businesses, most catering to vice, but there was also a gunsmith and a pawn shop. The Volinski Syndicate kept their Dust Exchange in a low-roofed, prefabricated building with an overhead garage-style door. The members of the gang wore easily recognizable old style pilot coats that looked to be made from real leather and had shearing-lined interior. They kept their collars flipped up, and most carried Lancer style laser pistols in holsters with silver stitching.

"They don't care much for subtlety, I suppose," a man in workman's clothes said. They were outside the beer garden, which was really just a booth for the server and an awning to shade the customers. Not that it was really needed. Although Vicksburg was only a hundred miles north of Camp Sherman, the temperature was much cooler, with a constant breeze.

"The jackets or the holsters?" Travis asked, his own weapons masked by his long coat.

"Both," the workman said with a smirk. Travis could just make out the ghostly lines of scars around the man's mouth, nose, and chin. "They look like they walked right out of a musical. I suppose it keeps 'em from shootin' each other."

"They must be gunslingers with those fancy rigs," Travis pointed out.

"I wouldn't know 'bout that. I try to avoid gun fights whenever possible. My name's Robert Rawlings, but everybody calls me Rooster."

"Travis. It's nice to meet you."

"You minin' Dust?"

"Thinking about it," Travis said. "I heard the action up here is pretty good."

"Lots of small claims," Rooster said. "But everyone is makin' money. Not as much as the Syndicate, but that's life. Am I right?"

"As I know it," Travis said, nodding before taking another sip of his beer.

"My advice friend? Keep your money tight and find another occupation."

"I thought you said everyone was making money?"

"Making it and keeping it are two very different things," Rooster said, before turning up his mug and finishing his beer.

One of the more popular establishments was a bathhouse, and for the successful miner there was a haberdashery, boot maker, and several tailors all plying their trade in Vicksburg. But the main street was reserved for entertainment. There was a dance hall, and a theater with dancing girls. Unlike Camp Sherman, there was a doctor, although Travis could tell the official looking license that hung on a converted coat rack just outside the sawbones's tent was a fake. A very good fake, but Travis had an eye for such things. One of the words in the fancy script was misspelled, not that many people would take the time to read it word for word, or notice that *establishes* wasn't spelled "estabelishes." Still, he thought a fake doctor was better than no doctor. And from the size of the solar panels outside the tent, Travis guessed that the physician probably had a medical scanner that did most of the work diagnosing and prescribing treatments. All the so-called doctors had to do was read what the medical device told him.

After loitering at the beer garden with Rooster and people watching through most of the afternoon, Travis marked his first fugitive. It was a man accused of robbery and vehicular homicide, although the death had come during the thief's escape when he had crashed a hover car into another vehicle, causing the death of the elderly occupant who happened to be a very wealthy man. His family had put up a one hundred thousand credit reward for Johan Liester to anyone who could bring him in for trial.

As the day wound down, the excitement in Vicksburg rose to a new level. There were street performers doing everything from juggling sharp knives to breathing fire. In one tent there was an old-fashioned Freak Show, and in another a group of actors put on short plays. But the real draw to Vicksburg was bare-knuckle brawling, and the Volinski Syndicate was making big money every night taking bets from the spectators.

Travis paid the ten-credit cover charge for the right to sit on the wooden bleachers erected around the fighting pit, although there were plenty of people crowding the gaps between the seats in hopes of seeing some of the action. An entire stable of fighters was in the little town, each one wearing tight shorts and a leather belt, but nothing else, including a handful of women fighters. They were all scarred and carried fresh bruises from their frequent bouts. They fought until one opponent was unconscious or couldn't continue.

"Isn't it great?" a man with wild hair and a stained miner's coverall shouted in Travis' direction between fights.

"Yeah," Travis said, trying to match the man's intensity.

"Sometimes they even fight to the death," the wild man crowed. "It's the best."

Travis disagreed, but he wasn't there to stand out, or make trouble. In his mind the fighting was barbaric. Not that he had an issue with combat sports, or even the occasional fistfight. But the fighters were obviously slaves who were forced to fight nightly, sometimes multiple times in one evening. And it wasn't a regulated boxing match, just two human beings trying to kill each other. Travis could only imagine what happened to people who lost too often, and he didn't think it would *the best!* Especially not for the loser.

He did however mark another wanted fugitive at the bare-knuckle brawl, a man wanted for kidnapping named Garcia Sanchez. He had thick black hair tied back in a ponytail, and a bushy mustache that hung down on either side of his mouth in an odd drooping fashion. His unusual looks would make him easy to find. The bounty on him was a cool one hundred thousand credits, and Travis hoped he would be easy to apprehend.

The plan was to identify where the men he wanted slept off their nightly rounds of hedonistic entertainment. Then, he could swoop in while the town was quiet, grab up the three most valuable fugitives, and get out of town. It didn't seem like it would be much of a stretch, especially as the night wore on. After the pit fighting wrapped up, the citizens and guests of Vicksburg began drinking in earnest. There were nearly a dozen brewers and distillers plying their trade in the town. No less than fourteen saloons lined the main streets. Travis found a seat at a low stakes card game in a tent saloon called the Fireside. It had a stone fireplace right in the center, and kept wood from somewhere near the shanty town burning late into the night. As the night grew colder, the drinkers and revelers stayed close to the fire, leaving Travis to sit with his back to the wall of the tent where he could watch the people coming and going.

There were plenty of women in Vicksburg, and not just prostitutes and dancing girls. Travis saw several come into the saloon and order drinks, which they consumed near the fire. Some wore mining coveralls, others had on workman's pants and coats. They were all armed, just like the men, mostly laser pistols slung low for a quick draw. And there were several shootouts that evening. One of the reasons most towns had a long, straight street was to make room for dueling shootists. It was no secret that gunslingers had big egos. To be able to draw faster than your opponent and hit what you were shooting at was not a skill everyone possessed. Added to that was the fear and nerve-jangling risk of dying in the process of a showdown. It made many people's hands shake, which only added to the degree of difficulty it took to shoot another human being down. But to run, or try and dodge the laser fire being aimed your way, meant that you were a coward. You might survive the shootout, but you would never outlive the black mark on your reputation.

Travis found a third wanted man sometime after midnight when he came ambling into the Fireside saloon. Travis was up nearly fifty credits in his game, despite the fact that the pots were small and he was hardly paying attention to his own cards.

Augustine Ward was hard to miss. The man wore a tight-fitting shirt with pearly buttons. His pants were tight too, the better to show off his two fancy pistols, each in their own gun belt. They were Tremont Strikers, laser pistols made for quick draw shootouts. They were shaped like ancient revolvers from long, long ago. Each was made of highly polished steel, with a bone handle that had little gemstones embedded. They weren't stun guns. The Strikes had only one setting, full power, and took a specially shaped power cell that was made exclusively for the fancy weapons. They could each fire four shots, and had a special grip pressure safety feature, which also made them a favorite for twirling, since they wouldn't accidentally go off without being held in the proper manner.

Travis was drinking what appeared to be whiskey and cola, but was really just cola without the spirits. A tall woman with thick makeup who wore a stretchy bodysuit served the drinks. He had slipped her a fifty credit note to bring him cola but call it a Lemmy. She gladly obliged, clearly thinking he wanted a clear head for the card game, but Travis was more interested in Augustine Ward. The gunslinger had a big reputation, but was wanted alive on Tusk Minor, a small moon in the Mammoth system, where he apparently ran out on a large loan issued by the state-owned bank. The government in Mammoth was known for crushing penalties, and Augustine obviously had no desire to face what would surely be life-long servitude for his debt.

It didn't take long for Augustine, who was downing shots of whiskey, to start twirling his pistols. When he was bumped by a frustrated gambler trying to get closer to the fire, the result was inevitable. Travis knew that men like Augustine Ward were always on the lookout for targets that would allow them to grow their reputation without taking on much risk. The man who bumped him was clearly a miner, and carried a heavy military pistol in a holster with a cover flap.

"Watch where the hell you're going!" Ward snarled at the man.

The miner turned. "You talking to me?"

"Yeah, I'm talking to you, you clumsy oaf."

"I'm sorry, mister."

"Sorry don't cut it round here, you stupid bastard."

"Whatever," the miner said.

Augustine shoved the man from behind. He stumbled and nearly fell headlong into the fire. When he whirled around, he found Ward with his pistol out and pointed at the miner's head.

"Do I have your attention now?"

"You're a damn coward shoving me in the back," the miner snapped.

He was too angry to realize the trap he was walking into. And Travis got to his feet.

"Hey, mister, you ain't leaving, are you?" one of the other players said. "We want a chance to win some of our money back."

"No," Travis said. "I ain't leaving."

In the center of saloon people had pulled back, everyone on their feet, watching the confrontation.

"Did you just call me a coward?" Augustine Ward asked, knowing full well what the miner had said.

"You're damn right I did. Put your dirty hands on me and I'll crack your nose, you skinny bastard."

"Oh no, you'll meet me in the street, you oaf. I'll show you who's a coward. I'll show everyone and having you pissing your pant leg."

He twirled his pistol and dropped it back into the quick-draw holster he wore on his right side. The miner looked at Augustine, then at the crowd.

Someone shouted, "You gonna take that from him, Lonzo?"

"Show him what a miner can do!" someone else urged.

Travis felt sorry for the man. He had just accused Augustine of being a coward and he didn't want to seem like one himself. But the offense wasn't so great that he wanted to kill Augustine either, and it only took one look to see the man was a gunslinger. It wasn't the kind of fight the miner was looking for.

"Well?" Augustine asked. "You comin', or are you too scared?"

The gunman had already won. If the miner walked away Augustine would crow about how intimidating he was. And if the man met him in the street, it would be Ward's chance to really show off his skills. It was madness, nothing short of murder dressed up as a shootout. Augustine could argue, if P2 was a civilized world, then the miner had accosted him in the saloon, and of course he drew first. Augustine Ward would be declared innocent, even though he was anything but.

Several people had their data slates out, filming the confrontation. Travis wanted to intervene. He could save the miner and take Augustine Ward prisoner, supposing he was fast enough to win the duel. But that would also blow his cover. He wouldn't just be seen as a bounty hunter in Vicksburg, but the videos being recorded would almost certainly be uploaded and spread across various platforms online. His face would be known wherever he went, and that would make his work twice as difficult. The reward for Augustine Ward was a hundred and fifty thousand credits, more than all the rest of his prisoners combined, and yet Travis knew he couldn't risk it.

Fortunately, he didn't have to.

"Why don't you stand down," a familiar voice said.

Travis had to strain to see a plain looking man step up beside the miner. He wore workman's clothes, and a black and white desert scarf. Travis wasn't sure, but he thought it was the man called Rooster, the one with signs of scarring around his mouth.

"Why don't you mind your own business?" Ward snarled.

The hand that shot out and slapped Ward moved so fast Travis nearly missed it. Ward was still staring down the miner and never saw it coming. It was a backhand, fast and hard, but not powerful enough to knock Ward down. It stung and enraged the gunslinger.

"I'll kill you!" Ward screamed.

"You're welcome to try," Rooster said.

"You think you're faster than me with that long-barreled anchor on your hip? Let's go."

"After you," the newcomer said.

"Hey mister, you ain't got to do this," the miner warned him.

The man with the scars turned, and spoke to the miner, but his eyes were on Travis. "It's no trouble, my friend. No trouble at all."

# 18

The call had come in earlier that day. Morgan had spent two nights in Vicksburg already. He found the town delightfully wicked. The food was bad, the selection of spirits limited, but absolutely nothing was off limits. He had spent both nights in a private tent, and each night he had entertained a different woman. Each was paid not just to share his bed, but to stay on his arm as he toured the different establishments in the town.

Morgan didn't like to attract attention, but he did enjoy having the best that money could buy. He didn't look like a rich man, not in his bland, work clothes. But he spent over ten thousand credits to hire the most beautiful escorts in Vicksburg. They ate real meat from actual animals at a small private dining tent normally reserved for the shot-callers of the Volinski Syndicate. But they were only too happy to roll out the red carpet when Iona Frost showed up, lackeys in tow, and explained exactly who Morgan was.

He sat in a private box with the best view of the nightly fights. He drank the oldest, most refined spirits from the saloons he visited. And he enjoyed the press and shuffle of being among the miners, treasure hunters, gunmen, and gangsters.

Iona Frost was not so pleased with his laid-back demeanor. She had urged him to head south, but Morgan knew it was only a matter of time before Travis was drawn to Vicksburg. It was too busy, and too full of murderers and thieves for him not to go there. Morgan was no expert, but he had seen several people who he was certain had rewards for the capture. She questioned him while he dined on beef spareribs with a dark-skinned escort named Veronica.

"You worry too much, Ms. Freeze," Morgan had said. "This is the place, surely you can see that."

"Maybe, but it would be faster if you went south," she had urged him.

"If you want him dead like that, why not just put a sharp-shooter on him?"

"You know why."

"Because then it comes home to roost, eh?" He chuckled. "The boss don't need that kinda heat," he continued with a rough imitation of Dice's voice and diction.

"We want it clean, and with no strings that might lead back to us," Iona said, clearly irritated with the assassin.

"Then let me do it my way," Morgan said. "He'll come here, and there will be plenty of time to bring the issue to a satisfying conclusion. You really should try the short ribs, my dear. They were frozen, it's true, and far from perfect, but really quite delicious."

"I'm not here for the food," Iona said. "We have a job to do."

"My job is to kill the bounty hunter," he said, flashing Veronica a wicked smile and delighting in the look of surprise on her face. "Your job is merely to watch me do it."

"And make sure it in no way traces back to my people."

"It will not. I know how to pick a fight," he said, with a

flourish of his fork. "You know, there are opportunities here that you might partake in."

"No thank you," Iona said.

"Your name is so fitting," he said. "Freeze, and you are so full of frost and bitterness."

She had left, not quite storming out of the small tent, but clearly unhappy with his attitude. But Morgan believed in enjoying everything in every moment, whether it was food, companionship, or murder. Whatever he did, he took great pleasure in it. His success and finances allowed him to avoid anything he didn't enjoy doing, so that his life was one of excess and extremes.

After two days in Vicksburg Iona returned, finding him in a drug lounge where he was coming down from the Dreamers, which left users in a semi-conscious, completely relaxed, euphoric state. She plied him with strong, bitter coffee, and got him walking outside in the cool air, but away from the main street.

"He's here," she told him when he was fully alert again.

"Already? That was fast," Morgan said.

"What do you intend to do?"

"I intend to watch him," Morgan said, saying the last two words as if they were the conclusion of a powerful argument.

"The Incendius Organization is paying you to kill him, not just watch him."

"And I will kill him, but if I simply go out and gun him down everyone will know why," Morgan said. "It cannot look like a hit. You, of all people, should understand that."

"We are paying you a lot of money," she said. "We're paying Vega Volinski a lot of money for the right to do it here. I think that entitles me to know what you're planning."

"To get close to him," Morgan said.

"He won't recognize you," she insisted. "You can walk right up to him."

"No, no, not that kind of close. I mean to befriend him. Get his guard down. Then, when the time is right, I'll kill him."

"But why?"

"It is for me to know the whys and hows. Trust in my reputation, Ms. Freeze. I never miss a target. I'm not sloppy, and I'm not rash."

He hadn't explained that getting close to Travis Hurts was part of what made the job interesting and the kill fun. It wasn't enough to simply take out the mark. He needed the target to know him, and even like him. He needed to see the deep, emotional pain in his eyes when he realized who Morgan really was, and that he was going to die by the Specter's hand.

"Just get it done," she said. "Otherwise, my people will have to step in."

"I don't work that way, Ms. Freeze. I'm an independent contractor after all. I'll kill Travis Hurts my own way, or no way. You interfere and I'll simply warn him about the hit and move on."

"You do that we'll kill you," she said in a stern, almost anxious voice.

"That would be fun, but there's no money in it. So why don't you just let me do what your Boss is paying me for?"

She stopped walking, but he did not. He had a photograph of Travis Hurts memorized. Finding him wouldn't be hard. They could casually bump into one another, become acquainted. And then Morgan would set the hook, and draw Travis in close. Morgan was already composing a story in his mind, a complete fabrication that would bond the bounty hunter to him. He couldn't help but smile at the exquisite agony it would cause when Morgan ripped that bond apart.

He found his mark at the beer garden. He looked no

different than most people in Vicksburg, but the long coat and wide brimmed hat were somewhat unique. They weren't designer brand clothing, but they did speak of more money than what most of the locals were wearing, including Morgan.

He gave the bounty hunter one of his favorite aliases. When he was young, an older boy had called him rooster and got the other kids laughing. But he didn't laugh when Morgan broke his nose, and he didn't tell a soul who did it either, not after Morgan threatened to kill him if he talked. He couldn't help but wonder if that boy, a man now, Morgan mused, thought of him every time he blew his nose.

After the beer garden Morgan had kept his distance. He followed Travis without being seen. It was a skill that came naturally to Morgan. He had the ability to blend in, look natural, and best of all, his was a face that was completely forgettable. After dinner at the chow tent, Travis went to the bare-knuckle brawl. Morgan skipped the Volinski's private seats, and instead lingered with the crowd on the ground. While they watched the fights, Morgan watched Travis. He took in every wince, and every look of compassion. It was a curiosity. Travis Hurts was in a violent line of work. His name, clearly the invention of someone in his ancestry, was literally a call to inflict pain. And yet he seemed to care about the fighters. He didn't know them; they were slaves from all over P2. Morgan had spoken with the man running the fights. He took in debtors with no other way to pay their loans and trained them to fight, promising that if they could win a hundred bouts he would set them free. Most couldn't keep track of their record after taking brutal shots to the head night after night. Those that managed to keep track he had killed. It was a savage business, but none were so entertaining that they gained the popularity that would keep them from losing a fight that ended up costing them their lives.

Morgan thought of the fighters like cattle. They were doing

what they were supposed to do. It didn't matter if they got hurt doing it. Nor was it a matter of significance if they lacked the will to escape, or the understanding that they could enjoy what they did, just as Morgan enjoyed his own brutal role in the universe.

When Travis settled at the Fireside Saloon, Morgan knew his chance would come. It was only a matter of time. He knew who Augustine Ward was, of course. The cocky gunslinger was a pathetic caricature of a true gladiator. He was all pomp and circumstance, his reputation built on gunning down the common man, like Lorenzo the miner.

"Hey mister, you ain't got to do this," the miner warned him.

Morgan turned, looking over the miner's shoulder and staring straight at Travis Hurts as he replied, "It's no trouble, my friend. No trouble at all."

The crowd pushed their way outside. At times, Morgan felt like they might run him over, and there was plenty of pushing. He let their hunger for blood infuse him, and he savored the sounds and smells as he went from the warm tent out into the cold, dark night. There were lights on either side of the wide dirt road that had been hard packed by thousands of feet walking on it, day and night, in such a short time.

As Morgan moved out into the darkness in the center of the road, he turned and looked for Travis Hurt. The bounty hunter was there. And Morgan couldn't be certain from that distance, but he thought he saw compassion on the lawman's face. It gave him a thrill, and he turned wide-eyed toward Augustine Ward.

"You're a gunfighter," Morgan said. "Admit it."

"What gave me away, farm boy? Hope you're ready to die."

Morgan had a delicious idea and seized it. "I'll bet ... I'll bet you've got a price on your head," he said in a high-pitched voice.

"You'd win that bet," Augustine said, squaring up and

running his thumbs down the gun belts, one sloping down toward each hip.

"How much they got on you, Ward?" someone from the crowd shouted.

"Hundred-fifty last I heard," Augustine said. "You looking to collect, farm boy?"

"Is it dead or alive?" Morgan asked, suddenly grinning, completely unable to contain his glee at the spectacle playing out.

He wondered if actors felt the same way as they stepped out onto the stage, or musicians when the crowd screams for an encore. Word had spread, and the people in other saloons came rushing out to see the showdown. There were men and women, many shivering in the cold night. There would be frost on the ground by morning, and the wind chill was dropping lower with every passing hour.

"Should I go lefty on this clod hopper?" Augustine shouted, playing to the crowd. There was a roar of approval and Ward put his right hand behind his back with dramatic flair.

"You really are sure of yourself," Morgan said.

"Doesn't take much to get the jump on a hick like you."

"Shall we then?" Morgan asked.

"Make a move, farmer!"

The air seemed to stop moving, and the sounds fell away into a kind of white noise behind Morgan. He held his hand out above the handle of his Widow Maker. It was not the flashy variety, certainly not like Augustine's shining weapons, or even like the little Slinger that Travis carried. Morgan had seen it just inside the bounty hunter's coat. It wasn't the lawman's only weapon. He had another on his left thigh, and something on his back. It wasn't clear what he was packing, but clear enough that he was taking no chances. If the people in Vicksburg knew who he really was, they would have ripped him apart. The crowd was in a frenzy, and Augustine was grinning at him, thinking that Morgan was easy prey.

For a moment they stood just staring, the whole world dissolving into meaningless noise around them. It was just Morgan and Augustine. The gunman seemed cocky; he was so sure of himself, even with his primary hand behind his back.

"You sure about this?" Morgan said.

"Don't run on me now, farmer boy," Augustine said.

"Enjoy this moment," Morgan said.

And then he went for his pistol. Augustine reacted with speed, snatching his little, shiny pistol and jerking it free of his holster, but that's as far as it got. Despite the barrel of his Widow Maker being twice as long as Augustine's, Morgan was fast. He pulled and fired in a rapid display of graceful movement that was hard to track with the naked eye. The laser flashed like lightning, illuminating the street and the onlookers for a split second. Then the laser bolt flash boiled the skin on Augustine's hand just above his thumb. It burned through the muscle and bone, hit the fancy handle of the little gun, and sent it flying away from the gunman's ruined hand with an ugly black scorch mark on the pale bone handle.

The crowd roared, and Morgan slowly put the big gun back in his holster. Augustine looked at him wide-eyed, unable to believe what had just happened. Then he looked down at his hand. Smoke was rising from the hole that stretched from his ruined thumb to the bones of his index finger.

"Want to go again?" Morgan said. "You can use your right hand this time."

There were howls of laughter and people screaming for more. People wanted to see Augustine go for the pistol on his right hip. And Morgan was ready in case he did, but the gunslinger was hurting. He didn't want to show it, but he knew the shock and pain wouldn't let him move as quickly as he was normally capable of. And there was fear in the man's eyes. From across the way, in the darkness of the night, Morgan could see it. He recognized it and relished it. His hand was steady above the grip of his Widow Maker.

Augustine Ward, famed gunman, quick draw artist, professional shootist, turned and ran. The crowds were pressed back on either side of the road. No one wanted to get killed from a stray shot. They booed the coward as he ran away, but no one tried to stop him. They were cheering for Morgan, and he turned, soaking up their raucous praise. He was looking for Travis Hurts, the bounty hunter, and his mark on P2. But he was gone. Not just lost in the crowd, which was flowing like a river. With the danger over, they were moving to embrace the champion. Someone called for drinks, another person pushed a scantily clad sporting woman in his direction. She pretended to fall and he caught her. She was breathing fast, her cheeks flushed. The crowd pressed in. It was going to be a rowdy celebration, and Travis was missing it all.

# 19

When Travis saw Rooster draw and shoot his long-barreled pistol, he felt a shiver of fear. The man was fast, maybe faster than anyone Travis had ever seen before. And the manhunter knew exactly what Augustine Ward was going to do. The man was cocky and bold, but there was little substance. He proclaimed himself to be a Renaissance Man, but in reality, he was just a killer. The ships weren't far down the dark street on Augustine's end of the road. So, Travis slipped back into the Fireside Saloon and hurried out the back. He circled around the businesses that lined Main Street and waited at the end, between the tents and the lot of aircraft.

It didn't take Ward long to appear. He was busy looking over his shoulder and didn't see Travis step from the shadows and throw his foot out. Augustine Ward's feet tangled, and he fell hard. Travis was on him in an instant, pulling the gunman's pistol from the holster as he put his knee down on the outlaw's back.

"Some show back there," Travis said.

"Who the hell are you?" Ward said loudly.

He was angry and near panic, but the pain of his wound had sent a shock through his body. The pain was overwhelming his senses and he couldn't think straight. Travis pulled the wounded hand back behind Ward's back. The man cried out in pain. There wasn't a lot of time, Travis knew. He might be the only bounty hunter in Vicksburg, but with a hundred and fifty thousand credit reward there would be others wanting to take Augustine Ward to justice. Most didn't have the means. They had come to Pergamum Prime on transports and had no way off world. Most of the aircraft in the nearby landing area were atmospheric craft. But there were a few who could take Ward to Los Mesa in the Chichijuan system.

"Take hold of this," Travis ordered, as he pulled of the bandana he kept tied around his neck. He wrapped it around Ward's wounded hand. "Grip it tight. That will help with the pain."

The gunfighter groaned, but did as he was told. Once Ward made a fist, gripping the bandana, Travis slipped a pair of plastic restraints over the hand and tightened it on the wrist.

"What are you doing?" Ward asked, his voice sounding disconnected.

"Taking you in," Travis said, pulling the gunslinger's right arm back and slipping it into the restraints.

With Ward's hands bound behind him, Travis stood up. He saw the shadows moving to his right, but pretended not to. He hooked the front of his duster behind his Slinger holster, then bent down and pulled Ward to his feet.

"Hey man, just let me go okay," Ward mumbled. "Do you even know who I am?"

"That's far enough," a gruff voice demanded.

"Let 'im go," another ordered.

"Not going to happen," Travis said.

He didn't want the other men to move into the light or size

him up. He drew and fired his pistol, two quick shots. They were true, dropping the two men quickly.

"Hey, you're fast," Ward said.

"If we don't get out of here fast, you're probably going to end up dead," Travis said as he pushed Ward forward.

They moved away from the main street. Most of the tents and shelters were behind them, but they had to move through a few. The ground was covered in coarse grass and weeds, and each step also kicked up dust. Following them wouldn't be difficult, even in the dark. The moon was a crescent sliver, with thousands of bright stars overhead. And without much in the open plain to cast a shadow, they were visible. So was the corral. As busy as Vicksburg was, the tent city was only a few hundred yards from the corrals to the landing area at the far end.

Travis got Ward jogging. When he refused at first, all Travis had to do was slap the gunman's ruined hand. He yelped, not unlike a dog, and didn't resist any more after that. They made it to the corral without running into anyone else. There was no time to saddle Macy. He threw the blanket across her back, then pushed Ward up onto her. He was leading them out of the corral, Ward leaning hard on Macy's neck, when three men came toward them out of the darkness of the town.

"Hold it," a female voice said. "We'll take them off your hands."

"Sorry, that's not happening," Travis said. "We don't want trouble."

"Then give up the gunman," the female said. "Otherwise, these boys are going put you in the ground, Mister."

Travis slapped Macy hard on the horse's backside. She had been on the weaker side when he traded for her, but a few days of sweet oats had given her strength. The horse jumped forward, breaking into a gallop away from the town, as Travis dove back behind the corral fence. It was made from a variety of materials, but the gate was mostly stacked rock, and a metal cross beam. Lasers shot toward where Travis had been standing. A few bolts hit the rock support and blasted little bits of grit into Travis' face.

"Get that animal!" the woman yelled. "He's getting awa—"

Travis had pulled his Kicker. It was about the length of his forearm, with a fore and after grip. He brought it up and fired straight into the woman. She fell back with a scream.

"Fiona!" one of the men shouted, while the other cut loose with his pistol. Eight laser shots turned the rocks of the corral support into a chipped mess, but none found Travis. The shooter cursed as he emptied his power cell. He was just starting to swap it out when Travis shot him with the Kicker. Unlike his Slinger, which knocked a person out cold, the Kicker had more kinetic power, and left the person fired on awake and aware, but unable to move most of their body.

The last man didn't bother shooting. In the darkness it was hard to judge distances. He was a big man and he charged Travis. He dove straight at the pile of rocks. They were held together with a mixture of clay and straw, but the laser blasts had weakened the mortar. The rocks went flying while both stones and the big man crashed hard into Travis. They all fell to the ground in a heap. Travis could barely breathe with the big man on top of him. He had lost his grip on the Kicker, and the big man was raising a sledgehammer-sized fist. All Travis could do was snatch up a rock and swing it hard. The big man's fist hit the stone, knocking it away, but snapping several bones in his hand at the same time. The big man howled in pain. Travis bucked him off to the side, and scrambled to get his footing. A wild slap caught one of Travis' feet and threw it into the other, tripping him again. The horses were neighing and bucking on the far side of the corral.

Travis could feel the danger all around him. He rolled over just as the sound of knife leaving sheath was heard, a menacing whisper in the darkness. Travis saw the shadow of the man, like a mountain even on his knees. He drew his Slinger and fired two shots. The big man went back, and two horses charged out of the open corral. They just barely avoided stepping on Travis.

He rolled to his knees, got to his feet, and looked around for his Kicker. The weapon, having recently been used, still showed the power display on the rear. If not for that tiny, digital display, Travis knew he would have lost the gun. There were voices drawing nearer from town. The manhunter grabbed the Kicker, leaped over the body of the big man, and ran away into the night.

He was breathing heavily and exhausted by the time he caught up with Macy, who had stopped running when Augustine Ward fell off her back. She was calmly munching grass when he arrived.

"What a mess," he told her.

The horse blew air through her flapping lips in reply, as if she understood him exactly.

"Let's go find our bounty."

Travis didn't bother trying to ride Macy without a saddle. He was a decent horseman, but he wasn't good enough to ride bareback. They found Augustine Ward a short way off from where Macy had been waiting for Travis. He used his smelling salts to get the outlaw conscious and on his feet. Then they walked five miles through the dark night to reach the ship.

"You got another one," Ava said. "I thought you weren't going after anyone that time out."

"Plans change," Travis said. "This guy was on the run."

He locked Augustine into the cage next to Bill Teagan. Travis had already removed the outlaw's gun belts and taken the goods from his pockets, including a pack of Dreamers and a skinny roll of credits.

"I better get that back," Ward said.

"He's got a hand that needs attention," Travis said. "But you better make him stick them out through the bars behind his back."

"That bad?"

"He's a killer, Ava. You don't want to take him for granted. You don't want to underestimate any of these people. How are you doing?"

"Not bad. I'm halfway through the training simulation. Who knew flying was so fun?"

"Not me," he said with a smile. "You wouldn't run off and leave me, would you?"

"Can I get the reward for these people without you?"

Travis shook his head and smiled. "You need an FRS license, it's in the fine print."

"Figures," she said with a little grin. "I guess I'll wait. But you know what they say, a gentleman never leaves a girl waiting."

"Is that a fact?"

"It is," she said.

It was playful banter. Ava was coming out of her grief because of the sudden change in her circumstances. But it would only take one memory to send her spiraling back into the pain and terror of losing her husband the way she did. Still, Travis thought it was good to see her smile.

"You've been walking all night," she guessed. "I've got food ready in the galley. Come get some while it's hot."

"That sounds great," Travis said. "And listen to you, in the galley."

"Hey, if I'm going to be an ace pilot, I need to know the jargon, right?"

"Of course," he said.

"Sit down. Let me get you a plate."

He watched her pull a pan of hot biscuits from the little oven. They came in frozen pucks, but plumped up to be flaky and delicious in the oven. She had precooked sausage patties warming in the microwave. It wasn't as fancy as he might get from a cafe, but after the night he had, he was grateful for it.

"It's good to fix a meal for a man again. It's too bad you don't have any real food on this ship."

"Never knew I needed it," he said.

"We could get some when we get off world," she said. "This isn't much of a kitchen, but you'd be surprised what a person can do with the right ingredients."

"About that," Travis said. "We need to make a decision."

"Okay," she said, "just let me take these biscuits out to the others. I'll be right back."

He ate his breakfast gratefully. Never, since his mother had been killed, had anyone ever fixed a meal for him that he didn't pay for. Travis had dated women in the past, but his job kept him on the move and things rarely got past friendly first dates. And no one had ever stuck around long enough to cook for him. Of course, Ava Lynn Baxter was his employee, not his lover, and she had made the food for the prisoners, not him. Still, it felt really good after a long, hard night to sit down in a nice clean place and enjoy a hot meal.

"I'm back," she said. "Your new prisoner's already asleep in his cell. Can I wait to see about his hand?"

"Yes, it's cauterized. He got shot and it left a pretty nasty wound, but it's not bleeding."

"I love this kind of talk at mealtime," she said, rubbing a hand down her belly. He could practically see her thinking that she would raise her child with good manners.

"Sorry," Travis said.

"What do we need to decide?" she asked.

"Should we stay or go?" he asked.

"The cells aren't all full," she said. "I thought you wanted six prisoners."

"I did. And only three of those four have rewards for their capture," he explained. "If we leave now, we'll get about two hundred and thirty thousand in reward money."

"Wow, really?"

Travis nodded. "That's twenty-three grand for you, plus travel. Sandra's wanted on Lennon Four, and Augustine is wanted on Los Mesa in the Chichijuan system. Those are both excellent worlds. Either one would make a fine home for you and the baby."

"What if we stay?" she asked.

"I marked two other outlaws," he said. "We could up our reward money to a little over four hundred thousand credits."

"That's an extra seventeen thousand for me," she said.

"A few more days here, a few more trips to other systems, but you'll have more seed money to get you started somewhere."

"How dangerous is it?"

"Depends," Travis said. "Maybe I can stroll back into town, maybe not. It was a pretty hot run out of there."

"Is there anywhere else we could go to get other outlaws?"

"Not that I know of," he said. "And while I could round some others up, probably, they might not be offering as much in reward money. It would for sure take more time. A few weeks probably."

"What would you do if I wasn't a consideration?" she asked.

"Stay," he said. "But you are a consideration. I might not even be able to stay, if I'm being honest. But I'd like to go back and see."

"Then go," she said. "I'm happy to leave whenever you're ready, but I don't want to inconvenience you. And you've already been more generous than you can imagine. Gosh, just sleeping on a real bed again. You have no idea how wonderful that is for a pregnant woman."

Travis smiled. "Glad you like it," he said. "When I bought

this ship, I knew I would need a partner, but there wasn't time to find one. I owe the bank nearly seven hundred thousand credits. And my first payment will be due soon. You are making this trip possible."

"What can I say, I'm pretty awesome like that."

Travis stood up, and suddenly had the impulse to take Ava into his arms. It was a strange, heady feeling. She was close enough that he could have reached out and touched her. He wasn't used to women being so close, and his desire made him feel a little dizzy.

"Are you okay, Travis?" she asked.

She really was attractive, he thought. Not beautiful like a movie star, and not seductive the way Sandra Mayfield could be, but he felt himself longing for her in a way that he had never felt in all his life. She was tall, nearly as tall as he was. Not slender, and not curvy either, other than her belly. She had a sturdy frame, not masculine, but not dainty. And he found her in that moment to be almost irresistible.

"Just tired, that's all," he said in a soft voice.

"You could stay. Sleep on the bed, I'll wash the sheets this evening."

"No," he said, stepping back. "If I don't go back they'll know it was me that stirred things up last night."

"Are you sure it's safe?"

"No such thing as safe," he said. "But it's not stupid. Thank you for the breakfast, Ava, it was lovely."

"You're welcome," she said, looking at him with a mix of surprise and suspicion.

He had already swapped out the batteries in his Slinger, but he picked up a fresh set for both the Slinger and the Kicker. Then he left the ship and didn't look back. He had a long walk back to the camp, and he needed the time to clear his head.

# 20

Iona Freeze was furious. The assassin Dice hired was showboating his quick draw skills while the mark disappeared into the night. Fortunately, Orvil's man Prescott had found Travis' ship and was keeping eyes on it. She wasn't surprised that Travis had gone after Augustine Ward. The gunslinger was a wanted man with a hefty reward for his capture. It was the reason Travis Hurts was on P2 in the first place. And if he left, they would be in a fix.

"I don't understand," Orvil said. "Why do we care about this bounty hunter?"

"He must have taken someone important," Reg said.

The trio from the Incendius Crime organization was huddled inside one of the shelters run by the Volinski Syndicate. It was costing them a thousand hard credits a day, which was outrageous for a shack with only one narrow camping cot, a tiny electric heater, and a battery-powered lantern. Maybe, Iona conceded, it was better than sleeping cold in a tent. She was surprised how cold it got at night in the boom town. But still, she thought the entire operation was costing too much, and taking way too long.

"You don't understand how the law works," Iona said from the doorway where she watched the locals going about their business.

"You get arrested, you go to jail," Orvil said. "How complicated can it be?"

"There are laws about how people are prosecuted," Iona said. She didn't mind educating the low-level henchmen. They worked for her, and she had ambitions of taking over at some point, when the timing was right. Dice only cared about his people earning, but she wanted more. She was a woman of vision, and when she took the reins, she would ensure that everyone was focused on the same goal of being the most powerful organization in the galaxy.

"That's the craziest thing I ever heard," Reg said.

"But it's true," Iona said. "Do you know who Lawrence Pescitory is?"

"I've heard the name," Orvil said with a shrug.

"He's a made man. Operates a crew in the Commerce Ring. Got in hot water over tax fraud, and a money laundering beef. Then a cop got himself shot, and everyone's looking at Lawrence."

"Sounds like a frame up," Orvil said. "I don't miss having law jamming me up everywhere I go."

"But here's the point," Iona persisted. "The prosecutor can throw spaghetti at the wall to see what sticks, doesn't matter if it's true or not. They'll take Lawrence into court, tell a good story about how he killed an innocent policeman, and how the bounty hunter had to track him down across three different systems because Lawrence was desperate and on the run."

"Those dirty bastards," Reg grumbled.

"But that's where their laws come into play," Iona said. "You see, the bounty hunter doesn't just hunt fugitives down and turn them in for a reward. He testifies about it. He can talk about what they did, maybe even what they said when he caught them. He can even submit evidence he found on them."

"Or planted on them," Orvil interjected.

"But ..." Iona let her companions lean in to hear what she was saying, "only if he testifies."

They understood what she meant, but she elaborated.

"If the bounty hunter is out of the picture, he can't submit evidence, he can't talk about what happened, and he can't repeat what his mark may have said during the capture."

"Which means the prosecutor loses a big chunk of her case," Orvil said with a nod.

"It's not a slam dunk," Iona said. "Lawrence Pescitory is still in police custody. They want him to flip, but he's no rat. Their case didn't fall apart against him, but there are some pretty big holes if the bounty hunter isn't around to talk. Lawrence is an earner. He and Dice go way back. Our lawyers are pretty confident they can punch enough holes in the case to get him off, but the boss wants to be sure of it."

"So, we gotta stop this bounty hunter," Reg proclaimed.

"But we can't be anywhere near it," Iona pointed out again. "If rumors start flying that we were somehow involved, the judge might bend the rules to favor the prosecution."

Orvil got to his feet, grinning. "Who can blame us if this bounty hunter dies at the hand of an infamous killer, in someone else's territory?"

"Exactly," Iona said. "Which is why Black should have done the deed already."

"He's piece of work," Reg said.

"Not what I expected at all," Orvil agreed.

"He's a psychopath. Who can say what makes a guy like that

tick?" Iona said. "Maybe it doesn't matter where the bounty hunter dies, but here there's no law to investigate it, and no one that would dare testify about it. If Hurts goes back to a civilized system, we could have a problem."

"Prescott said he's on his way back," Reg said, "with the horse and the mule. That's good, right?"

"Maybe," Iona said.

"He said he got a pretty good look into the back of that ship," Orvil said. "The bounty hunter has cages in there."

"But he can't say how many," Iona reminded him. "We know there are at least four prisoners in there now. He could be going back to town to sell his animals before he takes off for good."

"Prescott can take him down if that's the case," Reg said.

"A sniper shot will look like a professional hit." Iona shook her head.

"So maybe we let the animals out of the cages," Orvil said. "Make it look like someone escaped. They killed the bounty hunter and his lady friend on the spaceship."

"We don't kill innocent women," Iona said. "You know the code."

"I'm just saying," Orvil pressed on. "If someone finds 'em slaughtered together, they won't think we did it. Not if there's evidence that one of his prisoners broke out and took revenge."

"It would be better if Black does the deed," Iona insisted. "But it doesn't hurt to have a backup plan. Reg, go find our contract hitter."

"You want him here?"

"No, just make sure he's out there doing what we are paying him to do."

"Got it," Reg said.

He slipped out into the cold morning air. Iona had picked up a wool poncho from one of the venders in Vicksburg. It served as a garment and her blanket when she slept. Normally, she enjoyed showing off her physique. It could be alluring and intim-idating, as needed, but most of it gave the impression that she was not a typical woman. She was strong, disciplined, powerful, not the type of person to take for granted, or to get on the wrong side of. In her mind, there was nothing better than seeing a man draw back in fear. But the poncho was warm, and it had certain advantages when it came to carrying weapons that you didn't want people to see.

"You know it's possible the town will do the job for us," Orvil said.

He leaned against the wall and lit up a thin cigar. Iona hated the smell of it, but everyone on P2 smelled. The town itself reeked of trash and sewage. Iona wasn't the type to wear perfumes, and she preferred the cloying smell of the tobacco to the odors of other people.

"They might," she agreed.

"If they catch on he's a licensed bounty hunter, they might beat him to death. I've seen others get dragged out into the wilderness, or strung up from the nearest pole and left there to rot."

"You paint quite the picture," Iona said.

"I don't mean to overstep," he replied. "I'm just saying, maybe a rumor gets the job done. There's people at the corral asking questions."

"Because of a few missing horses?"

"Because there's evidence of a fight. Two men on the far end of town were found stunned. There's evidence of heavy laser fire at the corral. People saw the flashes in the night."

"But no bodies," Iona said. "Whoever was involved got their wounded, or their dead, out of town."

"Still, it looks bad. Wouldn't take much to have people wondering why the bounty hunter left town, and why he's coming back. Someone could be paid to say they saw his ship, or saw him taking Augustine Ward that way."

"Yeah, that might work," Iona said. "If he stays around town long enough, we could get the crowd worked up tonight. I'll tell Black he has until sundown, after that ... anything goes."

# 21

It was a long walk back to town. Travis led Macy and Tuck. Neither animal seemed to mind the walk, but Travis felt bone weary. Worse still, he knew there would be questions when he reached Vicksburg. And he was in no mood for an interrogation.

Around a dozen people were near the corral. Most seemed busy, either seeing to animals, or working to fix the gate, but a few were clearly watching him approach. When he was still forty yards out a pair of rough looking characters stepped toward him. One was a large, barrel-shaped man with a thick black beard, the other was lanky and tall. They had on the sherpa lined bomber jackets that all the members of the Volinski Syndicate wore, and had pistols on their gun belts.

"That's far enough, stranger," the bigger man said. "You want to tell us what you're doing?"

"Besides wasting the day tracking down my animals that some fool set loose last night?" Travis growled.

It wasn't hard to act angry. Travis could be a grumpy character when he got tired.

"You see what happen?" the skinny man asked.

"All I saw were my animals missing when I came to see about 'em this morning," Travis said. "This town needs a stable."

"Won't be here long enough for that," the big man said.

"The mine played out?" Travis asked, feigning a sudden sense of urgency, as if he were going to miss the boom.

"Always does, sooner or later. How do we know you didn't cause this trouble last night and just ride out and back to hide your involvement?" the big man asked, stepping in front of Travis to block his progress.

"Hell, if was going to do something like that I'd probably take my saddle," Travis snarled. "That's mine right there on the fence."

The two men glanced over at the saddle Travis was pointing at.

"Don't prove nothin'" the skinny man snapped.

"Who died and made you two the law in Vicksburg?" Travis said.

"Nobody died," the big man said. "Not that we can tell. But there are people missing. Someone took Augustine Ward. There were witnesses."

"Do I look like I'm hiding a prisoner somewhere?" Travis said. "I don't even know who you're talking about."

"You a miner?"

"I'm a gambler," Travis lied. "I was at the Fireplace last night until the shootout. After that I got some sleep and when I checked on my animals this morning, I found 'em missing."

"And you just set out into the wild and found 'em huh?" the skinny man asked.

"I can follow a track," Travis said, trying to sound bored. "Now, I'd like to get these animals some oats and water. I wouldn't mind a meal myself, but if you're set on running me off I'll just take my saddle and be on my way."

"Nah, it's better if you stick around, Mister," the big gangster said.

"Fine," he replied. "If you don't mind."

They stepped aside and Travis tied up his animals inside the corral before getting them some oats from the bag that was under his saddle. He strapped on feed bags and let the horse and mule eat while he fetched water for them. He was exhausted, but he wasn't the type to put off chores until later. He would catch up on his rest once they were in hyperspace.

He got a few sideways glances and outright suspicious stares, but Travis ignored them all. He was just finishing with his animals when Rooster showed up.

"There you are," he said. "I've been looking for you all morning."

"I had to go get my animals," Travis said. "Some fool left the gate open on the corral."

"No surprise there," Rooster said. "That gunslinger was running for the hills. He probably stole a horse. Glad it wasn't yours."

"You and me both."

"I was about to get some grub. You hungry?"

"Starved," Travis admitted.

"Good. I'm buying. Did you see the show last night?"

"You mean the shootout where you outdrew a gunslinger and shot his gun out of his hand? I think everyone in town saw it. If they didn't, they've heard about it by now."

They were walking down the main street. Rooster leaned close and spoke softly.

"You want to hear something funny," he said. "I wasn't aiming for his hand. I was trying to kill that cocky bastard."

"You got lucky?" Travis asked. Rooster nodded.

"Every dog has his day. I guess mine was yesterday."

Travis chuckled, then said, "I'm still wondering why you stuck your neck out for that miner to begin with."

"I've known him for years," Rooster said. "We do some business occasionally. I run deliveries for some of the miners who don't like getting cheated by the Syndicate."

"Yeah, but you could have been killed," Travis said. "From what I hear, Augustine Ward is the real deal. A professional gunfighter."

"It might have turned out different if he wasn't so damn cocky," Rooster said. "Who draws left-handed? I'm fast enough, but I don't always hit what I'm aiming at. But I got plenty of free drinks at the bar after the showdown. My fifteen minutes of fame I suppose."

They went into a tent with a sloppy sign painted on an old, rusty frying pan that said *Meat and Tators*. A woman with a limp was waiting on the tables, which were long with plain benches. She brought them both a plate of fried pork chops and fried potatoes, along with two mugs of cold beer. They both set into the food with gusto, neither man talking while they ate.

Eventually, Travis pushed his empty plate away and drained the last of his drink.

"You want more?" Rooster asked. "I don't mind paying."

"Nah, I'm good," Travis said.

"I don't think you believe me," Rooster said, leaning forward. He still had his knife and fork, one in each hand, but his food was forgotten. And he had a mischievous look in his eyes.

"About the food?"

"About the gunfight," he said.

"It's a little hard to believe you could out draw someone with that big pistol of yours."

"You carry a little piece?"

"Not like that one you took off Ward," Travis said.

"I know how to protect myself," Rooster said. "Living on a

157

world like this, moving items as valuable as Dust ore, you learn to."

"But you carry a shooter with an eight, nine-inch barrel?"

"Nine," Rooster said. "It's called a Widow Maker. Titanium alloy, four/twelve shot power cell. Looks big, but it's light."

He drew the pistol, checked the safety, then handed it to Travis. He took the gun and was surprised at how light it was, and the balance was very good, but Travis still thought the barrel was too long for a quick draw. He gave it back.

"Nice weapon," Travis said. "I don't like lethal shooters, but to each his own."

"I like to have the option," Rooster said. "In my line of work, you never know what kind of trouble you might run into."

Travis nodded, as a big man entered the cafe tent. There was no doubt as to his identity. Frank Lee Voss was wanted on Grimwal Grand for multiple murders. He was a professional gunman, more of a mercenary than a quick draw artist, the type who didn't balk at killing. The reward for Voss was half a million. He was what Fugitive Recovery Specialists dreamed of, the kind of apprehension that would do so much more than merely pay the bills. Half a million, combined with the rewards for the prisoners Travis already had, would pay off his bank loan for the *Purgatory*. The only problem was, Frank Lee Voss knew Travis on sight. Fortunately, there wasn't much light in the tent. A cold front was pushing thick clouds into the sky, and the cafe's canvas structure was stained with old grease smoke. It made for a gloomy setting. Still, Travis looked down at the table, so that the brim of his hat hid his face from Voss.

The big man sat down at a different table, with his back to Travis, who breathed a little easier.

"You okay?" Rooster said.

"Yeah, I'm fine," Travis said. "Just saw an old acquaintance I'd rather not run into."

Rooster turned around and saw Voss' wide back, then whispered, "That guy?"

Travis nodded, his hand instinctively checking the handle of his Slinger. He wasn't as worried about having to out draw Frank Lee Voss as he was getting out of town alive. There were plenty of people up and about. With Augustine Ward missing, people would be nervous. There was just no way to make a play on the gunman and get him out of Vicksburg without the locals turning against Travis.

"I took him for a few hundred back in Camp Sherman," Travis lied. "He wasn't happy about it."

"Took him?"

"Playing cards," Travis said. "That's what I do."

"You're a card sharp?"

"Professional gambler, if you don't mind," Travis said. "I don't cheat."

"I should hope not," Rooster said. "That's a sure way to get dead fast in these parts."

"I was playing last night at the Fireside before your spectacle got everyone riled up."

"My apologies," Rooster said with a grin that made it clear he wasn't the least bit sorry.

"I usually play for small stakes," he said. "I don't need much. Fifty here, a hundred credits there. Life is better when people don't lose more than they can afford to lose."

"Including you?"

"Especially me," Travis said.

"But the big guy didn't know when to quit?"

"No. And he didn't take it kindly when I left the game."

"Sounds like a sore loser. Let's hope he has a short memory."

They left the cafe and ended up at a saloon with decent drinks and pretty girls. Travis joined a game and lost track of Rooster. The day wore on. Travis was tired and had trouble concentrating on the game. He lost nearly a hundred credits himself before calling it quits just before sundown.

There was tension in the air. He had overheard more than one group of people in the saloon talking about Ward, or what they thought happened at the corral. There were plenty of rumors, and much talk about witnesses, but Travis knew it had been too dark to see faces. Nor had there been much opportunity for anyone to ascertain who had been involved without checking the trio of people Travis had stunned with his Kicker.

Just like with cards, Travis knew the time was nigh that he got out of town. His plan had been to wait until just before dawn to take two more prisoners. He even had a running list of wanted men in his head that he had seen in Vicksburg. Garcia Sanchez and Johan Leister both had decent rewards for their capture. Travis was certain he could take them down too, that wasn't the problem. The issue was getting them out of town without the locals catching on before Travis and Ava could get off world. Not that Travis expected a boom town with no law enforcement to put together a posse and go after him, but he didn't want to take unnecessary chances.

There were four prisoners in holding cells on his spaceship. If Travis was killed, what would happen to them? He hadn't expected to feel a sense of responsibility for the outlaws in his custody. It was one thing to be known as a stand-up guy who treated his prisoners with respect. But it was a whole different thing knowing that if something happened to him, the prisoners on the *Purgatory* could be in serious danger.

Not to mention Ava Lynn Baxter. Travis couldn't stop thinking about the woman. She was a widow and pregnant with another man's child. He didn't know how long she had been grieving for her husband, but he knew it wasn't longer than it took to have a baby. And he was not a stable, reliable man who could be counted on to support a family. His job chasing outlaws was always changing. He might pursue a prisoner across several worlds and for many weeks before catching up to them. Sometimes he didn't even earn enough reward money to cover his expenses. And with the *Purgatory* he would be gone on longer hunts, for multiple outlaws. It was a greater risk with greater reward, but he couldn't seriously think of raising a family.

The truth was, Travis was in a dangerous profession. He knew it, and didn't mind it. Living a long life just wasn't something he had ever valued. He liked the hunt, liked the adventure of going to new places all the time, putting his future, and his very life, in his own hands. And there had been plenty of close calls. He had the scars to prove it.

But that was no life for a lady, not to mention a child. She wanted a fresh new start, and deserved someone who would be there for her through thick and thin, not leaving all the time to chase fugitives. He could take a job as a local law enforcement, but that didn't hold much appeal for Travis. Many never even drew their weapons in their entire career. Writing tickets and settling domestic disputes simply wouldn't hold his attention for long. And without the mental stimulation, he would begin to resent his life.

The best thing that he could do for Ava Lynn Baxter was to get her safely off Pergamum Prime. Whatever his feelings were, and how difficult it might be to let her go, he knew that it was for the best. He wanted to give her what he could. Life had dealt her a bad hand, but it didn't have to be a losing hand. Not as long as Travis had anything to say about it.

He had made up his mind to find a way to get one more prisoner. The temptation to capture Frank Lee Voss was hard to resist. But he told himself whatever opportunity came his way first he would take it, then get off P2 while he was able.

# 22

"I want it done now," Iona insisted.

"The timing isn't right," Morgan said.

"I don't care about timing. Do your damn job."

"No," he said simply, without the least bit of animosity in his voice. If she was making him angry, he wasn't showing it.

"You are refusing to do the job you were hired to do?" Iona said in a threatening tone.

"If you insist that it be done today, then yes I am," Morgan replied. "I know what I'm doing, and how these things should be done. If you want to ruin the entire operation, be my guest."

"You won't be paid."

"I don't care."

"We'll come after the money you already took."

"I'll return it," he said, still calm and relaxed. "But if you want to threaten me, I find actions much more compelling than words."

"And if he leaves," Iona argued. "Then what?"

"He won't," Morgan said. "Destiny has bound us together, certainly you must see that."

Morgan Black didn't actually believe in destiny, or fate, or even in God. He didn't worry about the future, or waste time with regrets about the past. He was fully invested in the present, even in the conversation with Iona Freeze. She was a hard woman, but he liked that about her, and found her much more interesting than her boss. Dice was a common thug, perhaps smarter than average, but that wasn't saying much. Most criminals weren't masterminds, after all. But Morgan did enjoy heightened emotions; fear, anguish, hostility, even lust, they all made him feel more alive. It was like the emotional overflow from others was soaked up by Morgan, who relished the deep feelings.

"What I see is my target walking around ... alive when he should be dead."

"His death is a foregone conclusion, Ms. Freeze. What we are doing now is weaving a memorial symphony. Tell me you won't remember this event for the rest of your life? Wouldn't you rather it be a grand spectacle? This is the dance of death, and you should embrace it to the fullest."

"I embrace results," Iona said. "And I expect nothing less than exactly what was called for."

"There are a million ways to die," Morgan argued. "It will happen."

"Unless he decides to leave the planet," she pointed out.

"He won't leave," Morgan insisted. "Your own people say his ship isn't full. Why would he leave with empty cells on board his ship? That's just bad business."

"You don't know that," she said.

"I have spoken with him," Morgan said. "We shared a meal this very day. A dreadful culinary exercise, but the conversation was exquisite. At one point I even handed him my own gun. Had he but known the danger he was in, or the opportunity that sat before him, he would have slain me without hesitation, but he

163

didn't know. It's a heady, intoxicating thing to wield such power over the life of another person."

"You had time to eat with him?" Iona asked.

"Indeed. The first of what I hope will be several such opportunities."

"You're out of your mind," she snapped.

"Actually, I'm at the top of my game. Think of it, my dear, we've been seen together. People will think we are friends. And while no one on this world will care who killed Travis Hurts, word will spread. Killed by his friend, they will say. Saw them eating in the cafe just a few days before, they will whisper. Must have been a quarrel, they will guess."

"You're mad."

Morgan continued as if Iona hadn't interrupted him. "What they will not say is that Travis Hurt was assassinated. They will not dig into his life and discover that he apprehended one of Dice Jester's lieutenants and oldest friends, or that he was scheduled to give testimony in Lawrence Piscitory's trial next month. They will not assume that the Incendius Organization had anything to do with Travis Hurts' death. Those two ideas won't even be in the same sphere of their minds. I believe that is exactly what I was hired to do, and if you will stop trying to make me into a run of the mill gun thug, that is what I shall deliver. As promised, on this planet."

She looked like she might cut his throat. There was no telling what nasty little tools of death she could be hiding under the poncho she wore. Most people would have been frightened, or at least intimidated by her furious stare, but Morgan felt energized by it.

"One more day," she said, almost as if it hurt her to say. "By this time tomorrow he will be dead."

"I can probably arrange that," Morgan said, silently wishing he had more time.

She spun on her heel and stormed out of the tent that Morgan had rented. It was an old military issue officer's field tent, tall enough for a person to stand in the middle, sloping down to a little desk on one side and a narrow cot bed on the other. He watched her go, then checked his weapon. The Widow Maker had a full battery charge, and he carried another in a little case that fit into his pocket.

He gave the woman enough time so that it wouldn't be obvious to anyone who wasn't watching the tent closely that the two of them had been together at all. He resented that Dice had sent his lapdog to micromanage the job that Morgan had been hired to do. He was not a prospect hoping to make his bones in the Incendius Organization. Nor was he an unknown. Rather, Morgan Black was the very best at his craft. Killing was easy; anyone could commit murder. But assassination was an art form, and Morgan was at the top of his game. A well-paid, highly successful, assassin for hire.

He strolled through the clusters of tents until he reached Main Street. Normally the afternoons were the warmest part of the day, but the clouds were thick and it was starting to rain. The cold drops pelted down on his workman clothes. Morgan realized that his one regret about the job was that he couldn't appear to Travis in his usual attire. In truth, the bounty hunter wouldn't recognize him in his normal black garb, including the face mask that hid his features. He might remember the Widow Maker. It was a custom weapon, but not the only one of its kind in the galaxy. The long-barreled laser pistol was based on an earlier design, but made with highly superior materials. Not that the details of the weapon were of much interest to Morgan. But it was his trademark, just as much as the black cape and mask. Travis would see that long barrel pointed in his direction and would understand in that moment the depths of Morgan's betrayal. It would be a sweet moment to savor, and lock in his memory. It would also be the last thing Travis Hurts ever saw.

# 23

As it had the evening before, the town seemed to swell with people as the sun went down. The cold, rainy weather only made it seem rowdier in the boom town. Main Street and most of the tent establishments were full to bursting. As soon as it was dark, Travis returned to the corral and got Macy saddled up.

"We may have to make a run for it," he told the horse and mule. "It's best if we're ready when the time comes."

The bare-knuckle brawl was held inside a huge tent on the opposite side of Main Street from the corral. There were lights mounted on the front, near the main entrance. A guard, paid by the owner of the tent, made regular trips around the outside of the huge structure. Travis stood in the darkness, less than fifty yards from the tent and the guard. With the thick clouds, there was no light but the small lantern the guard carried. It gave only a small circle of light around him, and left the world in darkness beyond its glow. That, combined with the cold rain, which began to sting as the drops partially froze as they fell, caused the guard to pull his collar high and pull his hat down low. He walked with his head down, merely making the rounds without really watching for anything or anyone that might be lurking in the dark.

"Looks like the weather's in our favor," Travis said.

The horse looked at him as if to say he was crazy. Travis hurried to the side of the tent and ripped up one of the dozens of stakes that held the tent flaps down. Returning to his mount and mule, he positioned them in the darkness. After tying their leads to the stake, he drove it into the ground so that the animals wouldn't wander off.

The guard passed again, and once again saw nothing but the ground in front of him. Travis returned to the tent and used his knife to cut a small hole in the canvas. It was thick and stiff, resisting his knife at first. But once he got the blade through, it cut easily enough. Travis made a short gash in the canvas, just big enough to look through. He peered into the tent. The bouts had yet to begin, but there were a few spectators loitering inside.

Travis left the rear of the tent, circled wide, and approached from Main Street. The hard-packed road was softening in a thick mire that swished around his boots. The half-frozen rain bounced off his hat and duster. He wasn't the only person moving toward the fight tent either, and the weather made people hurry. Most pulled their hats low, and hurried from one structure to the next.

"Trav?" a familiar voice said.

He turned and found Rooster hurrying toward him. "Evening," Travis said.

"A mighty fine night this is turning into," Rooster grumbled. "My tent doesn't have any heat. Makes me wish there was forest out here. There's nothing to burn but dried animal dung. And that's one stinky mess I do not relish being stuck in a tent with."

"Why not sleep on your ship?" Travis asked as they paid the cover charge to get into the fighting tent.

"And miss all the action?" he asked.

"Mud, freezing rain," Trav said, "and stinking fire smoke."

"Yeah, there probably isn't even any dry dung to burn tonight."

They shuffled in and found seats near the edge of the bleachers. Early wasn't early enough, the first few rows were already taken, but Travis managed to get a seat right on the edge of the fourth row, which was close enough to the ground that he could hop down when he needed to. The plan was to take out anyone with a reward for their capture that he could. He had casually circled around the ring of bleachers until he spotted the slit he had made in the side of the tent. All he had to do was sit and watch for his opportunity.

"I like watching the fights, but ..." Rooster said.

"But what?"

"Well, I hate to complain, but the fighters? Come on, man. Those poor souls are living hard."

"Agreed," Travis said.

"Would you fight if it was open to the public?"

"Me?"

"Yeah, you're a pretty big guy," Rooster said. "My money would be on you in a fight."

"I prefer not to if I can avoid it."

"A professional gambler must run into a fair share of violent people," he insisted. "Do you watch the fight to learn new moves?"

"No, just for the entertainment value."

"And the fast money?"

"I don't bet on the fights."

"Wait, what? You said you're a gambler."

"I gamble at cards," Travis said. "You have to know these fights are fixed."

That got more a few sidelong glances. Most of the people

around them were eager to see the action, and hungry for blood. Travis knew they didn't want to hear about the fights being fixed. But with one man running the show, it was a foregone conclusion in Travis' mind. He made money from the ticket sales, but the real grift was in determining the outcomes of the bouts before they were ever started.

"Wait, you're saying they tell the fighters to win or lose?" Rooster said, pretended that the idea had never occurred to him.

Travis shrugged.

"Hold on, the Syndicate is covering the bets," Rooster continued. "What good is it for the proprietor to rig the contests?"

"He's in league with them," Travis said quietly. "The fights are rigged. The Syndicate knows the outcome and sets the odds accordingly. The proprietor gets a cut of the winnings. Betting here the odds are all on the house."

"But if you know that, can't you predict the winner?"

"It's like playing roulette," Travis said. "You can bet red or black, and you've got a fifty-fifty chance of winning."

"But if you know the odds, can't you predict the outcome better than half the time?"

"Perhaps," Travis said. "But what good does it do to put a hundred credits on a fighter that's a four to one favorite? You risk a hundred to only win twenty-five? Like I said, it's a sucker's bet."

"So bet a thousand," Rooster said, laughing at the absurdity of the idea.

"You could, but what's to stop the Syndicate from signaling for your fighter to lose?"

"Oh, what a wicked, wicked scheme," Rooster said.

Travis felt an odd sensation. He couldn't say what it was exactly. Rooster was a loud, gregarious person. But that didn't make him a bad person. He had stepped in to save a friend from

Augustine Ward, which was noble, but the fact that he could outshoot the shootist was completely against the odds. And the fact that he seemed thrilled by the idea of the Syndicate working in league with the fight master to rig the bouts was a major red flag. Travis wondered why the man was so eager to be friends.

The tent was filling up fast, and it was loud inside. Before Travis could figure out what Rooster's angle was, he saw Frank Lee Voss. The gunman was two sets of bleachers away, spitting copious amounts of dark tobacco spit into a cup. Travis hoped the gunman would get up and move around the back of the bleachers, but he wouldn't hang all his hopes on the big reward. Travis did as he vowed to do, and found both Garcia Sanchez and Johan Leister in the crowd as well. He felt like a spider who had spun a web. All he had to do was wait for the first of the wanted men to fall into it.

The fights started and occupied their attention. Rooster, who rarely stopped talking, was busy cheering for the pugilists. In the very first fight one of the men used the crown of his head to open a gash above the eye of his opponent. There were no rules, no official to reprimand a fighter, or call the fight because of the wounds of the other. Instead, they kept fighting, the blood from the gash flowing down the fighter's face until it was covered in red. The patrons were screaming and cheering the fighters on. It was a rowdy show, and the only good thing about being in the tent to Travis was that he wasn't outside in the cold rain.

"There he goes!" Rooster shouted. "He's done it!"

The man with the gash had prevailed. After pushing his opponent back, he landed a quick hook that caught the head butter right on the tip of his chin. The man's entire body stiffened and he toppled sideways like a cut-down tree. Sometimes the fighters followed their opponents to the ground and continued pummeling them. Travis thought that maybe the thrill of the fight was too great, and they simply couldn't stop inflicting damage, but the man with the gash over his eye just turned away, lifting both hands and circling the pit, engaging with the crowd who cheered his name.

"Not a bad show," Rooster said.

"That cut's certainly real," Travis admitted.

"A gash like that could take weeks to heal. A little flesh glue and some makeup could cover it though."

"Until the next fight," Travis said.

The crowd was cheering the names of the next two fighters. Rooster had to lean over and shout into Travis' ear to be heard.

"It might all be fake, but the crowd's enthusiasm is contagious."

"You're a madman," Travis told him.

Rooster threw back his head in response and howled like a wolf. In almost any other place it would have been completely inappropriate, if not downright crazy. But in the fighting tent on P2, it was completely normal. People were cheering, chanting, screaming in a frenzy as the fights progressed. The next two were scrabbling bouts with fighters who clearly didn't want to be in the pit. The crowd booed them and threw garbage at them.

When a pair of buxom women in sequined body suits that revealed more flesh than they covered went into the pit to clear the debris, Garcia Sanchez got up from his seat and headed for the rear of the bleachers. Travis felt a stab of disappointment. Frank Lee Voss was ogling the women and drinking from a flask. Part of Travis wanted to stay and wait for the man with the half million credit bounty on his head. But an instinct deep inside of Travis told him to get out while he could. Greed was sure to get him killed.

"I had too much to drink," Travis said. "I'll be back."

"The next fight's about to start," Rooster said.

"I'll hurry," Travis said, before slipping off the bleachers and onto the dirt floor.

A weight seemed to lift from Travis' shoulders. He wasn't going to make enough money to pay off his ship in one sweep, but he would still make good money. In fact, even after paying the first payment on his ship, and refueling, he would have more money than he had ever made at any one time in his life. And he would be getting Ava off P2. He could live with that. In fact, he felt pretty good about his decision.

It was dark at the back of the tent. A few people were hurrying back to their seats after relieving themselves outside. Travis pretended to be looking for his seat as Garcia Sanchez approached. The man was short, but wide-bodied. He had thick shoulders and big biceps. But it was the long hair and thick mustache that were his most recognizable features. Had he cut his hair into a different style and shaved off the mustache, Travis might not have realized who he was. The man was wanted for kidnapping. He had taken a wealthy man's trophy wife, held her for ransom, and then tortured her. She wasn't hurt badly enough to be at risk of dying. Sanchez had disfigured her, focusing on her face, and then after her husband paid him several million credits, she was released.

The press didn't write about it, and doubtless no one said anything to the husband, but everyone talked about it in private. Would he lovingly care for his hideously disfigured wife? Would he stay by her side through the countless surgeries it would take to return her to some semblance of normality? Was his love for her more than skin deep?

It was not. The wealthy man quietly sent his wife away, and instead focused all his attention on finding the man responsible. He was funding the reward for Sanchez's capture, and Travis was going to deliver.

His Slinger would have done the trick, but not without attracting attention. He could have hit Sanchez over the head, but that would risk permanent damage to the vile man. It might not have been any less than he deserved, but Travis didn't pass judgment. He turned over his prisoners in as good a shape as possible. Which meant that he needed a more discreet way to disable Sanchez.

The shorter man walked past Travis, and in the darkness never saw the Storm 50kv stun wand he pulled from a hidden pocket in his duster. The handheld baton was only seven inches long, but the nodes at the end delivered fifty thousand volts of electricity to the target they were pressed against. Travis activated the device by pressing a little switch on the side and then stuck it against Garcia Sanchez's lower back. The shorter man froze, his back arching, his grunt of pain completely overwhelmed as the crowd cheered for new fighters entering the pit.

Travis grabbed Sanchez by the arm, holding him up when the stun wand finished delivering its charge. As Sanchez sagged, Travis grunted with the effort of holding the shorter man up. He was dense with muscle and heavy. Travis dragged Sanchez, who looked like a drunk who had passed out, to the tent. It only took a few seconds to find the slit. Travis looked out, saw nothing, and then stuck his knife blade through the opening and sawed his way down until the slit was big enough to step through. He went first and then pulled the unconscious kidnapper through after him.

The irony of the situation wasn't lost on Travis. He was kidnapping a kidnapper. But the urgency of the situation was such that Travis didn't have time to consider the social ramifications of his actions. He dragged Sanchez away from the tent and toward his horse and mule. He was almost there when someone shouted at him.

"Hey! What are you doing?"

It was the guard. He was holding his lantern up high, letting the edge of the light reach Travis and the animals.

"My friend passed out," Travis replied.

The rain was mostly ice by that point. It no longer stung, but pelted. The guard had a gun out and was pointing it in Travis' direction. He looked angry, perhaps at being lied to, or maybe just because he was stuck out in the freezing rain.

"You stop right there or I'll send you to hell, Mister," the guard shouted.

Perhaps it was the light that was shining through the hole Travis had cut into the tent, or maybe the guard shouting, but someone stuck their head through the hole. The guard turned to look. At the same time Travis dropped Garcia and whipped out his Slinger. The small, almost delicate weapon delivered a stun beam and a flash of light. The guard was knocked into the tent, ripping the hole even larger. Travis bent down and pinned Sanchez's arms to his back. He was in the middle of putting restraints on the kidnapper when Sanchez suddenly rolled over. Travis was taken completely by surprise. In the cold wet downpour, he lost his grip, then his balance, and went down into the mud.

Garcia Sanchez was an animal. He leaped on top of Travis, his hands pushing the bounty hunter's chin back. Travis felt his head sinking into the mud. It was so deep that it could be submerged, and the cold, wet sludge felt as though it were sucking him down into the depths of hell. Panic made Travis try to rip Sanchez's hands from his throat, but the shorter man was too strong. His forearms felt like they were made of steel cables, and Travis only managed to shift the man's focus from his chin to his throat. It was as if someone had thrown a switch and sucked all the air out of the world. Bright sparks appeared in Travis' vision. Despite Sanchez's weight on his body, Travis felt himself grow light. It was a swoon coming on, and Travis had just enough time and insight to pull his knife and stab the kidnapper. The blade only went in half an inch before it wedged between two of Sanchez's ribs, but it was enough to send the kidnapper rolling away.

Travis dropped the knife and grabbed his own throat as air rushed out of his lungs and then back in. He coughed and sputtered. Sanchez got to his feet. He had one plastic restraint on his left wrist, but otherwise his hands were free. Still, it must have been enough for the kidnapper to realize that he had come within a hair's breadth of being caught. He started to run.

Sitting up was hard. Everything hurt, and Travis felt weak. The mud seemed to have a hold on him, but Travis wrestled his way loose and sat up. People were pouring out of the tent but he ignored them. He got to his knees and could just see the shadowy figure of Garcia Sanchez running for his life. Travis pulled his Kicker from the holster on his left thigh. It had more range than his Slinger. The laser flashed, illuminating the rain drops for a split second. In the flash of light Travis saw Sanchez arching from the pain. His entire lower body would go numb. It might not stop him from crawling in the mud, but Travis was certain he could catch up. Unfortunately, the fight wasn't over. Travis just didn't know it yet.

# 24

Iona wasn't at the fights. She found them to be sad and predictable. Her own organization ran a number of sports promotions. And they had a strong sports betting racket on over twenty worlds. The planets that made sports betting illegal were by far the most lucrative. Perhaps it was because there was less competition, but Iona thought that the poor saps who gambled on every aspect of every professional sporting event were simply more enthralled with doing something illegal. They were business owners, academics, and politicians, the most respectable people, men and women. Yet they loved the way doing something illegal made them feel, and the Incendius Organization was right there to help them do it.

She knew that Morgan had gone into the fighting tent with Travis Hurts, so she and her two companions stayed close. They lingered at the outdoor cafe. A fire had been built using some sort of synthetic fuel inside logs made of stainless steel. There were thousands of tiny holes in the fake logs, allowing the flames to leap up and dance in the cold night. There was no smoke and no odor from the faux campfire. They drank coffee laced with liquor which warmed them from the inside, and waited for something to happen.

"What's going on back there?" Reg said, after Travis stunned the guard.

They hadn't seen the shooting, but they clearly saw the flash of light.

"Lightning maybe," Orvil said. He was reluctant to leave the fire.

"That was a laser flash," Reg said. "I'd bet my left—"

"Go and see," Iona said, cutting the crude remark off before Reg could finish.

The two men pulled up the collars on their coats and hurried off toward the tent where the fights were held. It only took them a moment, and then Orvil waved for her to join them. She tossed the remnants of her drink out of the mug she was holding and stepped out from under the cafe awning. Her boots squished in the muddy road. She wondered why no one had thought to put boards out. The entire camp would be filthy from walking around in the muck.

At the corner of the fighting tent she saw Travis on the ground, being choked. At first, she wasn't sure who it was. The man on top, the man doing the choking, had long hair that was covered in mud. She could see the muscles in his arms bulging.

"That's him," Orvil said pointing. "The bounty hunter."

Iona felt her heart leap. This was better than she could have hoped. Travis Hurts killed by one of his own prisoners in front of dozens of witnesses. There were more coming through a hole cut in the tent every moment. They would save half of Morgan Black's fee. The fool's reluctance to do his job would pay off to the Organization's benefit. Better still, she could leave. And not just the filthy boomtown of Vicksburg, but the entire planet. She could go back to where she was most useful. She might be underappreciated, but at least she was feared among her own. Fear was more useful than appreciation, at least in her mind.

Then Travis pulled his knife. She saw him stab the long-haired man choking him. When the blade caught on Sanchez's ribs she knew why. It was a classic mistake in fighting with a knife. The blade had to be shoved in horizontally, so that it would slip between the bones of the ribcage and reach the vital organs. Of course, that kind of rational thinking while all the oxygen is cut off from your brain was nearly impossible, and the stabbing had the desired effect.

She watched Sanchez get to his feet and run away. It seemed to her a cowardly act. Why not finish the fight? But she wasn't in his mind to know who he was, or what motivated him. Instead, she watched Travis Hurts, the problem that simply wouldn't go away, get to his knees and shoot the running man in the back.

"Kicker," Orvil said in a low tone. "Even after nearly getting killed he won't shoot someone with a real gun."

"Hey! I know you," a booming voice echoed across the crowd, like the dying peels of distant thunder. "You're that bounty hunter!"

That sent a murmur through the crowd. Iona saw Morgan Black pushing through the crowd. There was very little light, even though someone had found a lantern, probably the guard's, and was holding it up. The rain made it seem darker. It was falling harder, the size of the frozen drops increasing. Fortunately, the bigger they got the less solid they became. They were like small ice balls formed by lots of little slivers of ice. They soaked more, and hurt less. Iona was shivering from the cold, or the excitement, she wasn't sure which.

"You can shoot a man in the back," the booming voice said. "Let's see what you do face to face."

"That's Frank Lee Voss," Reg said. "He's damn good with a gun."

"Fantastic," Iona said, as the crowd moved away from the hole in the tent to give the shootist and the bounty hunter room to work their pistols.

"It's good to see you Frank," Travis said. "You're worth a lot of money."

"You won't live long enough to collect," the gunman snarled.

Iona saw Morgan on the edge of the crowd. He was moving slowly, getting into position. She realized what was happening. The assassin was moving in for the kill shot. She wouldn't let him claim the kill, not after the runaround he had put her through. For all his reputation as a stone-cold killer, it seemed he was just a coward after all.

"Go start the transport," she ordered Orvil.

"What?"

"Go, get the transport ready. I'm leaving."

"Right now?"

"Yes," she said.

"You," she poked Reg in the side with a hard knuckle. "Tell the Volinski Syndicate we appreciate their hospitality. Then get yourself back to our territory."

"Yes Ms. Freeze," he replied, as Orvil stalked away angrily.

She couldn't blame them, they wanted to see the fight. They wanted to see Travis Hurts gunned down. So did she, so she slid sideways, angling to get a better view. She didn't care about Frank Lee Voss. The gunman meant nothing to her. All she cared about was seeing Travis Hurts die.

†††

Morgan had known something was wrong when Travis slipped away before the start of the next fight. It wasn't just that moment, it was the entire evening. He seemed distant, and their conversation was forced. Morgan didn't mind the discomfort between the two men, although he felt they were more alike than either of them would willingly admit. Still, he stayed in the moment, and accepted the strange discomfort his target made him feel.

He had watched from the shadows as Travis took down Garcia Sanchez. The bounty hunter was smooth, and prepared. It pained Morgan to admit he had been wrong. Maybe Travis planned to come back after taking his quarry to the ship he kept a few miles outside of town. Or maybe he would fly away and make Morgan look like a fool. The assassin couldn't let that happen, which was why he started sending people out through the hole cut in the back of the tent.

When he had appeared himself, there were dozens of people from the fighting tent, and more coming around the sides. Frank Lee Voss was a loudmouthed brute, but he was also good with a gun. Maybe if it hadn't been raining, and Travis hadn't just been nearly choked to unconsciousness, the bounty hunter could take the gunman down. But Morgan wasn't exactly sure, and he wasn't going to take the chance. To him, it wasn't about completing the contract. The money and even his reputation took a backseat to his desire to carry out the hit in the way he envisioned it. Seeing Travis gunned down by a random outlaw simply wouldn't do. It would be like stopping a book in the middle and never finding out how the story ended. Morgan would write the ending, and he would write it in blood.

He eased his Widow Maker out of its holster. It wasn't easy to do with the gun's long barrel since Morgan didn't want to be seen doing it.

"You can shoot a man in the back," Voss bellowed, his voice strained. "Let's see what you can do face to face."

Excellent, Morgan thought. He wanted Voss focused on Travis. In fact, he wanted everyone focused on the bounty hunter. The truth was out, and Travis was done in Vicksburg.

Fortunately, he had the good sense to be prepared. Morgan could see Travis' horse and mule tied up just a few paces away from the bounty hunter.

It was all a sudden and unexpected twist in the way that Morgan had envisioned things going. But he thought the story was better that way. He knew what he had to do, and exactly how he wanted to do it. The secret was to not get into a rush. He had to let things play out, and step onto the stage at just the right moment, when the drama was at fever pitch.

"Good to see you, Frank," Travis said, and Morgan could hear the fatigue and strain in the bounty hunter's voice. "You're worth a lot of money."

Morgan could often go with very little sleep. A few hours a night could see him through for weeks at a time. But Morgan knew that Travis had spent the previous night chasing down Augustine Ward. He had been up for hours by midday, already stretched to the breaking point. Iona Freeze had her henchmen watching him through the afternoon hours. Travis didn't sleep, but played cards instead, keeping up appearances. Morgan wondered why he didn't simply pay a sporting woman for her company, then sleep in the little alcoves in the saloons or brothels where the women plied their trade. But Travis was probably too self-righteous to avail himself of the easy pleasures to be had in a town like Vicksburg. And then there was the issue of the woman on his ship. Morgan didn't know who she was, but he knew enough about Travis Hurts to know that he traveled alone. He had done plenty of research on the lawman before taking the job Dice offered.

Travis had to be bone weary, which was another good reason that Morgan couldn't let him go toe to toe with Frank Lee Voss. The gunman was average height and thin, with dark, leathery skin, and a deep voice.

"You won't live long enough to collect," Voss snarled.

They were feeling each other out. Voss was only fifteen feet from Travis, who had holstered the Kicker. It was much too heavy and bulky for a quick draw. His hand was steady over the handle of his Slinger. Morgan wanted to see the showdown. It was what everyone around him wanted. They were eager for blood. The fights had started things, but they weren't as thrilling as two men locked in mortal combat. Travis didn't look worried. But that might be simply resignation. As tired as he probably was, he might just be ready to die and have it over with.

"What are you waiting for, then," Travis said. "Pull that Slayer and have at it."

"I do, you die," Voss said.

"It's nothing I haven't heard before," Travis said. "Men like you, killers, are never as fast as they think they are. Take Augustine Ward for example. He got beat, now he's locked up and facing life on a penal colony."

"He was a peacock," Voss replied. "He never took on anyone of substance."

"And you have?" Travis said. "Do you just kill colonists and farmers trying to make a living? Don't you ever get tired of doing other people's dirty work? What'd those people on Grimwal Grand ever do to you? They weren't gunslingers or shootists. They were innocent. But I'm going to give you a chance they never had. Walk away, Frank. You go your way, and I'll go mine."

"The hell you say," Frank Lee Voss shouted.

"It's that or we go to shooting and I ain't no farmer, Voss. I'm a hunter of men, and I've seen it all. You draw on me, and I'll put you down. Plain and simple. It's up to you."

"You're the one gonna be worm food," the gunman said.

Morgan saw the muscles in Frank Lee Voss' shoulder tense. It was just a tiny, subtle movement, but to the trained eye it was crystal clear. And Morgan knew what it meant. Voss was on the verge of going for his gun, and that was a possibility that Morgan couldn't let happen, even if Travis was talking an excellent game.

He leaped forward, holding up his Widow Maker by the barrel, and smashed the butt of the handle down on Frank's head. The gunman collapsed, the crowd gasped, and Morgan spun on his heel in the mud, holding his pistol properly and ready to shoot at anyone who might try to stop them. Travis Hurts was his mark, and his kill, no one was going to snatch it away from Morgan Black.

"Easy, easy there," Morgan said. "My friend won't kill you, but I'm not as forgiving as he is."

"Rooster?" Travis said.

"Hello friend. I thought I might lend a hand."

"He's a bounty hunter!" someone shouted.

"A lawman," someone else yelled.

"Better get your prizes and get us out of here before things get ugly."

Travis didn't argue. He pulled Frank's pistol, a dark, medium-sized gun called a Slayer. It had a short, but larger bore barrel that was big enough that Morgan could have put his index finger inside the muzzle. It was a weapon known for having only one purpose, hence the unofficial title.

He dragged Frank Lee Voss toward his mule, just as an indignant woman in a dark, heavy dress with a gold satin sash tied around her waist stepped forward. There was a pistol sticking out of it, and she didn't reach for it, but instead pointed a finger at Morgan.

"Step aside," she ordered. "That lawman ain't going nowhere."

"You willing to bet your life on that?" Morgan asked.

Perhaps it was his threat, or maybe his broad smile, but the woman stepped back. Few people, no matter how hard or how good with a gun, were able to stand under Morgan's intense gaze. He relished their fear, and there was plenty of it. Many of the folk in the crowd were hard scrabble people, miners and treasure hunters, just looking for a good time. They didn't care if an outlaw was captured, as long as it didn't interfere with their fun. The real issue was the members of the Volinski Syndicate. They should have been on the scene, stopping Travis from taking someone out of their territory. But they were nowhere to be seen.

"Rooster, you better come with me," Travis said.

"I wouldn't have it any other way," Morgan replied.

He backed up, keeping an eye on the crowd. The horse and mule hooves made sucking plops in the mud. The rain was coming down harder, the show was over, and people, tired of being wet and cold, began to slip back inside the tent. Morgan holstered his pistol long enough to hop onto the mule's back behind the prone body of Frank Lee Voss.

"Now that was one hell of a good time!"

# 25

Travis was woozy, but adrenaline was pumping through his veins. And Macy, the faithful steed, seemed to lend him strength as he climbed into the saddle. The crowd of onlookers seemed disappointed, and many were already returning to the fighting tent. Two men had held off the crowd, but they weren't looking to get in on the action. They were simply hoping to see something strange and spectacular. He couldn't really fault them; it was human nature after all. But he felt a sense of profound relief flooding through him.

Riding into the darkness with Frank Lee Voss spread unconscious across Tuck's back, Travis couldn't help but wonder about Rooster. The man had once again risked his life to help someone in trouble. It should have been an admirable trait, but instead it felt wrong. Of course, if he knew the value of the reward for Voss' capture, he may simply want a cut. Travis wasn't opposed to that, since he hadn't planned to capture Frank Lee Voss, and even with just half his reward money it would be a huge increase in what he earned on the trip.

Looking around it was hard to see in the darkness, but he

didn't think anyone was following them. He reined Macy in as they approached Garcia Sanchez, who was trying to escape by crawling on his elbows. The man wouldn't be able to walk for hours, and with his body numbed by the Kicker he wouldn't be hard to restrain.

"I don't see any trouble," Travis said.

"Me either," Rooster replied. "I will say that you are a man of surprises. You're a bounty hunter?"

"Fugitive Recovery Specialist," Travis said, getting down from his horse.

Rooster hopped off the back of the mule and shook his head. "Isn't that the same thing?"

"I'm a licensed member of law enforcement."

"You're not improving your social standing," Rooster pointed out. "Around here, a bounty hunter is more respectable."

Travis was accustomed to being the perceived bad guy. He was a hunter of men, and there was something about it that didn't sit well with some people. Not that he worried too much what anyone thought of him. He was never in any one place for long, and the few people who really knew him understood not only what drove him to his career, but what kind of human being he was deep down. In many ways, Travis Hurts was trying to give the galaxy the justice that was denied to him as a child.

"Sanchez, put your hands behind your back," Travis ordered as he stood over the crawling fugitive.

"Screw you, man. You stabbed me."

"You were choking me to death."

"I wish I had succeeded," he growled, but he put his hands behind his back. He already had a plastic restraint around one wrist, and it wasn't difficult to get the other one through its loop and tighten them both down.

"Two for one, not bad," Rooster said. "What now?"

"Now I take them back to my ship and get off this world."

"You've got a ship?"

Travis nodded as he put restraints on the still unconscious Frank Lee Voss. There wasn't time to do a thorough search. Travis did a cursory pat down of the outlaw, removed a knife, money roll, and a tiny bag with little pills inside it. Rooster helped Travis lift Sanchez up and lay him beside Voss on Tuck's strong back.

"Looks like I'm walking," Rooster said.

"You can go back to town if you want," Travis said. "There's no use in sticking your neck out on my account."

"That ship has sailed my friend," Rooster said. "I'll stick with you, make sure you get airborne without getting shot full of holes first."

"Thanks," Travis said, still not sure if Rooster was being neighborly, or if the man had a hidden agenda.

"Besides, I want to see this ship of yours. You've got other prisoners, right?"

"I do," Travis said.

"Holy smokes, did you capture Augustine Ward?"

Travis nodded. "He's on board the *Purgatory*."

"Purgatory, oh man, that's the perfect name for a bounty hunter's ship. You are the real deal my friend. Tell me what happened with Ward?"

Travis shared the story of the gun fight on both ends of town. It wasn't all that glamorous in his mind, but Rooster seemed thrilled by the details.

"Man, I thought I lived on the edge. You could have been killed."

"Yeah, I suppose so," Travis said.

He was leading the horse and mule, walking beside Rooster. Exhaustion was setting in. His legs felt weak and trembly beneath him. It was hard to see in the darkness, the wind and rain were getting colder every minute. But Travis was also exhilarated just to be alive. It wasn't lost on him how close he had come to death. If he hadn't stabbed Garcia Sanchez when he did, he might not have had the strength to do it at all. He had been maybe two seconds away from blacking out. Then there was the gunfight with Frank Lee Voss. The man was a killer. He wasn't a fancy gunslinger like Augustine Ward, but Travis knew the really good gunmen didn't need to brag. Travis was pretty good himself, but that didn't mean he wouldn't have gotten killed in the showdown.

"Hey, I meant to say thank you," Travis said. "You probably shouldn't have jumped into the fight like that, but I really do appreciate it."

"My pleasure," Rooster said. "We only get one life to live, and I intend to make the most of every minute. Besides, watching the fights got me all riled up."

"The crowd nearly turned on us," Travis pointed out. "You could have been killed."

"Me? What about you, lawman. You were about to throw down with a wanted outlaw. I mean, I know that's how you make a living, but how do you know you were fast enough to beat Voss?"

"I don't know," Travis said. "But that's the risk, and it's why there is a reward for bringing him to justice. No one thinks it's going to be easy."

"And you don't mind taking the risk?"

"It's part of the job," Travis said.

"There's easier ways to make money, my friend."

"I've got a short attention span," Travis said. "I need a lot of variety, otherwise I lose interest."

"Sounds like you've got a death wish."

"It's as much about who I am, as what I do," Travis said, still scanning the dark countryside for any signs of danger.

"What does that mean?"

"It's a long story," Travis said with a sigh. "Suffice it to say that my childhood was rough. Some people see that as a liability, but it's always seemed like an advantage to me."

"Because you aren't afraid of the bad guys?"

"Oh, sometimes I'm afraid, but I learned a long time ago that there's no benefit to shrinking back in fear."

"Sometimes fear protects us from doing stupid things," Rooster pointed out.

"I'm not talking about base jumping, or drag racing," Travis continued. "I was raised around guys like that."

He pointed a thumb over his shoulder toward the two men on Tuck's back. Sanchez was cursing softly, and Voss had started to moan. Travis knew that soon he would need to stand Frank Lee Voss up and force him to walk. It would be better for Sanchez too, but it wouldn't be possible for hours yet. The Kicker put a man down and kept him down, that was the appeal of the weapon.

"So, you know how they think," Rooster said.

"And what they're capable of," Travis said. "I put my experience to good use. I benefit and society benefits."

"And the bad guys get what they deserve."

"That's up to the legal system. My job is just to see that they face whatever they've got coming."

"And you don't worry that sometime, somewhere, a bad guy is going to gun you down?"

"It's probably inevitable," Travis said.

"But you're fast with a gun."

"There's always someone faster."

"And you aren't afraid of dying?" Rooster pressed.

"To be honest I don't think about it much," Travis said. "If I die tomorrow, I'll go to my maker knowing that I left the galaxy a little better than I found it."

The walk through the night was cold and miserable. It

wasn't long before they were both hunched in their coats trudging along in silence. They stopped for a short rest and Travis tied Frank Lee Voss to Tuck and made the gunman walk.

The sun was coming up by the time they reached the *Purgatory*. Travis was relieved to see the ship. They had made it without incident. The hike through the darkness in the freezing rain had been taxing, and took nearly twice as long as it should have, but they made it.

"That old thing," Rooster said. "That's your ship?"

"That's her," Travis said.

"I like a vessel with a little more style."

"In my line of work, it's better not to stand out."

"That makes sense," Rooster replied. "You have to keep a low profile. I, on the other hand, need to project an image of success. I just hope those local yahoos haven't done anything to my ship."

"Are you really leaving town?"

He shrugged his shoulders. "I doubt anyone will want to do business with me now. Word travels fast and plenty of people will be dragging my name through the mud."

"I'm sorry for that," Travis said. "But I appreciate your help. Let me split the reward money for Voss with you."

"That's not necessary," Rooster said.

"He's wanted on Grimwel Grand for half a million credits," Travis said. "I wouldn't have him in custody without your help."

"Half a million? Really?"

"I can show you the posting for his capture."

"Oh, I believe you," Rooster said. "You're an honest man, other than pretending to be a gambler and lying about everything."

They both chuckled as Travis opened the rear hatch. Despite the early hour, Ava was waiting just inside. Three of the prisoners stood at the bars, watching to see who Travis had caught. Only Sandra Mayfield seemed uninterested.

Garcia Sanchez was starting to regain feeling in his legs, but he couldn't walk on his own yet. The man had a splitting headache from hanging on Tuck's back through the night. He also had a wound that needed attention, but Travis planned to see about that once they were in orbit. He didn't relish spending one more moment on P2 than absolutely necessary.

"Ava Lynn Baxter, meet Rooster," Travis said, introducing his two companions to one another.

Travis had explained her situation to Rooster, leaving out his own feelings of course. He knew there was no way to be with Ava, if she even felt the same way. So he left his affections for the woman out of the explanation.

"It's a pleasure to meet you, ma'am."

"Call me, Ava, please."

"I'd be happy to," he said.

"Rooster lent me a hand getting out of Vicksburg. Once we get these prisoners on board we'll get off the ground."

Ava opened the last two cages, while Travis led Frank Lee Voss inside. The gunman was stiff and obviously searching for a way to get free before his fate was sealed, but Travis had his gun out. The Slinger wouldn't kill him, but no one relished getting stunned for no reason. They didn't remove his restraints or soaked clothing. It was warm on the ship, and they could see to the prisoner's comfort once they were safely off P2.

"One down, one to go," Travis said.

"I can start the preflight checklist," Ava said. "I was about to start cooking, but if we're leaving ..."

"Yeah, it can wait," Travis said.

"Rooster, would you like a tour of our little ship?" Travis asked.

"I wouldn't say no," he replied with a smile. "And if that offer of a hot shower still stands ..."

"It does," Travis said. "We can put you down closer to Vicksburg. I don't want to land in the lot, but you'll be within sight of your ship."

The rain had settled into a cold drizzle, and both men were soaked through. They helped Sanchez off the mule and half carried him into the ship.

"How long you gonna keep us locked up like this?" Adam Turney demanded to know. "It ain't fair."

"I think you better get used to it," Travis said. "Odds are, you'll be spending the better part of your life behind bars."

"I'm going to kill you, lawman," Frank Lee Voss said. "Maybe not today, or tomorrow, but it's coming."

Travis ignored him. "Ava can show you the shower," Travis said to Rooster. "I'm going to release the animals."

"You don't want to sell them before you leave?"

"No," Travis said. "I just want to get off this miserable planet."

"All right, I understand," Rooster said.

Ava appeared in the doorway that separated the cargo hold from the engineering space. "Everything's ready," she said, the excitement in her voice undeniable.

He couldn't blame her. The moment she had been hoping for, probably dreaming about, had finally arrived. They had a full ship, which meant maximum profits, and they were leaving P2. Civilized planets awaited. Travis hadn't added up how much her cut of the reward money would be, but he knew her portion from the capture of Frank Lee Voss would be fifty thousand credits, which was more than the full reward of some of the other prisoners.

"Show Rooster the shower. I'm setting the animals loose, and then we'll go."

She nodded. Travis thought she looked beautiful in that moment. He liked making her happy. It occurred to him as he walked down the rear hatch ramp that a man could do a lot worse than spending his life making a good woman happy. It was something to think about, he told himself.

Macy was waiting. Travis pulled the saddle off her back. She neighed.

"That's right girl. I'm setting you free."

The horse looked at him with soulful eyes.

"Sure, I'd take you with me if I could," he said, removing the bit from between her teeth and the bridle from around her head. "But I think you'll be pretty happy out here."

He turned to the mule. "You watch out for her, Tuck," he said, removing the mule's bridle as well. "The two of you have earned some loafing time. It's cold here, but there's plenty of grass."

The sack of oats was still half full. He sat it on the ground with the mouth rolled back so the animals could get into it. They both bent their heads down and began to eat. Travis felt a sense of lightness in his chest as he carried the saddle back toward the ship. In the dull gray morning light, he never saw the laser beam that hit him.

# 26

Iona felt the betrayal. It was like a cold steel blade slicing into her back, scraping on her ribs, as it punctured her soul. But she came from a world of betrayal. Loyalty was part of the code her people, members of the Incendius Organization, lived by. Unless a person could rise up in the ranks through betrayal. Merit was good, earning was better, but betrayal was the fast track to the top. She knew that well enough. The one good thing about being a strong woman was the fact that no one ever trusted her. She didn't bat an eye seeing those around her fall, as long as she was lifted on the heat of their destruction. But it was a rare thing that she felt the bitter taste of being betrayed.

Travis Hurts was seconds away from death, and Morgan Black had ruined everything. It was freezing cold outside, but her fury burned so strongly that she didn't even notice. The crowd was dissipating, as their morbid curiosity waned. Iona had to push down the desire to draw her own weapon and gun the bounty hunter down. But Morgan black had his weapon leveled and ready. She might be able to shoot him before he shot her, but the odds were against her gunning them both down. And there were still enough witnesses behind the tent to spread the story that a woman had done the shooting. She was one of the few females deeply involved in organized crime. It wouldn't take the authorities long to discern that Iona had slain the bounty hunter, which was exactly why Dice had hired an outside contractor.

She watched the two of them move away from the fight tent. The lantern was lowered, the space grew dark. Iona turned and walked back toward the main street of the muddy little town. It didn't take long for Reg to return, and Vega Volinski was with him.

"Things did not go your way," the gangster said. Unlike the rest of his henchmen, he wore a long leather coat with a huge collar turned up against the wind. It had the same sherpa lining, and he had a close-fitting skull cap made of synthetic wool over his large, bald head.

"They rarely do when outsiders are involved," Iona said.

"My people did not interfere, as per your wishes," Vega said.

"No, I wasn't talking about your people. I have no complaints on that score. Your hospitality will not be forgotten."

It was a double-edged comment. The shack she had been overcharged for, and the generous distribution deal that Orvil had negotiated, were not in the Incendius Organization's favor. She would not forget that they fleeced her when she needed to do some work in their territory. But she doubted Vega understood the veiled threat.

"You are leaving now?"

"Leaving town, not your territory. Not until the bounty hunter is dead," she admitted.

"What do you need?"

"My people will handle things. We'll take the lawman at his ship."

"Just don't leave a mess for my people to clean up," he warned her. "That was not part of the deal."

She nodded, and the head of the Volinski Syndicate moved back the way he had come.

"What now, boss?" Reg asked. He looked as angry as she felt.

"Get your hoverbike and follow us out to Hurts' ship," she said. "Orvil will be in contact. We're done waiting."

"Damn straight," Reg said. He was a local man, just a tough guy that had proven himself to Orvil and the local crew. He meant nothing to Iona, nor did she respect him, but she liked his enthusiasm.

The transport was running when she arrived. Orvil hadn't heard the news and she explained the frustrating turn of events.

"So, we aren't leaving?"

"We're going after them," she said. "Get us moving in the right direction, but swing wide. I want to be in place when the bounty hunter arrives."

"What about Black?" Orvil asked.

"His time is up," she snapped.

"Maybe he's just waiting for the right moment," Orvil said. "He still might get the job done."

"If he doesn't, he dies," she said coldly. "We use your plan. Make it look like one of the prisoners got loose and killed the others."

"Works for me," he said.

She knew he would step up once she acknowledged his role in coming up with the plan. He was an earner, his cooking lab turned out enough dreamers to keep half the organization's crews supplied. He oversaw the distribution too, vetting the smugglers getting the narcotics through customs and onto various worlds where it could be sold to the masses. They ran half a dozen boom towns like Vicksburg and Camp Sherman, and made a tidy profit exchanging hard currency for Dust and treasures. But like every other member of the organization, he dreamed of more. He knew that Iona acknowledging that the plan to deal with Travis Hurts was his would give the gangster a boost with the higher ups.

They flew for an hour, going in a very wide loop before settling three miles beyond the *Purgatory*. Reg had followed them on a small, one rider hover bike. It wasn't a silent machine, but not as loud as a wheeled vehicle, and nothing like the noise from the transport, which had heavy duty repulsers and turbo thrusters.

"You two arm up," she ordered. "Then hike into our position."

"You taking my bike?" Reg asked, clearly uncomfortable with the idea.

"You have a problem with that?" Iona said.

Orvil hit his underling on the arm. Reg looked at his boss with trepidation, not fearing for himself, but for the vehicle.

"No," Reg said at last. "That's fine."

She climbed onto the bike, ignited the two small repulsers and sped away. Hewy Prescott was exactly one mile away from the *Purgatory*. Iona hid the hoverbike in a clump of bushes and joined Prescott, another of Orvil's local workers, near a rock the size of a large pumpkin. It wasn't much cover, but at that distance, and with Prescott stretched out on the ground, there was little chance he would be seen. The sniper had a Lexton High Impact laser rifle with a big hunting scope. It was more than enough to take down a person at that distance.

"Anything?" she asked, going to her knees beside the sniper.

"Nary a thing," he replied. "It's quiet. Been quiet except for the prisoner he brought in yesterday morning."

"Good. He's on his way now," she said. "I'll take this position. Leave the rifle."

"My pleasure," he said. "I been freezing my rear off out here for days."

"It won't be for nothing," she said. "We take care of our own."

He grinned in the darkness.

"You, Orvil, and Reg get ready to move in once I take Hurts down. Orvil knows the plan. We'll move the ship to neutral territory and leave it for the locals to find, eventually."

"You're the boss," Prescott said.

He disappeared back the way she had come, and Iona looked through the scope. The ship was too far away to see in the darkness, but the scope had night vision. The rectangular ship was easy to find. It was the only thing on the open prairie except for grass and the occasional shrub.

After a while Orvil crawled out to make sure she was okay. She was wet, cold, and mad as a hornet. He got his marching orders, and three outlaws began a slow crawl toward whatever might conceal them once the sun came up. Iona was glad that Orvil was smart enough not to bunch up behind one bush or rock. Instead, he and the other two tough guys spread out. She guessed they were as close as a quarter mile from the ship when she finally spotted two men leading two animals. They were so far out that she couldn't identify them, but she was certain it was Travis Hurts and Morgan Black. What she couldn't understand is what had changed the assassin's plan to kill the bounty hunter? Did they have some kind of link in their past? Or maybe they knew the same woman at different times in their lives? She didn't think two people could know each other that well in the short amount of time they had been together, but something had changed. Not that Morgan Black was anything but a wild card under the best of circumstances. He had no loyalty to her, or the Incendius Organization. She knew he was a wealthy man, not filthy rich, but certainly not living paycheck to paycheck. The money that Dice had already paid him was more than most people working honest jobs made in an entire year. A man with no ties to their organization, and no need for money, was a man she didn't trust. They had no dirt on Morgan Black, and so he had no reason not to betray them.

Iona kept the rifle trained on the two men. She watched them approach the ship, finally coming into focus. In the gray dawn light she was able to swap the scope back to regular vision and identify the two men. She could even see their prisoners, one on the mule, one staggering along behind it.

"There you are," she said.

Her men had strict instructions not to advance on the ship or commence the attack until she fired the first shot. She took her time, watching as they took the prisoners on board. She saw the woman from Camp Sherman, the pregnant widow, on board the *Purgatory*. She saw Morgan Black go further into the ship where she couldn't see him any longer. Then she watched as Travis Hurts saw to the animals all alone. He was such a fool. Did he really think he was safe? Men had certain advantages that she didn't have, especially in the criminal life she had accepted as her own. But sometimes those innate advantages caused them to have blind spots too. Travis Hurts, like most men, simply assumed they would get away with whatever scheme they cooked up. The bounty hunter thought he was safe. He thought he had won, and would ride off into the sunset with a ship full of valuable captives. The fool had no idea the man in his ship with the widow was the most dangerous assassin in the galaxy.

Maybe it was the widow woman, she mused as she focused the crosshairs of the rifle scope on Travis Hurts. Maybe they both knew her from an early point in their lives. Or maybe there was a kinship no one had found in their digging through Travis Hurts' life story. Iona knew he was raised by a murderer. His father killed his mother, leaving him a helpless victim in the foster system. Who knew what abuses he had endured growing up. At a young age his father returned, kidnapped him from the foster parents who were raising him, and fled to a moon in another system. Any law enforcement officer with half a brain could have tracked them down, but most criminals who flee the planet are forgotten about. And with no one who actually cared for the foster kid, there was no one to press the police to find him.

Travis was raised by his father, until he turned his old man in to the police and set out on his own. It was a gutsy move. Iona had checked on his father, who was still on Lucerine, a hard penal world that was about as close to hell as a person could get in life. She didn't envy him, or the hatred he must harbor for the son who betrayed him. Maybe she would send Leon Hurts a message letting him know his son was dead. Iona felt a sense of satisfaction at that thought, as she breathed in a short breath, held it to steady her aim, and fired.

# 27

The laser beam hit the saddle and burned through it to Travis's hip. His duster had heat-absorbing fibers that would save him from a short range, low power laser shot. It didn't keep the beam from leaving a nasty burn on Travis' hip, but it wasn't a kill shot. In fact, the wound was only skin deep. The kinetic energy knocked him down. He hit the ground and rolled toward the ship, slapping the controls as he crawled under the vessel. The rear hatch closed, and the security features engaged.

For the first time since landing on P2, Travis drew his Ranger around on the harness hidden inside his long jacket. It was a full size tactical repeating rifle with a Xenatron High Capacity power cell. It didn't have variable power, and couldn't be set to stun. It was a lethal weapon, with a full forty shots available with the Xenatron HC battery.

Three men rose up, seemingly out of nowhere, like demons being summoned from the underworld. Only they were outlaws with laser pistols, which they fired as they ran. Most of the shots were wild, not so much aimed at him as pointed in the general direction. Some hit the ground, others hit the ship. The *Purgatory* had heat resistant tile shielding covering the hull. It was meant to protect the vessel from the friction heat of entering a planet's atmosphere, but they also did a good job of deflecting the laser beams of small arms fire. The ship sat on landing struts that held the vessel nearly three feet off the ground. That left a small gap for the outlaws to shoot at. They were bold until Travis raised his Ranger rifle and shot back.

His first shot hit a man with lank, greasy hair, and filthy clothes. The beam knocked him backward while simultaneously burning through his chest. Hewy Prescott was dead before he hit the ground. Travis would have joined him in the afterlife if he hadn't moved when he did. To get his Fugitive Recovery license he had attended a host of special training seminars while working for the Rosenthal Detective Group. He learned how to shoot, but also the importance of moving in a gun fight. His instructors would say, "Stay still and die fast," over and over to the students until it echoed in Travis' mind anytime he was in a fight.

As soon as he made his initial shot he rolled to his left. A powerful laser beam, from far beyond where the other two outlaws had come from, ripped past him. It was barely above the ground, singeing the tips of the tall, fibrous grass. As Travis stopped his roll, one of the outlaws slid down, feet first, only thirty yards out from the ship.

Travis fired first and missed, as he tried to shimmy and shoot at the same time. The outlaw, a skinny man in a dirty black coat, returned fire with his laser pistol. He blasted two wild shots. One hit the ship, the other was close enough that Travis felt the heat. But it was the last of the charges in the outlaw's weapon. He turned and started running away. Travis fired again, hardly aiming. The shot scored a burn across his thigh. The outlaw fell, but bounced back up as quickly as possible and hobbled away.

Travis rolled again, this time coming out from under the ship. The last of the gunmen was on the opposite side of the *Purgatory*. The mysterious sniper was too, but that didn't mean Travis was out of danger. He jumped up onto the side of the ship, grabbing the utility rails beside the fold-out wings. There were small hand- and footholds that allowed him to climb up onto the vessel. The ship seemed to be flat on top, but was actually rounded. He slithered up the side and peeked over the top. He could see something in the distance. It was too far out to be recognize or even tell exactly what it was, but it was the only thing Travis could see that might be the sniper. He raised his rifle and fired nine fast shots. The beams peppered the area. A mile was about the Ranger's maximum range, but it was enough to get the shooter moving. Travis saw someone scrambling back. They were running away. At the same time, he felt the vibration as the airlock on the far side of the ship began to cycle.

"That's it," a gruff voice. "You move and you die, bounty hunter."

Travis froze. The voice was coming from behind him. He glanced back. The third outlaw was pointing a gun up at him. Travis thought it might be possible to leap forward and slide over the rounded roof of the ship before the man shot him, but it was doubtful.

"Throw down that rifle, Mister," the outlaw said.

Travis let go of the Ranger and it slid off the side of the *Purgatory's* roof.

"Now that Kicker," the outlaw instructed him. "Two fingers, nice and slow. Pull it out of the holster and drop it too."

Travis had no idea what was happening on the far side of the ship. Had someone he hadn't seen gotten in? What was happening to Rooster and Ava? He should have been more on guard. With so many prisoners in his custody it was only rational that their compatriots might be looking to spring them.

He pulled the Kicker out of the holster just as instructed. He let it fall. Oddly enough, even though he was facing the threat of almost certain death, he was thinking how bad it was for his weapons to be on the wet ground. He would need to disassemble, dry, and clean them. Laser weapons didn't much like getting wet, and a wet weapon could be deadly to its user.

"Now you come on down," the man said. "Ain't no use in trying anything stupid. This is the end of the line for you. Better start thinking about your lady friend and what you want to happen to her."

Travis managed to turn and get a look at the man. He was in nicer clothes than his companions, but still soaked, with little bits of grass sticking to his trousers and jacket. Travis was hoping he might get a chance to pull his Slinger before the man saw it. But at that very moment Rooster came strolling around front of the ship.

"What kind of man threatens a wom—"

Rooster had his long-barreled pistol out, but wasn't aiming it at the man. He held it casually at his side. The moment he spoke the outlaw turned and fired. The shot hit Rooster in his left shoulder. At the same time Travis went for his Slinger. The outlaw turned back and fired at Travis, but missed wide. Travis fired too, and missed, his shot going just over the outlaw's head.

*Stay still and die fast.*

Travis flung himself forward. The outlaw shot again, but Travis was already dropping to the ground. He landed hard in the muck and rolled. The outlaw fired again, but couldn't track Travis fast enough. The lawman returned fire, hitting the outlaw center mass. He fell to his knees, dropping his pistol, alive but unconscious from the Slinger's stun shot.

The mud, just a few inches of it, had softened Travis' landing enough that he wasn't injured in the fall. He crawled over to where Rooster had been spun around and was lying face down.

"No, no, no," Travis said, fearing the worst. He rolled his friend over and Rooster groaned.

"Oh, that hurts," he said.

"You're alive. Okay, that's ... that's good."

He pulled back the workman's coat. It was a rugged, canvas type synthetic on the outside, with a simple felt lining. There was a blackened hole at the shoulder, and when Travis pulled the coat back, he found a similar burn through the shirt, but smaller. There was a third degree burn on Rooster's skin, but the laser hadn't gone deep enough to be deadly.

"What are you wearing?" Travis asked.

"Insurance," Rooster croaked. "It's supposed to absorb the energy."

"It worked."

"Doesn't feel like it," Rooster said.

Travis had a burn on his hip too. It was painful, but not debilitating. He helped Rooster up.

"Any idea who they were?"

"No," he said. "Never seen them before."

"There's still a couple out there," Travis explained. "We have to go now, before they come back."

He helped Rooster past the body of the dead outlaw, stopping only long enough to retrieve his weapons. Travis was tempted to scan his face and search the criminal database, but there was no time for lingering. He opened the rear hatch and they hurried inside.

"What the hell, lawman?" Frank Lee Voss shouted. "What happens to us if you get yourself killed."

Travis ignored him. The hatch was closing. The angry gunman hit the bars of his cell. They boomed, but didn't budge.

The others joined in, shouting and testing the limits of their cages. Travis turned and raised his Slinger.

"Ain't no prohibition against keeping you unconscious until I take you in," he warned them. "Settle down, or I'll do it for you."

"Coward, give me a gun and we'll see what kind of man you are," Frank Lee Voss snarled.

Travis fired in an almost careless fashion, shooting from the hip. The Slinger made a ~*Voip!*~ sound as it shot a stun beam straight into Voss' chest. The gunman was thrown backwards. He crashed hard into the bars between his cage and Augustine Ward's, before he slumped to the ground.

"Anyone else like to lodge a complaint?" Travis asked.

No one spoke but Rooster. "I like your style," he said.

"Come on, we'll get you fixed up."

Ava was waiting in the living quarters. She looked terrified, but when she spoke, she seemed calm.

"What do you need?"

"Take us up?"

"Me?" she asked.

"Yes, fast."

"Got it," she said.

He saw her hurry to the pilot's seat on the right side of the cockpit. Travis helped Rooster into the reclining lounger, and then grabbed the first aid kit that was stashed under the counter in the galley. He came back with a burn relief spray in a tiny can. He emptied it into the wounded man's shoulder.

"Thanks," Rooster said. "That helps."

"I can take you to a medical center," he offered.

"On this planet? No thank you. The only doctors here are the ones that failed out of med school or lost their licenses."

"You can stay with us," Travis said. "If you want."

"Be a bounty hunter like you?"

"Fugitive Recovery Specialist," Travis corrected him.

Rooster laughed a harsh little bark of a laugh. "I don't think so," he said. "Just take me to my ship. I'll be fine from there."

"You sure?"

"I've had worse, believe you me. This is nothing. I'll be right as rain before you know it."

"All right. And Rooster, thanks for being there for me."

"My pleasure, Travis," he said.

Travis turned and headed for the cockpit. He didn't see Rooster, AKA Morgan Black, easing his Widow Maker out of his holster.

# 28

Iona was running. She wasn't a coward, but somehow, she had missed the bounty hunter. The rifle was to blame. The scope obviously wasn't sighted in correctly. Her first shot was a hit, but it was low and off center. She tried to correct with the second shot, but aimed too high. The third shot while the coward hid under his ship should have been perfect, but the timing was off.

After that she saw Prescott fall, and Reg running away. The momentum in the fight was changing. She got off one more shot before the bounty hunter disappeared from view. A few moments later, while Iona was scanning for him, the confounded lawman appeared on the roof of the ship and peppered the ground all around her with laser fire. If there had been suitable cover, she would have waited to get another shot, but she had always listened to her intuition. She told herself she should have listened to it about Morgan Black. At that moment, with laser fire kicking up dirt and rocks all around her, that quiet inner voice had told her to run. And she didn't need to be told twice. The ambush had failed, and it was time to fall back and regroup.

She ran to the hoverbike and drove it back to the larger transport. She left the small vehicle and got the larger transport started. At almost the same time the *Purgatory* lifted off. She saw it rising straight up into the air. She considered taking another shot with the sniper rifle, but there was little chance it would do any damage. Plus, she didn't want to attract the bounty hunter's attention. Odds were good his ship had weapons, and she preferred to strike from a place of overwhelming power, not the other way around.

After watching the ship take off, Iona drove toward the scene of the attack. Reg was staggering toward her, clearly wounded. What she didn't know was whether he was injured from the battle, or if he had hurt himself running away like a coward. She drove right up beside him, and he leaned on the transport.

"He got me," Reg said. "My leg's on fire."

"That why you ran?" Iona asked, her voice as hard as titanium.

"My pistol ran out of power," he said, suddenly worried.

"And Orvil?"

"They got him," Reg said.

"Then I don't suppose I need you for anything," she said.

His eye grew large with fear as she pulled out her small pistol. The gun made a flash as it fired a laser that burned its way through Reg's chest. He was still holding the door of the transport as he fell forward. He made a gagging sound, followed by a shuddering groan. Iona wondered for a moment if she would have to shoot him again, but he exhaled a long, slow breath and died. Nothing was going right, she thought, but she was tying up the loose ends, and ensuring that no one would contradict her story, whatever she decided that would be. It felt horrible to lose, but she wasn't down for the count. She would get back on her feet to fight another round. And it felt empowering to be putting the pieces in place, or taking them out as the case might be.

Reg was still holding onto the transport as she sped away. The sudden movement caused his body to spin. He bounced against the side of the transport twice before finally falling to the ground. She glanced in the rear camera feed and saw his body lying still and lifeless in the tall grass. His dirty coat was coated with mud and debris. She could just make out the laser hole in his back. Iona didn't tolerate failure, and Reg had run from the battle. It would have been better for him to stay and fight. Under different circumstances, she would have made an example of him. And in her own narcissistic focus, it never occurred to her that she had done the same thing. In her mind, the reality of the battle was changing. Facts meant nothing to her, only perceptions. She didn't think of herself as a coward for running. She had done the prudent thing by saving herself. Reg, on the other hand, had shown his true colors by fleeing. Nor did she believe he had emptied his pistol and taken a real wound. The scorch mark on his trousers could have come from anything, she decided. He was a coward that needed to die. And taking care of him had been as common to her as emptying a bag of garbage.

The dark clouds above mirrored her own emotional state. Iona was angry. She knew that Dice would be too, especially if there was a hiccup with the drug supply. And he would blame her. Dice Jester wasn't stupid. He knew she was ambitious, but he also recognized her talent. What Iona needed was a believable way to spin the story, and a reliable man on the ground making sure nothing interfered with the production of one of their most lucrative products. When word got out that Orvil was dead, the wolves would begin circling. They all wanted the lab, every cartel, syndicate, and OC crew on the planet. And many would rather see it destroyed than let someone else run it. She would need one of her most ruthless and efficient people to oversee the protection of the lab, and she knew just who to send.

There were two bodies left out in the empty field. She drove right past Prescott, but stopped near Orvil. He was a made man. Finding him dead out here, in the middle of nowhere in the Volinski Syndicate's territory, would raise some major red flags. She got out, but left the transport running. Orvil lay on his side, his legs folded under him, his gun lying beside him. She rolled him over, saw where his clothes were darkened from the stun blast, but there was no laser burn. Putting her fingers to his neck she could feel his pulse was strong. The lawman had stunned him. Prescott was dead. She had driven past him and saw the wound. His eyes had been open and staring up vacantly. But Orvil was alive.

"You have to be the luckiest man on the planet," she said.

Iona worked out with heavy weights on a regular basis. She was nearly as strong as most men. Orvil wasn't small, but he wasn't heavy with muscle or fat. She sat him up, stooped down and flipped him over her shoulder. Then she carried him to the passenger seat of the transport and flopped him into it. He would be sore when he woke up, but sore was much better than dead.

Orvil was still alive, and that changed everything. He would need to focus on the drug production and ensuring that no one came against them. They had failed, but no one needed to know that. Morgan was the traitor, and all Iona needed to do was shift the focus of Dice and his Capos to that one fact. She would paint an undeniable picture of the cowardly assassin. Her own failures would be minimized, while Morgan's would be amplified. Orvil wouldn't contradict her. Revealing her failure would be to admit his own. That was all the leverage she needed over him.

After climbing back into the hovercraft and taking the controls, Iona thought about what she should do next. Vicksburg was to the north, but there was nothing for her there. She had already ended her stay with the Volinski Syndicate leader. To go back would be to acknowledge her failure. She would have to do that with Dice, but no one else. There was work to be done. After regrouping, Iona would find a way to fix the mess Morgan Black had made. He was on her list. The bounty hunter too. And while she was at it, she would snuff the widow woman just because she could. That wicked thought made her smile in a savage, horrible kind of way. She turned south, pressed the throttle forward, and raced away.

†††

Vega Volinski kept his personal quarters on a modified hoverbus, essentially a double decker public transport ship that had been found in the rubble of Laverton, one of the mega-cities that had once populated Pergamum Prime before the alien invasion and war. What had once been full of passenger seats had been converted to a portable home and tech headquarters. P2 was a planet that had lost much of its former technology, but Vega was a firm believer that modern tech found on other planets would give him an edge in the struggle to control as much of the war-torn planet as possible.

His lieutenant was a mousy man with frizzy hair, bad breath, and some very dark hobbies named Damien Sellers. He was also a tech whiz, and was currently operating a drone hovering five hundred feet above the plot of land where the *Purgatory* had been. It was a small drone, no bigger than a sparrow, but with a high-resolution camera, and the ability to broadcast the video feed back to Vicksburg.

"Well?" Vega asked as he poured himself a cup of coffee and wrapped his thick robe a little tighter around his broad shoulders.

"You were right," Damien said. "It just went down."

"And you got what we needed?"

"Oh yes," he said. "They never even looked up. I got close ups of everyone's face, especially Freeze."

"They killed the bounty hunter, then?"

"No," he said with a chuckle. "The fools botched it."

He gave a brief recap while the video he had recorded of the ambush played on a big display screen.

"So where are they now?" Vega asked.

"I have no idea where Freeze and her lapdog have run to. Probably off world. But here's an interesting bit of information. The *Purgatory* flew straight up, and then began a slow descent."

"Where?"

"Just outside the city," Damien said, referring to Vicksburg.

"Here? They're coming back here?"

"Looks like it."

"Oh, this is a prize," Vega said. "Round up the troops. Let's show the lawman just what we think of his kind."

"What do you want done with the footage?"

"Can you alter it?" the crime boss asked. "Make it look like Iona Freeze and her rabble succeeded in killing the bounty hunter?"

"Sure," Damien said. "And if you capture his ship, we can make a real production of it."

"I just need to show that the Incendius people were behind the assassination. We'll leak it to the dark web, but make sure the right people find it."

"So, the law does our work for us," Damien said with a wicked chuckle. "They're so easy to manipulate."

"Dice Jester and his pack of fools will lose ground all across the galaxy. And we'll be waiting to take it. Starting with his cooking lab."

"Sounds like a plan, boss. What do you want me to do?"

"Make sure everyone is armed, and find a way to keep the bounty hunter's ship on the ground."

"Can do," he said, getting to his feet and hurrying from his usual spot in their gang headquarters. "We'll be waiting outside for you, boss."

"Excellent," he said. "I'll be right out."

Vega pulled off his robe and picked up a Pulser Industries tactical assault weapon. It was a military grade, automatic laser rifle. He couldn't help but grin with the anticipation of using the weapon. There were so few opportunities for a real fight on Pergamum Prime. The criminals existed in a delicate balance, holding certain territories and resources. He couldn't challenge the Incendius Organization outright. That would make the Volinski Syndicate vulnerable. Orvil and his pack of fools could ally with other groups to crush Vega and split up the Volinski territory. It was better to wait until an enemy showed their weakness, then he could chip away at their resources. But the assault rifle was made for more direct fighting. And he was finally going to get a chance to use it.

# 29

Ava Lynn Baxter was flying a ship. It wasn't a simulation. She could feel the pull of gravity as the *Purgatory* rose up into the air. Her heart was pounding with the exhilaration of being in control of something so big, so powerful. It was something she felt was lost forever when her husband was killed. What had started as an adventure had dissolved into a nightmare that she felt powerless to escape from. Had it just been herself, she might have merely accepted her fate. But it wasn't just her. She had a baby, a precious little child growing inside her. She could feel it moving, and her love for it was fierce. For a long time she grieved for her loss, but even more painful was the realization that she could do nothing for her child. On P2 she had been alone, penniless, and completely out of options. She spent all day long scrubbing clothes just to have enough credits to feed herself, and with the baby inside it was never enough. But there were no options. Camp Sherman had been the closest settlement, and it had taken her nearly a week to get there on foot. Going anywhere else had seemed impossible.

Then Travis had come along with an offer that seemed too good to be true. She would have turned him down, except there was something about him, something honest and good. Ava had always been a discerning person. And she had been won over by the earnestness of the lawman, not his credentials, or the fabulous benefits of safety, food, money, or the promise of getting off world. So far, everything he promised had been true. She was out of the worn-down tent she had been living in, and in the safety of a starship. It had only one living space, and that was quite small, but Travis had generously given it over to her. She had gone from sleeping on the ground to sleeping in a real bed, and a comfortable one at that. She had gone from barely having enough food to having more than she could eat. Despite the fact that there were wanted killers just two compartments from where she slept, she felt safe.

Yet, beyond the rich rewards she enjoyed, it was the empowerment that made the real difference. She fed the prisoners on board the ship, and did a little first aid. He hadn't asked her to, but she also cleaned the vessel. In her mind, anyone could do those things. It was when he encouraged her to learn to fly the ship that things really changed for Ava. She had gone through the training simulations, sometimes redoing the more difficult modules several times. It wasn't enough to pass each section, she needed to ace it. And with plenty of time on her hands she had done just that, honing her skills and really learning the abilities until she had a firm grasp on both atmospheric and space flight. But it had all been simulations. She had never flown before.

While Travis saw to his friend, he had given her probably the greatest gift she had ever received. It was a gift of trust. Of course, her husband had loved and trusted her, but he was so wrapped up in his inventions that she sometimes felt neglected. Silently she chided herself for feeling that way. He had been a good man, just maybe not as attentive as she would have hoped. But the thrill of flying had surpassed everything that came before it. Her grief, and her fears receded in the exhilaration of controlling the powerful aircraft. The ground fell away below her, and soon the ship was enveloped in the clouds.

Suddenly, without warning, the ship burst through the clouds and into the dazzling light of the sun. Below the clouds P2 was a drab and dreary place. But above the clouds the world looked completely different. The gray clouds were bright white, and gilded in golden sunlight. The sky was clear, everything was bright and cheerful. She brought the ship to a stop, letting it hover above the clouds while she surveyed the incredible world she had discovered and let the sunshine on her face.

"Beautiful," Travis said.

He was standing just inside the cockpit, and for the briefest instant she thought he was referring to her. Ava never thought she would ever feel good again after her husband was killed. And romance was simply a thing of the past. It never even crossed her mind that she would ever have feelings for someone again. And yet, she couldn't deny the fluttery feeling inside her when Travis said that one word.

Of course, he was referring to the clouds. They were beautiful and majestic. Ava had heard of people living in enclosed dome cities on gas giants. She had seen high resolution holograms of the swirling, colorful gas clouds on those worlds, but she had never thought of living there. But looking out the *Purgatory's* front view screens, she thought it might be wonderful to see such incredible, natural beauty every single day.

"It is," she replied. "It's like a completely different world up here."

"Yeah, too bad we have to go back," Travis said, moving over to the pilot's seat on the left-hand side of the cockpit.

"Back?"

"To Vicksburg," Travis said. "Just long enough to get Rooster to his ship."

"And then we're leaving?"

Travis nodded. "Straight to orbit. We'll set course for the nearest system that has a reward for one of the prisoners. We'll resupply there too. You can pick out some groceries, and start making plans."

"Plans?"

"Where you want to live," Travis said. "I didn't get a chance to tell you. We got Frank Lee Voss."

"The outlaw with the big reward?"

"Half a million," Travis said. "You'll have over eighty-thousand credits to get you started. That's enough to do just about whatever you want. It might not go far on a core world, but there are a lot of good planets where eighty thousand is a decent yearly wage."

She felt a pang of disappointment. Of course, he was anxious to get rid of her. She was just his employee, nothing more. She had watched over the prisoners while he did his work, and with that job done, her part was over. It was a bitter realization, and she felt tears stinging her eyes.

"I'll let you take us down," she said, getting to her feet and moving to the door.

"Okay. Are you all right, Ava?"

"Fine," she said, rubbing a hand over her stomach. "This little thing is standing on my bladder."

"Oh, yeah, that's something ..."

He seemed almost embarrassed. She slipped out of the cockpit and went straight to the bathroom, chiding herself for thinking that any man, no matter how good, would want her while she was carrying her late husband's child. The tears came hard and fast. She told herself it was hormones. She had found herself bawling watching one of the entertainment vids on the ship one evening. Her physical reality was changing so much. Her stomach seemed to grow bigger each day, and she hadn't been lying about needing to use the bathroom. The child inside her pressed on organs and fluttered around so much that sometimes it was hard to sleep.

"Get ahold of yourself," Ava whispered, not noticing in her rush to the bathroom that the cabin where Travis had left his friend was empty.

# 30

Morgan could have done the deed right then and there. He could have killed Travis and his lady friend with quick shots to the back of their heads while they were chatting away in the cockpit. But that wasn't Morgan's style, and he knew better than to go shooting his pistol inside an aircraft. It wouldn't do to finish the job, only to die himself in a crash. Besides, he was almost feverish with anticipation of looking into Travis' eyes when Morgan revealed who he really was.

His shoulder hurt, but he could deal with pain. In fact, his mind was able to compartmentalize the pain and simply lock it away. He still felt it, especially when he moved his left arm, but it wouldn't impede him in any way. The cabin of the ship was neat, clean, and functional, but it had no sense of style. There was almost no decor, just bare bulkheads and plain furniture. It almost seemed sad to Morgan, who thought of it as a prison cell. Only the key to the cell was hanging by the door that led to the engineering space. He got to his feet, grabbed the key, and slipped back through the engineering section. The big Holstead

FTL drives were silent, but the quad repulsers hummed, and he could see the wings locked in their horizontal positions for flight in P2's thick atmosphere through small windows on either side of the ship. But Morgan wasn't interested in the aircraft, or the engines. He went on through to the cargo section where six poor souls were locked up with no hope of escape.

Morgan stood in the doorway for a moment admiring the way the cells were crafted. It was a timeless design, welded steel bars for walls, heavy duty doors. There was just enough room in each of the holding cells for an adult to lay down with their head toward the door, and their feet nearly touching the solid back wall. Each one was wide enough that a person in the center was out of reach of the person in the adjoining cell.

He didn't think of himself as an outlaw, or even a criminal. Morgan Black was an artist with a unique skill set that allowed him to thrive unseen in the galaxy. Known, but unknown. Without his mask and black attire, he could mix and mingle in civilization without anyone knowing that he made his living, a small fortune really, killing people. Not that he really considered it killing. He did kill, but he was more than just a murderer. Anyone could commit murder, as he often thought to himself. He was an artist of death and terror, known by many names such as The Man In Black, The Wraith, The Specter, The Ghost Gun. Each of his many aliases were like a layer in a rich tapestry that he was crafting.

Immediately to his left was a woman. He could have released her. The key was in his hand, and he had the power to offer any of the fugitives their life back. In the woman, who sat huddled in the corner, wrapped in a blanket, he saw a kindred spirit. She too was a death dealer who lavished pain on her victims, relishing the exquisite agony of their demise. But he left her where she sat, preferring a more precise and certain outcome.

"Hello Frank," Morgan said, turning to his right.

"I know you?" the gunman asked.

"No, I'm no one important. But I do have an offer for you."

"Don't trust him," Augustine Ward snapped, holding up his wounded hand which had been wrapped in a thick bandage. "That bastard conned me into thinking he was just another rube, when all the time he was a shootist."

"What kind of offer?" Frank said, ignoring the other prisoner.

Morgan held up the key. "Freedom," he said simply. "If you can be patient."

"What the hell does that mean?"

"It means I have a plan that involves you waiting until I am off this ship before you wreak havoc upon it and your captors."

"I can do that, mister," a sad, mousy man in what looked to be little more than rags said. "I'll kill that bounty hunter for you. Do it with my bare hands if I have to. Just unlock my door."

"Don't listen to him," said Garcia Sanchez, who was still bleeding from the wound in his side. "He couldn't fight his way out of wet paper bag. Let me go, and I'll kill whoever you want."

"I'll kill you," the pathetic looking individual said as he reached through the bars and grabbed Sanchez's arm.

Even wounded, Sanchez was stronger than Adam Turney. He yanked his arm, which Turney had not expected. The sudden movement pulled him off balance, and his face crashed into the bars of the cage between them. He let go of Sanchez, grabbed his own face, and fell onto his backside.

"How long we talking?" Frank asked.

"Not long," Morgan replied, ignoring the other prisoners. "Maybe just an hour."

"You want me to kill the Bounty Hunter?"

"No, he's mine. But his lady friend ..."

"The pregnant woman?"

223

"That a problem?"

"Hell no," he snarled. "I'll snap her neck."

"Good," Morgan said. "Give me maybe ten minutes after the bounty hunter and I leave the ship. Then do your worst."

"What about them?" he asked with a jerk of his head toward the other prisoners.

"Do whatever you like with them," Morgan said, as the turned and looked at Sandra Mayfield. He had no idea who she was, or what she had done. And he felt no affection for her. He wasn't drawn to her beauty, or moved by the fact that she was a woman among some very bad men. "But you can let her go," he said. "I think that's for the best."

"Whatever you say," Frank replied.

Morgan slipped the key into the lock. It turned easily, the lock disengaging and the door opening slightly, but Frank took hold of it and pulled it closed.

"Ten minutes," he said.

Morgan nodded and headed back toward the living quarters. He hung the key by the door and was sitting in the lounge chair as the ship descended back through the clouds. Down, down, down, he thought to himself, back to the gates of hell. His heartbeat sped up, and he could feel a tingling sensation as he thought about revealing himself to Travis. It was going to be one of the most exquisite moments of his career. He had killed so many they began to blur together, but the moment when Travis Hurts realized his friend and partner was the most notorious killer in the galaxy ... well, that would make the bounty hunter's death one that Morgan Black would never forget.

# 31

The *Purgatory* flew down through the clouds without any trouble. A storm might have caused havoc with the electrical systems, and strong winds could make controlling the ship difficult. But there were no winds, no thermal updrafts, just thick clouds and drizzle. They spiraled down in a smooth descent. Travis was at the controls. He could see Vicksburg below. The world was a grey, dreary landscape, but the city was like an ugly scar. The greasy tent covers were blotches of brown, the muddy streets were almost black. People hurried from shelter to shelter, almost like an infestation of vermin.

Travis was no one's judge. What people did was only his concern once the law had been broken, and the guilty had been assigned a bounty high enough to get his attention. He didn't chase down every criminal that popped up on his database. He was more interested in the runners, in those who committed crimes on several worlds; who were, in his estimation, career violators who would cause loss, pain, and outrage wherever they went. Most were destined to die in the same manner in which they had lived. It was never surprising when a body was found, obviously the victim of murder while involved in criminal activity. Most people wrote them off, thinking they would get what they had coming to them. Travis knew better. Death was not enough. They deserved to face the people they hurt, to know that those people, the supposed victims, had in the end gotten the upper hand. The criminals might enjoy the spoils of their foul deeds for a short time, but they would rue them for the rest of their natural lives as they slaved away on penal worlds.

In his mind, Travis was both rescuing the wanted felons from where their life of crime would ultimately lead, and supplying justice to those left wounded and scarred by the criminal's actions. It was not a glamorous life. He didn't stick around after turning in an outlaw to be thanked by the families of their victims. But he had grown up around men and women who had no regard for anyone other than themselves. They were abusers, takers, narcissistic gaslighters, who found some sort of sick amusement in the suffering of others. His father had been as bad as anyone. To cross him would result in a beat down, which Travis learned by hard experience. His father had been like a powder keg, primed to explode at any moment and for no reason at all. Travis had tried to fight his old man a few times, before learning that it was better to just defend himself from the vicious attacks until he could escape. Eventually he escaped permanently, while his father, wanted for various crimes from theft to murder, was sent away.

Travis' mother had been Leon Hurts' first kill, but not his first crime. What she saw in him Travis couldn't fathom. Maybe it was just a fling, but soon she was pregnant and Leon Hurts had laid claim to her. No one would help her, no one would take her in. She didn't have the means to escape his clutches, and eventually he beat her to death. That crime had sent him to prison, but only on a twelve-year sentence, of which he only served nine years and a few months. He had reappeared in Travis' life like a recurring nightmare. He was just a boy at the time, only ten years old, having never known true familial love or nurturing. The foster care system on Traegen Major was sketchy. Foster parents shuffled children in and out of their homes. The children were put up in various shelters and group facilities. It was at one such state-funded group home that he had first learned about his father. A cruel older boy had looked up the information online and even printed Travis' father's mugshot. He and the older boys in the group home had taunted him with the story and the picture for months. A year later, having landed in what was a stable, if poor and slightly dysfunctional, foster family, Travis began seeing his father in various places. It was like having visions of a ghost. Travis didn't know his father at that time, but he knew what he looked like. Seeing that man in a variety of outfits, in an array of places, made him sometimes wonder if he was losing his mind.

In foster care there was always talk of how things could get worse. Juvenile detention facilities were a step down, but there were also asylums for the insane. Travis and the other children called them crazy houses, or loony bins, but they were the last place any of them wanted to end up. Travis was so afraid of those government funded facilities that he never mentioned his "visions" of seeing his father. But they weren't visions. Leon Hurts was out of the penal colony and back on Traegen Major for one purpose, to get his son. And so it was that while walking home from a school function in the dead of winter, when the days were short and people hurried to and from their destinations with little concern of anything other than staying warm, Travis had been snatched off the street.

His father immediately moved them to Rote Nine. If Vicksburg was given the chance to grow into a permanent city, it would resemble the place known as the "Sprawl" on Rote Nine.

There were dozens of cities full of hard men and women who worked in the mines, or in the shipyards. The Sprawl consisted of structures made from all types of materials, with no safety codes, no oversight. They sprang up because there were ample materials for building them, and because the hard-working blue-collar people needed a place to spend their money. They were hard drinkers, gamblers, con artists, and criminals. It was the perfect place for Leon and his son Travis to start over.

Leon didn't work, but he did run a successful con game that supplied enough money to feed himself, his son, and his litany of bad habits. There were always other people around the shack that they called home. Mostly men, but a series of women that Leon called girlfriends. They were all just like him, takers, selfish and cruel adults only too happy to torment Travis. And Leon didn't mind. If anyone ever complained, his father would explain that he was simply toughening the boy up. And so, he was. Travis learned to fight, to be wary, to protect himself. He had nothing of value, and no prospects. There was no schooling other than hard experience, and no love. But being alone in such a dangerous and scary place motivated Travis to improve himself. He was mostly self-taught using the public computers in the nearby city of Wabash, which consisted of a post office, a library, a few businesses, and a transit station. The library was open to anyone, and had computers available. Travis didn't have a permanent address living in the Sprawl, or any ID, but living in the foster system had taught him that most adults responded to politeness and good manners. For Travis it had all been an act, whether he was being polite to the librarians, or being tough to his father's friends. He learned to play the roles he needed to play to get what he needed to get.

One day Travis discovered his father's stash of hard currency, mostly bills which weren't always accepted, but there were coins too. He kept his stash in what looked like a bottle of cleaning supplies. That alone should have been a dead giveaway, since they lived in a shack that had never been cleaned. But the bottle had a twist off top, and the emergency funds were stashed there, where no thief or criminal would think to look. So, after seven hard years of life with Leon, Travis devised his plan. It took weeks to collect what he needed to get his official ID paperwork. But once he had that, he traded everything he owned of value, which wasn't much, for enough credits to buy passage off Rote Nine. Then he waited for his father to do what he eventually always did, which was drink and smoke himself into a stupor. Then Travis put his old man in an old wagon, the kind children play with. Travis had found it in the junkyard and repaired the wheels. It wasn't perfect, but it would roll. With his unconscious father in tow, Travis delivered him to the authorities in Wabash. Their job was keeping the Sprawl out of the city, and not much else, but Leon was a wanted felon. They kept him in custody and Travis stole his father's stash of hard currency and left for a better life.

It had always seemed right to him, ever since taking his father to jail, that other people deserved that same treatment. And when Travis discovered that, in some cases, a person could actually be compensated for catching outlaws and returning them to justice, he knew he had found what to do with the rest of his life. It seemed a bit strange to be returning to Vicksburg, since he already had a ship full of criminals, some of whom were worth more than he had ever collected before. Yet he would no more turn his back on Rooster than he would spit on his poor mother's grave. Without Rooster, Travis would be earning much, much less, and would almost certainly have been captured by the crew that ambushed him outside the *Purgatory*. The very least he could do was to help his injured friend back to his own ship.

He landed near the shanty town's lot of hovercraft and

atmospheric vessels. There were only a couple of true spaceships in the lot. One was a sleek, black spacecraft owned by Rooster. Travis had spotted it from the air. When they landed, it was only a hundred and fifty meters from the black ship, with maybe four or five vessels in between. He wouldn't be staying long, and left the ship running. When he stepped into the crew quarters, Ava was just coming out of the bathroom, and Rooster was already on his feet.

"Ava, I'm taking Rooster to his ship and I'll be right back," he said.

"And I'll be here waiting," she said.

Her eyes were red and puffy. Travis felt a pang of sympathy for her, although he had no idea why she would be upset.

"Are you ..."

She waved him off and went into the cockpit, clearly not interested in talking about whatever was on her mind. Travis could respect that. He decided that she was probably still grieving for her husband. They were on the verge of leaving his final resting place, and Travis guessed it was probably an emotional time for Ava.

"You ready, Rooster?"

"Quivering with anticipation."

"That must be the painkillers in that burn spray talking," Travis said.

"I appreciate you seeing me safely to my vessel," Rooster told him. "I'm a bit light-headed. I used to be able to stay awake for days and hardly notice, but I'm not as young as I sometimes think that I am."

"It's been a long haul," Travis agreed.

There was no need for Rooster to lean on Travis. His wounded shoulder wouldn't keep him from walking, but Travis still felt an obligation. There was always the chance that there could be trouble from the people in Vicksburg. He quickly swapped out the power cells on three of his weapons.

"You expecting trouble?" Rooster asked.

"No, but you have to always be prepared in my line of work."

"There's probably a handful of wanted men still in town," Rooster said. "You could lock them in the bathroom."

"No, he couldn't," Ava called out from the cockpit.

Both men laughed. They went out through the airlock on the side of the ship. It didn't have a ramp, but it wasn't much of a jump either. Travis' boots splashed in the mud. He would have to give all his clothing a major cleaning once they were out of the Pergamum system.

"I suppose this is goodbye," Rooster said.

Travis reached into his pocket and pulled out a flexible card with his name, and a scannable code.

"That's my contact," he said. "Send me your banking info, and I'll send you half the reward money for Voss."

"That isn't necessary," Rooster said, taking the card.

"It's only fair," Travis insisted. "I wouldn't have him in custody if it weren't for you."

"I suppose you're right," Rooster said with a chuckle. "I could use a vacation too. That money should cover it."

"And then some," Travis said.

They were only thirty paces from Rooster's ship. He pulled a gadget from his pocket and opened the rear hatch.

"Please come inside and let me show you—"

Before he could finish his thought, several men in dark brown leather coats stepped out from behind his ship. They were all armed, but one, the obvious leader of the pack in a longer jacket that nearly reached his knees, had a military issue automatic laser rifle. Travis felt his heart leap into his throat, and suddenly he wished he had never gone back to Vicksburg.

"Well now that you've dealt with that pesky problem from

off world," the big man with the big rifle said. "I'd like to introduce you to the Volinski Syndicate."

Travis didn't need an introduction. There was plenty of materials from law enforcement sources about the various organized criminal groups operating in multiple systems. The Volinski Syndicate was known to be filled with violent drug dealers that even had ties to human trafficking.

"No need," Rooster said in a cheerful voice. "We were just leaving."

"No," the man said. "My name is Vega Volinski, and this is my town. I'm afraid we're going to have to insist you stay for awhile, maybe forever."

"What is it you want?" Travis said, thinking maybe one of the criminals he had taken in was under the Volinski Syndicate's protection. "Did I pick up someone you want back?"

The gang members chuckled at that. Travis had already picked out a good place to take cover. Just half a dozen steps away was a converted double decker transport. It sat flat on the ground, and offered plenty of cover. He just needed to get to it.

"You know what's funny, lawman?" Vega asked. "It's that you're not half as smart as you think you are."

Beside him Rooster stiffened. There were five gang members that Travis could see. And he could have bet good money there were more behind him, but he couldn't afford to turn around and look.

"Careful," Rooster said, the cheerfulness suddenly gone from his voice.

"Oh, should I watch what I say?" Vega said with a wicked smile.

"You might end up on my bad side," Rooster said.

Travis wanted to ask him what he was doing. Fighting was courageous perhaps, but they didn't stand much of a chance against so many gang members. It was better to try and buy their way out of trouble. But Travis didn't have a chance to tell his friend that.

"I'm not worried about you," Vega said. "Lawman! Do you even know who you are partnering with?"

Travis turned and looked at Rooster. He was breathing fast, his face an unreadable mask. Travis saw that his hand was in his pocket, manipulating something. Alarm bells seemed to go off in Travis' mind. An outlaw doing something he couldn't see always made him nervous. But this wasn't an outlaw, it was an ally, a friend.

Vega Volinski cleared his throat and said in a loud voice, "That's Morgan Black you're standing with."

For an instant the world fell away. There was no sign on Rooster's face that the shot caller for the Volinski Syndicate was telling the truth, but his eyes told the tale. Travis felt a heavy lump form in his throat, and his guts felt like they had turned to cold water inside him.

Could it be true? Morgan Black, the infamous killer, was the same jovial person he knew as Rooster? It seemed impossible, but in the span of an instant he remembered Rooster gunning down Augustine Ward, literally shooting the pistol from the gunslinger's hand. And his clothing that looked like what any other miner or treasure hunter might wear had laser resistant fibers just like his own duster.

"Shouldn't have ruined the surprise," Rooster said. Or was it Morgan, Travis thought. He was in a daze, his mind running to catch up and make sense of what was happening.

A sudden blaze of laser fire erupted from the sides of the black ship that Travis had been escorting his friend to. It vaporized four of the five gangsters, including Vega and his military rifle. Their bodies didn't stop the powerful lasers, which blew large chunks of muddy ground into the air, and blew apart a small hovercraft. The explosion rocked Travis out of his daze and sent him sprinting for the cover of the converted transport.

Rooster, no Morgan Black, the infamous killer, raced in the opposite direction. He had nearly reached the ramp to his ship when he drew his long-barreled laser pistol and shot the last of the five gangsters in the face. The man's head snapped back, his features blackened by the powerful laser blast, which had burned through his face, his skull, and into his brain.

At almost the same time, laser fire from behind them flashed through the gray light. Travis, still looking at Morgan Black, saw the assassin smiling. He looked almost giddy, as he ran up the ramp and into his ship, leaving Travis all alone with the remains of the Volinski Syndicate.

# 32

Ava Lynn Baxter was still scolding herself for getting emotional. It didn't make sense, but she was suddenly flooded with very strong feelings for Travis Hurts. She barely knew the man, she told herself. Yes, he was handsome, in a plain sort of way, but it wasn't his looks that made her feel so weak in the knees. Maybe it was his rugged nature? Or perhaps it was how seemingly capable he was? He was generous, kind, yet unflinchingly cool in the face of danger. She had seen him reacting to the ambush. The *Purgatory's* exterior camera system was extensive, with high resolution video. She just happened to be watching when the attack occurred. There was something sweet about the way he looked after his animals. Ava Lynn had seen plenty of cruel men abuse their horses and mules on P2. But not Travis. He had spoken to them and removed their tack, feeding them the remainder of the oats as he set them free. And then he had been shot. In that moment she felt as if her heart was going to stop. Rooster had seen it too. They were waiting for him to return to the ship so they could leave, and when Rooster saw the ambush, he too sprang into action. Like minds were often drawn together, and they were both men of action in the face of danger.

She had seen Travis respond to the attack with knowledge and bravery. He had slain one attacker, run off two more, and stunned the fourth. The danger had passed and he had come through unscathed. Which was odd, she thought, since he did get shot. That thought made her want to take another look at Travis. She brought up the *Purgatory's* extensive camera list. It projected onto the front view screen, above the digital instrument panel touchscreen. She usually kept the selected cameras on the prisoners in the cargo hold, and that's what came up first. Her mind was on Travis, and she started to select a different video feed when she saw one of the prisoners open the door to his cell.

It wasn't difficult either. He didn't jimmy the lock, or throw his weight against the door, he simply pushed it open. Her blood ran cold at the very sight of it. The man was lanky, with narrow hips, long arms and legs. He went straight into the engineering space. Ava changed the camera feed to the engineering compartment. There wasn't anything happening in that section of the ship that she needed to keep tabs on, and rarely looked at those feeds. It popped up just in time for her see the man moving straight for the door to the living quarters. Fear stabbed at her heart and got her moving.

All she could think about was the gun that Travis had shown her. He called it a Deck Sweeper. She had to get it, and hurried from the cockpit into the living quarters, but she was only halfway to the hidden compartment by the door that led to engineering, when it swished open. She wanted to scream, but who would hear her? The ship was well insulated.

"Well, what do we have here?" the man said.

Ava didn't respond. Instead, she took a step backward. If she could get to the cockpit, she could lock its door. There was no way to know if would hold up to someone trying to get inside. And once there, she didn't know what she could do to escape the man. He was an outlaw, at least six inches taller than she was, and clearly up to no good.

Her backward step launched the man into motion. Ava tried to turn and run toward the cockpit, but got only a few steps before he caught hold of her long hair. He yanked her backward so hard she thought he must have broken her neck. Her feet flew up, and she crashed to the deck hard enough to bruise her body, but all she could think of was how grateful she was to have fallen on her back instead of on her stomach. Her maternal instincts were kicking in. She knew she had to protect her baby.

"First I'm going to wring your neck," he said as he stepped over her. "And then I'm going to burn this ugly ship to the ground."

He was in the process of reaching for her throat when Ava Lynn threw both of her feet up into his groin. She had grown up with brothers, and her father had taught her the basics of self-defense. Ava had never been in a fight before, except for scuffles with her brothers. But she was determined that the outlaw would not hurt her baby.

The lanky man groaned in pain, but didn't move from standing over her. His hands moved from reaching for her throat to grabbing his damaged privates. And Ava, once in motion, had no trouble kicking him again. The second kick was even harder than the first, lifting the outlaw off the ground. He fell forward, his hands and midsection coming straight onto her face. She felt her nose get mashed, but she threw him forward and at the same time slid down to get free of him.

"You bitch," he groaned.

But Ava was no longer listening. She rolled to her hands and knees, got one leg up, then the other. She was still a few months from the end of her pregnancy, and hopping up off the floor quickly just wasn't possible. But she got to her feet just as the man was getting to his knees. She wanted the gun, but she couldn't be sure of getting it before he got to her again. That left two choices. Risk going for the gun, or lock herself into the cockpit. Her mind seemed locked, unable to process facts in a rational fashion. But her instincts were in full swing, and she stepped forward and kicked the outlaw hard in the ribs. He flipped onto his side, grasping for breath.

That should have given her time to get the gun, and she started for the hidden compartment, but he reached out and grabbed her foot. She tried to yank it free but couldn't in time. Her body was too far forward, and she fell, just barely managing to twist onto her side to protect the baby.

"I'm going to kill you!" the outlaw screamed.

Ava's hip was throbbing with pain, and her neck felt stiff. The outlaw still had a firm grip on her left foot, but her right was free. He crawled toward her with a look of hatred in his eyes. She lashed out with her right foot, smashing the heel straight into his nose. Her own nose was running, she could feel it spreading across her upper lip. His burst with blood, like water from a kinked hose when it gets straightened. He let go of her, but she wasn't finished, and kicked him again. His teeth cut through his upper lip. There was more blood, a lot of it. But she kicked again, knocking his head sideways. Then she pushed herself backward, across the deck, toward the doorway leading to the engineering space.

The outlaw was hurt. His nose was crooked and gushing blood. His upper lip was already twice its normal size, and blood was dripping into his mouth. He had to spit it out. He groaned as he tried to get to his feet. Fortunately, he was no faster than Ava. She got onto her hands and knees, pulled herself up using the door jamb for support, and then pressed the door to the hidden compartment. It swung open just as it had when Travis showed it to her. She grabbed the shotgun and turned just as the outlaw was stumbling toward her.

There was no time to slide the safety forward, aim and shoot the weapon. Instead, she swung the metal barrel into the outlaw's outstretched arm. He reared back, screaming in pain and rage.

"Damn it, you broke my arm!" he snarled.

The arm was hanging at an odd angle as he held it close to his body. Ava didn't care how hurt, or how bloody the man was. He was still a threat to her baby. It was all she could think about -- every fiber of her being was intent on stopping the man, of eliminating the threat. She pointed the gun at Frank Lee Voss. He was close, barely out of reach of the weapon's barrel. She flicked the safety forward just as he lurched toward her.

Pulling the trigger was simple, but the result was powerful. The gun jumped in her hands. She had the stock against her shoulder, and it felt like the weapon had kicked her the way she had kicked the outlaw's bloody face. It sent her staggering back against the wall.

It also sent Frank Lee Voss backward. His head was whipped back, and he flipped, his long gangly legs flopping over his body. The rubber pellets weren't meant to kill, but at point blank range they shattered bone and flayed the skin of his face. He lay twitching on the deck, just as the ground shook from the laser barrage outside the ship. Ava felt it, knew that the outlaw was no longer a threat, and knew she needed to help Travis.

Her husband had been outside their tent in the late afternoon the day he died. She had been feeling poorly. It was morning sickness that was lasting all day. She thought she had caught a virus, or eaten something that made her sick. So, she was resting in the tent, laying inside her sleeping bag. A cool breeze was blowing through and she had the tent's flaps open. She could hear the husband humming as he worked. It was a sound she often heard in her mind, and in her dreams. Ava had been dozing. She didn't hear the men approaching on horseback. She did hear the arguing, and was just about to get up and see what was going on, when her husband was shot dead. The only good thing about that day was that he didn't suffer.

Ava had feared that the men would take her captive and abuse her. She was paralyzed with fear and never moved from her sleeping bag. The men took the Dustincia mining machine and left. Ava stayed in the tent until night fell, too afraid and too shocked to come out. When she finally did, her husband was dead, and she knew it instantly. In fact, she had known it the moment the gun had gone off. The shot was to the heart, the beam burned straight through and out his back. No one could have survived it. He had been dead before his body hit the ground, but she still felt that if she had just done something, perhaps things would have ended up differently. She was determined not to make that mistake again.

She grabbed the bloodied outlaw by the leg and dragged him out of her living quarters. Blood trailed behind him, and he groaned, gurgling. She pulled him through the engineering space and into the cargo hold.

"Holy hell, she blew his face off!" Adam Turney shouted.

"Stupid fool," Garcia Sanchez growled.

"I could help you with him, if you like," Augustine Ward said, trying to charm Ava in to letting him out of the cell he was locked in.

She still had the rifle in one hand and had to drag Frank Lee Voss into his empty cage. Augustine Ward, the gunslinger reached through and latched onto the rifle with his good hand, but with his arm fully extended he didn't have much leverage. Ava did. She shoved the gun away, which just happened to flex Augustine Ward's elbow the wrong direction. He screamed in pain and the others laughed as Ava brought the weapon back to her bruised shoulder.

"Anybody else have something they want to try?"

The prisoners all backed up, pressing themselves to the rear of their cells. Ava locked Frank Lee Voss back in his cell. She didn't know if he would live or die. She left him on his side. Blood was still dripping from what had once been his nose. It was just a bloody mass in the middle of his face. His cheekbones were broken, but visible in places where the skin had been shoved off by the rubber pellets. His teeth were broken too, and his lips hung in grotesque strips.

Ava didn't care that his reward was for half a million credits, or that he might die. She ran to the back of the ship and hit the button to open the rear hatch. All that mattered was getting out of the ship and helping Travis if she could. But in her heart, she feared that he was already dead, just like her husband.

# 33

Travis rotated his laser rifle around and brought it to his shoulder. There were several gang members moving in his direction, but only two were in sight. They had laser pistols and were shooting in an almost casual manner, their hands low, the weapons held ready, and popping off a few shots just to scare out their quarry. None were shooting directly at Travis, which he found odd, but wasn't going to complain about. He was on one knee, his rifle up and ready to fire.

But he didn't shoot. Something was wrong, he knew that even though he couldn't put his finger on precisely what was wrong with the situation. His mind was humming, the sound in his ears so loud he could hardly think. His heart was pounding, and he felt an intense anger, but not at the men shooting at him, oddly enough. He was angry with Rooster. No, that wasn't right, he thought to himself. Not Rooster, there was no one by that name. It had all been a diversion, a clever con, or some kind of sick joke. The man he knew as Rooster was actually Morgan Black, better known to some as The Man in Black.

"Stupid," he said, his head buzzing with the danger approaching.

Actually, the sound was too loud. He looked up and saw a drone approaching. It had what looked like a small laser built into the bottom, the weapon rotating in his direction. Travis took off running down the length of the converted transport, but not in a straight line, he juked and dodged. His instincts were on point as the drone, getting louder and louder, fired a burst of laser beams at him. It was the proof he needed. Travis planted one foot in the soggy turf and cut like a pro football player avoiding a tackle. As he turned he brought his rifle up and fired. It was just a quick shot, with no real hope of hitting such a little target. It did make the drone flutter. The object didn't flinch, but the operator did.

There are times in a fight when a sudden opportunity presents itself. Travis had no idea that the converted transport was the headquarters of the Volinski Syndicate. But the door was right in front of him and he tried the handle. To his surprise the door opened. He dashed in, just as the gang members opened fire. Laser shattered glass, and punched through the flimsy siding of the converted transport. Travis dove to the floor. He was in a sitting area, with thick sofas. To his left was a kitchen area, and beyond that a bathroom. To his right was what looked like a control area. There was a man in a chair, ripping off the drone control headset that covered his eyes.

Travis saw the man pulling a pistol from his holster. It didn't matter that the man looked as though he had just touched a live wire that caused every hair on his head to stand straight out. Or that he had the skinniest arms and legs of anyone Travis had ever seen. The man jerked his pistol, and Travis, who had landed on his rifle when he jumped into the transport, had to roll onto his side to bring his weapon to bear. At that moment time slowed down. Travis had been in enough shootouts to know that he couldn't get his rifle up and trained on the man before he got shot. The skinny man was thick in the middle. He didn't wear the bomber jacket the Syndicate was known for wearing in that area, but Travis knew he was controlling the drone. And the man was going to kill him. Only his first shot missed. And instead of correcting his aim the excited man just kept firing. The sudden shooting brought another barrage from those outside the converted transport. Laser fire ripped through the vehicle again, and this time the strange man was caught in it. Travis didn't bother taking the time to consider how close he had come to dying. Instead, he crawled to the back of the transport, found a spiral staircase, and climbed up.

"Damien! Did we get him?" someone outside the transport shouted. "Damien!"

Travis reached the second level. It was divided into two compartments. The first appeared to be a lounge. There were sofas, a bar, and several monitors with video feeds from hidden cameras around the town. The windows were covered with drapes. Travis moved to one on the side of the transport that the gang members had been coming from. He peeked out, saw eight men. Four were in clear sight, the other four were partially hidden by a nearby repulser skiff, and a four-person off-road vehicle with big, knobby tires.

With a swipe at the curtain, moving it to the side, Travis had a clear view down on the gang members. He brought his rifle up and fired in one smooth motion. He was a damn fine shot and hit the closest man in the dead center of his chest. The laser shattered the window. The other gang members ducked instinctively. Travis kept shooting. His second shot hit another gang member in the shoulder, the blast burning down through his rotator cuff and into his chest cavity. The third shot winged another member of the gang who was turning to run away. He spun and fell headlong into the mud.

"You want me!" Travis shouted. "Come and get me!"

He dashed back down the stairs as the five remaining outlaws blasted the upper deck. But they were running out of power, and had to stop to reload the shooters. Back on the lower level, Travis could see two of the men behind the skiff. One was looking up, the other fumbling with a fresh battery for his pistol. Travis shot the one looking up first. The other man got his battery inserted and fired a wild shot that actually went wide of the entire transport. Travis shot him in the face, then ducked back into the kitchen, where the appliances and counters gave him more cover. There was a smattering of return fire, but their numbers were thin, and with only three left, they were waiting for something they could see to shoot at.

The big windows of the transport were all shattered. Travis had no trouble climbing out of one on the opposite side of the vehicle from where the last three gang members were waiting and watching. He circled through the mud to the rear of the vehicle, and from there quietly dashed to a sporty hovercraft with a clear bubble top. He dropped to one knee behind the rear of the vehicle where the body was tallest, then came up shooting.

The two men behind the off-road vehicle were hit, one in the chest, and one in the arm. The last gang member got a shot off in Travis' direction. It hit the bubble, which was made of some type of safety glass. The entire top shattered into little glass nuggets, but none of that stopped Travis from shooting the last man in the stomach.

The world was suddenly quiet. The only sounds were those of the two wounded men frantic to get to safety. By that point, Travis' fury had shifted from Morgan Black to the men shooting at him. He stood up and walked toward the nearest wounded man. He had fallen to the mud, his gun forgotten. Instead, he was crawling, thinking he might be overlooked and escape.

Travis kicked him hard in his side. The man flopped over onto his back, gasping for air.

The other wounded man had been hit in the arm, and was whimpering behind the motor of the off-road vehicle, which was mounted high in the rear with chrome accents and oversized components. The man wasn't looking at the engine, but rather staring right at Travis. The Fugitive Recovery Specialist had his rifle pointed at the wounded man on the ground. Normally, he might have taken them in. But he had no room, time, or patience for making arrests. He shot the man on the ground, silencing him, but making the other wounded man wail in fear.

"No, no, no!" he cried as Travis marched toward him. "Don't, please! I-I-I'll do whatever you want, Mister. Please don't kill me."

"You were going to kill me."

"I didn't have a choice."

"We all have a choice," Travis said.

He didn't recall pulling the trigger. His gun was down at his hip, the barrel pointing up at the wounded man's chest. He had a second weapon in the back of his pants. With an awkward jerk he brought it around, but Travis fired first. The shot lifted him off the ground and he landed with a splat in the mud. Smoke wafted from the hole in his chest.

Behind Travis someone was clapping. He turned and saw Morgan. Only he wasn't in workman clothes anymore. He was dressed all in black. His wide-legged garment fluttered almost like a lady's skirt in the wind. His half cap billowed behind him, clinging to his shoulders as if for dear life. He wore a low-fitting wide-brimmed hat that settled just above his eyes, and on his face was a black mask that covered his nose and mouth.

"Not bad," Morgan said. "Not bad, I must admit."

Travis turned, bringing his rifle around, but Morgan had his Widow Maker out. The laser blast hit the rifle right on the metal laser housing. The weapon flipped out of Travis' hands and hit him in the shoulder.

There were people from the town there by that point. They were staying well back to avoid the gunfire, but they were taking it all in. Some were even videoing the gunfight with their data slates held high. Travis felt a wave of fear, followed almost immediately by a wave of revulsion.

"You going to kill me now?" Travis asked, his fury quickly morphing into pain.

"That's the plan, yes," Morgan said. "I'm getting paid for it, rather handsomely I might add."

"By who?" Travis asked.

"Oh, you know I can't tell you that," Morgan said with a chuckle. "Trust me, Travis, this isn't the way I was planning things. It would have been much more intimate if I had gotten my way."

"Sorry to disappoint you," Travis said.

"Oh, you didn't. You have exceeded all my expectations. This was supposed to be a straightforward hit, just another dead lawman, but you somehow rose above all the obstacles thrown your way. I have to say, Travis, we could be friends, you and I."

"No, we couldn't," the lawman replied.

Morgan holstered his Widow Maker and spread his arms wide.

"We're not so different, Travis. We're both death dealers."

"I don't murder innocent people."

"What about that man you shot," Morgan said, pointing to the wounded man in the mud. "He was wounded, unarmed, no longer a threat to you. And yet you shot him in cold blood."

"That's not how I see it," Travis replied.

"But how would a jury see it? Would they say the man was an outlaw, a desperado in league with bad people who set out to gun you down? Would they care that he was one of fourteen members of the Volinski Syndicate trying to kill you and your friend? Or would they say you were just like me, a cold blooded, unfeeling, un-remorseful killer?"

Travis knew the remorse would come. It would haunt his dreams, and torture his soul. It wasn't the first time he had killed someone. There were times in his line of work where killing was unavoidable. But every life he took seemed to add a callus to his heart.

The people from Vicksburg were moving closer. Some had to step over the bodies of the slain to get close enough to see what would happen. No one was confused about who Morgan Black was. There were rumors about the man in black. Every so often video surfaced of the infamous assassin, usually on the dark web, of a gunfight. Travis had seen some, and knew Morgan liked to toy with his victims. He also knew the assassin was incredibly fast.

But so was Travis Hurts.

# 34

"Can you feel it?" Morgan bellowed. "It's electric."

"What the hell are you talking about?"

Morgan wanted to jump up and down with excitement. He had run into his ship to change. The stupid Vega Volinski had ruined everything. Morgan's plan had been a work of art, but it was as if some Neanderthal had slapped the paintbrush from his hand and rubbed his grubby fingers across the canvas. Killing him had been easy, but not really satisfying. It had come too fast, too easy. For a death to really mean something to Morgan, it had to cost him something.

He had thought to change and then run out and save Travis Hurts, but the lawman was nearly as deadly as Morgan himself. He had gunned down six outlaws and wounded two more. Morgan had watched with a growing sense of excitement as Travis finished off the last two men. He was tingling all over. His moment on center stage had come. The only thing left had been to deal with the bounty hunter's rifle.

Morgan had always been an expert shot. He didn't practice, it just came naturally to him. The Widow Maker's length

and balance were perfect for him, the weapon just an exten-
sion of his will. Travis had turned, and would have surely
brought his Ranger rifle to bear on Morgan. He might have
shot first and asked questions later. Killing the Man in Black
would have made Travis the most famous man in the galaxy.
So, Morgan disabled the rifle, ensuring that he would have a
fair fight.

"You should dial up that Slinger to full power," Morgan said.
"One shot should be all you need."

"I don't kill people," the lawman said.

"Not even me?" Morgan said with a chuckle. "You know
what they say."

"No, what do they say, Morgan?"

"Killing me will make you famous."

"Bringing you in alive won't be bad either."

"You've no more room in your ship," he pointed out.

"For you, we'll make room," Travis said.

Morgan laughed again. "I hope you'll release that poor
woman. Surely she's never hurt a soul."

"You're a sorry judge of character, Morgan," Travis said.
"That's Sandra Mayfield. She poisoned at least three husbands
that we know about."

"Poison! That is so wickedly clever. How long did they last,
her lovers, once she began the process?"

"I don't know," Travis said. "It wasn't quick."

"No, I knew it wouldn't be. She likes to watch them suffer.
Some of us do, you know. But not you, Travis. My guess is you're
the one who suffers."

"If you want to kill me, Morgan, best get to it."

The lawman pulled back the right side of his duster and
hooked it behind his quick draw holster. It was, surprisingly, a
very direct moment for Morgan. Almost as if he had been
slapped in the face. And he felt an icy shiver of fear. It was

agonizingly exquisite. He could compartmentalize his physical pain, but fear struck at his core in a way that pain could not.

"You surprise me," Morgan said, flexing his gun hand. "I'll admit, you're different. Not what I expected, but that's okay. It's been a long time since I had a victim that didn't squirm at the end like a worm on a hook."

"Jerk that Widow Maker and go to work," Travis said. "I'm sick to death of hearing your voice."

"I saved your life, lawman!" Morgan said. His composure had slipped, and his fear was making him angry. Was it possible that he wasn't as fast as Travis Hurts? The lawman had told Rooster there was always someone faster. Morgan had always been that someone. He feasted on the fears of others. It fed his senses like a gourmet meal, or a perfectly aged wine. Yet his confidence was slipping for some reason. He had just seen the lawman gun down eight of Vega Volinski's men. Those weren't quick draw showdowns, but still, it said a lot about Travis' ability with a gun.

"And now I'm going to save yours," Travis said. "Turn around, get on your ship, and leave. I won't stop you."

"Nice try," Morgan said with a chuckle, his confidence returning.

"Otherwise, I gun you down," Travis said. "I've seen you, Morgan. Remember? I know how fast you are. And I'm here to tell you right now, I'm faster."

"No one is faster," Morgan snarled.

"So go for that pistol and see what happens."

Morgan felt his scalp prickle with sweat. His breathing was shallow and his muscles were starting to tremble. Was it too much adrenaline, or was it fear? How could he know? For the first time in his entire life he wasn't certain. His tongue came out and darted across his lips in fear.

"You first," Morgan said.

"That's not how I play," Travis said.

"This is a dangerous game, my friend," Morgan said, trying hard to keep his voice steady. "You need every advantage you can get."

"No," Travis said. "I won't do it."

"You won't draw on me?" Morgan asked, feeling cheated, and outraged, and relieved all at the same time.

"You were right," Travis said. "You saved my life."

"And now you owe me," Morgan snarled.

"Which is why I'm letting you walk out of here, Morgan Black. You see, the people in this town saw your face. They have your shootout with Augustine Ward on video. It'll find its way to the planetary networks, and when it does everyone will know who you are. There won't be a safe place for you anywhere in the cosmos. Not anymore."

"You might be right," Morgan said, loud enough for the crowd to hear him. "But the truth is, I'll hunt down any person who posts that footage. They'll wake up and find me at the foot of their bed. I'll kill them, and I won't be quick about it."

"Does that usually work for you?" Travis said. "Just threatening innocent people's lives?"

"Yes," Morgan said. "It does."

"Well then, I guess it's up to me to stop you before you can hurt anyone else."

"But you can't, because you like me too much," Morgan said.

It was a stretch. He honestly couldn't tell what Travis' motivation was. Maybe fear, or maybe gratitude, or maybe he was just a good person at heart, Morgan couldn't tell. But he could feel the crowd getting closer. The job was taking too long. He needed to end it, to bring the failed game to a concise conclusion, and make sure everyone knew he was still the most terrifying death dealer in the galaxy.

"I don't like you at all," Travis said.

And to his surprise, Morgan was genuinely wounded by that statement.

"Whatever," he muttered.

Time seemed to slow down. He was going for his gun. It didn't matter that he was drawing first. His sudden, all-encompassing need was to kill Travis Hurts. It didn't matter that it was being recorded for the entire galaxy to see. He was an assassin, not a cult hero who had a code to live up to. His shoulders bunched, and his hand dropped to the handle of his Widow Maker. The gun was perfect, his draw was smooth.

Travis was going for his pistol too. Everything seemed to be a thousand times slower in Morgan's mind. He could see the little pistol sliding up the oiled holster. But his own weapon was already free, and coming up. There was just the tiniest jolt of relief. He was faster after all, still the fastest, still the deadliest. And the whole universe—

He never saw Ava Lynn Baxter. She had come around his ship with the deck sweeper in hand. She raised and fired the weapon. He heard the explosion as the old-fashioned gunpowder was set off inside the heavy weapon. But he felt the impact. None of the non-lethal rubber pellets punched through his clothing, which was designed to lessen the impact of a laser blast, but did nothing to stop the kinetic energy of a projectile weapon. They smashed into his arm and shoulder, peppering his chest and back. Some even hit his neck, leaving tiny welts in his flesh. His Widow Maker went flying from his grasp, and he was thrown headlong into the mud. The duel was over. He had lost. But only because Travis Hurts had cheated.

# 35

"Ava!" Travis yelled.

She was standing by Morgan's black ship. There was blood on her face and down her dress. His first thought was *the baby!* Had something happened to the baby?

He rushed to her side. She was swaying a little, her entire body quivering.

"Are you hurt?" he asked.

"No," she said. "Not really."

"The baby?"

She looked at him. And in that moment, with the townspeople yelling and screaming as they charged toward him, Travis knew that there was something there. She didn't just appreciate what he had done. She loved him for loving her child. Perhaps every parent appreciates someone who cares about their child, but Travis thought there was real love there.

"Is he ..."

"No," Travis said. "Just unconscious. We need to—"

But there would be no recovery this time. The crowd was angry. Their man had been gunned down, and not in a fair fight, but by a woman. He could tell by their shouts that they were furious, out for blood. Maybe they would have been anyway, no matter what the outcome of the fight had been, but in that instant Travis knew they had just one hope of survival.

"Get to the ship!" he shouted.

They both turned and ran. Travis had taken Ava by the arm. Her shoes were heavy with mud. The tape was coming loose and the sides were gapping open, letting the moisture in. Fortunately, no one was shooting at them. They sprinted back toward the *Purgatory* breathing hard, chests hurting from the effort.

"Get us out of here!" he shouted as they scrambled up the open rear hatch.

Ava dashed toward the front of the ship while Travis hit the button to close the rear hatch. A mob had formed and they were marching toward him. But he knew they could have done more. They could have drawn their weapons and made it a real fight for survival. Maybe it was the way he had faced down Morgan Black. Or maybe it was the dead bodies of the Volinski Syndicate that stayed their hands. They wanted him gone, that was all. So, they shouted and shook their fists, but no one pulled their weapons.

The ship lifted off the ground before the rear hatch sealed. When it did, Travis sagged against the wall. He had never been more afraid than he had been facing Morgan Black. He had tried every trick, every tactic he could think of to divert the evil killer. But in the end Morgan had gone for his gun, and he had been faster. If not for Ava Lynn Baxter, Travis Hurts would have died in the mud outside Vicksburg on Pergamum Prime.

✝✝✝

Morgan was still laying in the mud, struggling just to breathe. He had been shot with lasers before, and had endured torturous abuse as a child, but getting shot with the deck sweeper opened up a whole new world of pain.

The locals just watched him at first. He heard their whispered comments: *he's dead... won't survive this one... is he breathing?* Of course, he was breathing, but his cape had become like a death shroud. They couldn't see his chest moving in short little gasps. He wanted to rip his mask off. Normally, the slight increase in effort that it took to pull in air through the cup-shaped mask was just another thing that forced him to be present in each moment. But he was having enough trouble refilling his lungs with air. He would have removed it but there were too many people, too many witnesses.

And Travis Hurts had been right about one thing. He had been a little too brazen in his game. Taking down Augustine Ward had been sweet. No one was a faster draw than Morgan Black, but people had recorded the showdown. It might already be uploaded to the web of information networks. That would force him to make some cosmetic changes, which had always been inevitable.

"I got it!" someone shouted. "I got his gun."

That exclamation seemed to shake the crowd out of their cautious stupor. A fight broke out over his pistol, while others rushed in around Morgan himself. Someone pulled off his hat, and others yanked at his clothing. They all wanted a piece of the infamous killer. One bold spectator reached for his mask. Morgan responded like a viper when a predator gets too close. He didn't have his pistol, but he still had a small knife. It was a spring loaded, hydrogen steel blade, as sharp as a surgeon's scalpel. The blade popped out as Morgan swiped it across the wrist of the man reaching for his mask.

Blood, a scream of pain, followed by screams of fear, it was all music to his ears. The people were shouting and running. Morgan rolled to his knees. They squished down into the mud, made soupy by the crowds and by the blood that had been spilled as much as the rain. The landing area north of Vicksburg's Main Street had become a killing field. Morgan was in pain, moving hurt, his left arm sent waves of agony through his shoulder and neck when he tried to lift it. But he got to his feet. His hat was crumpled and filthy from the muck, but it was close enough that he could reach it.

Whoever had his gun hadn't dropped it when they ran. There hadn't been time to fully arm up when he changed into his iconic outfit. Normally he carried two back-up pieces, one in his right boot, another in a little fold of his cape. But on Pergamum Prime, what should have been one of his most memorable triumphs was ruined, leaving him hurt, humiliated, and on the verge of helpless. His knife wouldn't hold off the crowd for long, but his reputation might. He staggered toward his ship. No one moved to cut him off. The *Dymetr* was close. If he could get on board, the autopilot would get him airborne and safely away from the scene. He needed to run, to hide, to find a place to recover and plot his revenge. The fight wasn't over. Travis Hurts was good, but he had cheated. Morgan Black normally felt intoxicated after a kill, but on P2, as he struggled to escape, he felt only emptiness in his soul. There was no heady thrill, no gloating sensation or intoxicating sense of power. Instead, he just felt pain and anger.

He made it up the short ramp into his ship and closed the hatch. The crowds were fading back. Some had seen what the hidden lasers on his vessel could do. They would rally around his pistol, and it would become a trophy for the spectators, perhaps even a treasure in its own right. Nothing on the gun could tie back to Morgan. It was a custom weapon, one of two made specially for him, but the payment to the gunsmith had been death. Morgan had murdered the man with his own carefully crafted pistols, and then scrubbed his records of all mention of making them.

A simple order set the ship in motion. It rose up a hundred feet into the air and flew away from Vicksburg, moving north toward a range of mountains that were white with snow. Space would have been better. His black ship could practically disappear in the vast darkness between systems, but he would need to refuel and resupply before taking off on another long voyage. And what he needed more than anything at that moment was to rest and recover. The autopilot landed high in the mountains, on a frosty plateau that was sheltered by a towering cliff on one side.

Morgan set the ship's security settings to full alert. No one could approach the ship without his being awakened by the internal alarms. Her radar sweeps would pick up an approaching missile strike, her deflector shields would stop even the most powerful laser barrage. And the mountains themselves would deter most people. The plateau was about as safe a place as he could find. And that meant he could sleep. Everything hurt so much the pain was breaking free of his mental containments, wrecking the carefully arranged compartments in his mind. He needed to sleep.

A handful of pain killers were washed down with a gulp of brandy that scorched its way down his throat, then spread a sense of numbness throughout his body. He stretched out on his bed, normally so blissfully comfortable, but in that moment, it felt more like a bed of nails. Still, his fatigue, mixed with the narcotics, pulled him into a sweet oblivion where his shame, his guilt, his fears, and his disappointment couldn't reach him. Despite all that had happened, and in his mind, all that had gone wrong, he slept peacefully hidden in the mountains on Pergamum Prime.

# 36

His first thought was that someone was dead. There was a trail of blood running from the engineering space into one of the cells. When Travis looked in, he saw Frank Lee Voss unconscious and bloody, but still breathing. Beside him, in the back of his own cell, Augustine Ward was whimpering.

"What the hell?" Travis asked, not even aware that he was speaking out loud.

"Your friend let him out," Garcia Sanchez said.

Beside him, Adam Turney was sporting a bloody nose and a black eye.

"What happened to you?" Travis asked.

"This place sucks," Adam said, swiping at his nose.

"He had a close encounter with the bars of his cell," Sanchez said. "Maybe next time he won't be so stupid."

"Whatever," Adam grumbled.

"And him?" Travis asked, pointing at Augustine Ward.

"Your lady is a warrior, man. I don't know how she got the jump on Frank Lee, but she cranked Ward's arm pretty good."

"She broke it," he snapped. "It's killing me. I think she may have dislocated my elbow."

"You mess with the Bull, Ese, you gonna get the horns," Sanchez said. "Maybe you shouldn't have tried to grab the gun."

"You can't treat captives like this," Ward argued. "It's against the law."

"What law?" Travis said. "We're on Pergamum Prime. There's no law here. Isn't that what you like to say, Augustine?"

"I know you can't beat on us and expect a reward," he said.

Travis chuckled. "You better just get used to it. There's no easy life ahead for you."

"Bounty hunter, you know I can pay you more than the reward for me," Sanchez said softly. "You let me go, I'll double the reward money."

"From the ransom you got for kidnapping that girl?" Travis said. "No, I don't think so."

"You're making a mistake. They won't convict me."

"They already have," Travis said. "All that's left is the sentencing. I'm thinking you'll get the maximum at a maximum-security hard labor camp on a penal colony."

"Bastard," Sanchez snarled, but Travis had been around enough outlaws to know how dangerous they could be. There was plenty of space down the middle of the cargo hold that was out of reach from either side of the cages he had installed. He didn't have to check Garcia Sanchez's door; the short man's bulky arms and shoulders flexed as he tried to shake it open. The door held fast.

Travis stepped over and checked the others. They were all locked.

"How long you going to keep us here?" Bill Teagan complained. "I'm getting sick of this place."

"Don't worry," Travis said. "We're leaving P2 now. A few

more days and you'll be wishing you were back here in the lap of luxury."

"Yeah, this is a really wonderful place," Adam said.

"You say that now," Travis said. "Just ask Sanchez what they do to rapist murderers on a penal world."

Adam Turney's one good eye opened wide in fear. Travis stepped around the trail of blood that was fast congealing on the deck. Not that he was clean. His boots were coated in mud, and his clothing too. His duster weighed heavy on his shoulders, and Ava had left tracks right through the middle of the ship.

He went into the engineering space, then the living quarters, where the blood trail originated. It pained him to think of Frank Lee Voss getting that far. Ava's nose had been bleeding, which meant she hadn't avoided injury while putting the gunman down. He pulled off his muddy coat, realized his hat was missing, and decided the rest of him could wait. There would be time for cleaning up once they were safely in hyperspace.

Through the transparent steel section of the cockpit above the touchscreen instrument display, Travis could see that they were still in P2's atmosphere. The ship could only rise so high on the quad thrusters before the jet engines had to propel them up into low orbit. Ava looked over at him as Travis dropped into the empty pilot's seat.

"Do you want to talk about it?" he asked.

"No," she said quietly. "To be honest, I don't really remember much about it."

"I can watch on the ship's surveillance system. It's got playback capabilities."

"I didn't know that," she said in a soft voice.

"You saved my life, Ava," he said, just as they passed into orbit.

It always happened quickly. One moment they were in the

upper reaches of the planet's gravitational pull, then they broke free. Travis had to grab his seat to keep from floating up.

"Sheila, activate artificial gravity," he said.

"Artificial gravity activated," the computerized voice replied from the hidden speakers inside the cockpit.

"You can just tell it what to do?" Ava asked in surprise.

"The primary user can," Travis said, as he readjusted himself in his seat.

He was sore and tired, more tired than he could ever remember being in his entire life. It wasn't just the physical strain, but the emotional one too. The shock of learning that Rooster was Morgan Black had been a blow he knew he might never get over. Being conned by a career criminal was nothing a person should feel bad about. But it felt more like betrayal than merely falling for a con man's game.

On top of the fear and anger, Travis was wrestling with powerful feelings of affection too. Just being near Ava made him feel suddenly self-conscious.

"Lucky you," she said. "I really like this ship. It feels like home."

"You deserve much more than an old cargo ship," Travis said.

She looked at him, really peering deep into his eyes, and said, "What do I deserve?"

"Safety," he said, without even thinking. "Security, love, peace."

"And I can't have those things here?"

"It's just a ship," he said.

"It's your ship," she replied.

Feeling incredibly self-conscious, and not believing what he was hearing from Ava Lynn Baxter, he turned and activated the autopilot.

"Sheila, plot a course out of the system," he ordered without looking at Ava. He could feel her eyes still on him, and he wanted to seem confident, not weak.

"Navigation plot activated," the computer replied. "What is your destination?"

"Grimwel Grand," Travis said.

"Computing," the voice of the ship's operating system said.

Travis stood up and helped Ava to her feet. She was tired, her hair tangled, her chin, lips, and nose stained with dried blood.

"Did he hurt you?" Travis asked, still holding her hands.

"No, not really."

"You know, I've never met a woman like you."

"I just did what I had to do to protect my baby," she said.

"Were you protecting your child when you left the ship and came to help me?"

"I ... I just ..."

She was struggling for the words, and he leaned closer. He had kissed girls before, but not that many, and never any who he felt such strong feelings for. Ava Lynn Baxter didn't resist. Their lips met as if they were made to fit together. The kiss was soft, and sweet. Travis felt a tingling sensation shoot through his entire body.

When they pulled apart there were questions in both of their eyes. The ship was starting to break free from orbit, the main space engines thrumming to life.

"I'll clean up the mess," Travis volunteered.

"You've been awake for days," she told him.

"That's okay. I don't like putting things off."

"Then let me do it. You can sleep in the bed."

He shook his head. "You've been through a lot. Get yourself cleaned up. Don't worry about the rest."

She didn't argue.

Travis had plenty of cleaning supplies in the maintenance

section of the ship, most of it left from the previous owner, who was a stickler for cleanliness. The blood, while messy, cleaned up easily off the polished metal floor plates. Half an hour later Travis was in the shower, letting the hot water relax his aching muscles.

After drying off and changing into clean clothes, Travis found Ava preparing food in the galley.

"I never got the chance to feed everyone," she said.

"Smells good."

"I made plenty," she said.

It was all rehydrated space food, fortified with vitamins and minerals, but rarely having much in the way of flavor. But Travis didn't care, he was starving. After seeing to their captives, which included first aid for Frank Lee Voss, who was in a considerable amount of pain, and getting Augustine Ward's injured arm in a sling, they finally settled down for their own meal at the little table in the living quarters, just as the ship made the jump into hyperspace.

"We will arrive at the destination in seven hours," the computerized voice of the ship's operating system said.

"Thank you, Sheila," Travis said, his mouth full of food. "This is delicious."

"I added a little cumin and chili powder to ours. I hope it's not too spicy."

"No, it's perfect," he said.

"You should see what I can do with real food," she said with a tease.

"I would like that," he told her.

"You would?"

"Ava, I can't ask you to give up life on a civilized world."

"And you can't settle for life in one place," she said.

"I've tried that. I get restless, bored. I've scrimped and saved for a long time for this right here. My own ship, my own resources, the ability to go after the outlaws other people can't or won't pursue."

"What if ..."

"But you've got the baby to think about," Travis said.

"A baby on board a bounty hunter's ship," she said in an exaggerated fashion. "That's trouble you don't need."

"No, I ...". It was his turn to run out of words.

"I would never presume that you should take care of my baby," Ava said, sounding a bit constricted, like she was holding back strong emotions.

"Ava," Travis said. "Would you even consider a life here with me?"

He was terrified of her answer because it was an outrageous idea. The ship was built for a lone occupant. It might be possible to add a second bunk to the sleeping nook, but two people would be crowded in the little ship. Two adults and a baby seemed ludicrous. He didn't know what he was thinking, and he knew she would be crazy to even consider the idea. But he couldn't stand the thought of leaving her.

"Could we make that work?" she asked.

"It's absolutely crazy," he said. "And as you know full well, very dangerous."

"Travis, I don't want you to leave me behind."

"I don't want to leave you, not even on Kingsbury with all the money in the world."

"Then let me stay."

"I can't, it's too selfish."

"I have nowhere else to go."

"You can go anywhere," he insisted. "I'll give you every credit I've got. I'll come and see you every chance I get."

"It's not enough," she said, her eyes welling with tears.

"But you wouldn't want to raise a baby like this."

"Wouldn't I? We can't be a burden to you, Travis, but I ... I feel more at peace with you than I ever have with anyone else in my entire life. You have trusted me, before you even knew me. You gave me freedom, hope, and an opportunity to do something amazing."

"And you were nearly killed in the process."

"I'm tougher than you think" she said. "I survived losing my husband. I survived life alone on P2 for months. I found a way to survive. We were only in danger because Rooster let that prisoner out."

"Rooster was just a role he was playing," Travis said. "That was Morgan Black."

She reacted as if he had slapped her. She pushed back from the table, fear in her eyes.

"No," she whispered.

Travis nodded. "He's been hired to kill me."

"No," she said again.

"And he won't stop now," Travis said. "It'll be a matter of pride for him. You stopped him, Ava. I can't deny it. He was faster than me, and if it hadn't been for you, I'd be dead right now."

"Morgan Black?"

Travis nodded. "And he's not the only one. Outlaws don't linger on civilized worlds. Everywhere I go people will be trying to stop me. If circumstances were different, maybe I ... we ..."

She burst into tears. Travis didn't know what to think. He helped her to the bed, and before he knew it, she was asleep. He finished his meal, put their dishes away, and checked how much time they had in hyperspace. His heart was aching. He had come close to love, to having a family. The Man in Black made it impossible. There was just no way he could put Ava and her baby at risk.

He fell asleep in the reclining lounge chair. When he woke

up six hours later his body was craving more sleep, but they were in the Grimwel system. Ava was awake and in the cockpit.

"We're on course for the orbital station above Grimwel Grand."

"Perfect," Travis said. "I could use some coffee."

"I'll fix it," she replied.

He got on the comms and let the authorities know they were coming with Frank Lee Voss. An hour later, Travis was just inside the docking station. Medics were taking Frank Lee Voss away on a hover-gurney. Both of his hands were cuffed to the rails of the narrow bed. The Emergency Medical Technicians had scanned the prisoner's wounds. The chief of security was there as well. He stayed with Travis and Ava as the EMTs took Voss away.

"He's got some broken facial bones and teeth," the Chief said. "But he'll live."

"What about his face?" Travis asked.

"The Department of Corrections doesn't offer cosmetic surgery," the Chief said with a chuckle.

"Will that affect the reward?" Ava asked.

"Hell no," the security man said. "That bastard killed five innocent people. He's alive, and that's all the reward stipulates. I've already assigned the funds to your account, Travis. You two have earned it."

Travis wanted to say that the security man didn't know the half of it. He had pulled the video footage from the *Purgatory* and sent it ahead. If the security team had questions about how Voss got injured, they were answered by the video of Ava fighting him off. Travis had watched it too, both with horror and with pride. Ava continued to surprise him at every turn.

"Y'all sticking around for a while?" the Chief asked.

"Long enough to restock supplies," Travis said.

"Word gets out you brought in Voss; you'll be drinking free at the pub as long as you're in station."

"I'll keep that in mind," Travis said.

He wasn't a big drinker, and of course Ava couldn't drink because of the baby. Once the security chief left Travis checked his banking account. He had already received the half million.

"Do you have an interplanetary account?" he asked Ava.

She shook her head. "No, we never set one up."

"I can get you the money in hard currency," he assured her.

"Travis, that isn't necessary. I'll see about an account soon enough. We've got five more prisoners to deliver, remember."

"How could I forget?" he said.

They spent the next couple of hours shopping. Travis had the *Purgatory* refueled. Ava bought a rolling cart full of groceries, and Travis purchased a new Ranger rifle, and decided to spend a little of the reward money on a portable medical scanner. They also restocked their first aid supplies. Two hours after turning Frank Lee Voss over to the authorities in the Grimwel system, they set out for their next destination.

# 37

Word reached Iona of the shootout in Vicksburg by the time they were back in Incendius territory. People were already calling it the battle of Vicksburg. And there was video too, shaky, handheld video taken by spectators, that showed the dead members of the Volinski Syndicate, the showdown between Travis and Morgan Black, and even the infamous killer's gun.

"Maybe he didn't break his word after all," Orvil said in a weak voice.

He was suffering from stun sickness, and probably dehydration, but there was no time to coddle the man. Iona's plans had all changed. Their failure to kill Hurts was no longer salient information. She immediately sent word to Dice that Morgan Black had failed, but also that Volinski Syndicate territory was up for grabs on P2. She would stay on planet long enough to ensure that the Incendius Organization snatched up as much of it as possible.

Orvil was put right to work assembling his people. They

returned to Vicksburg and pushed out a group of Infada hard-liners to take control of the boomtown. Iona didn't care about anything else the Volinski Syndicate controlled, and there were plenty of other targets, which Orvil immediately went after with his people, but she wanted to control the narrative. What was surprising was the lack of cooperation she got from the locals. It seemed that Morgan Black's threat to hunt down anyone who shared video footage of his shootout with Augustine Ward had spilled over to those who took video of the battle of Vicksburg. By the time she had seized control of the town, even the person who uploaded the initial footage that she had seen was no longer willing to share it.

All the tech from the converted transport the Volinski Syndicate operated from had been stripped out of the old vehicle. And many of the witnesses to the battle had left town. Vicksburg still had a lot to offer the Incendius Organization. There was a lot of Dust to be collected and moved off world, but the boom town was tainted by the battle and the threat from Morgan Black. It would only be a matter of time before they would need to close up shop and move the town elsewhere. It was the way of things on P2.

An entire week went by before Orvil could report that all the Volinski assets had been collected. "We got their route through the mountains," he said proudly. "And the spaceport operating near Windham. That's where they were moving the dope, and we can do the same."

"Excellent," Iona said, although in truth she really didn't care. "What about the people you sent in search of Black?"

"Nothing," he said. "They're doing drone searches, and checking in all the larger settlements, but no one has seen him. There's no reports he's left the planet, though."

"He was wounded in the battle," she said, mostly to herself.

"Word is he survived," Orvil replied.

"But for how long?" she asked. "It's possible his ship crashed somewhere and he'll never been seen again."

"Maybe," Orvil said, sounding doubtful. "A guy like that doesn't just give up, you know what I'm sayin'?"

"You sound scared."

"I am," Orvil said. "I shot that bastard and he didn't die."

"He was wearing shielded clothing," she replied. "But you stung him. You were faster."

"I already had my gun out," Orvil admitted.

"Who else can say they got a shot on him."

"I thought you said we could never talk about it."

"We can't," Iona said. "If Dice were to know it would be the death of both of us."

"You didn't have to gun down Reg. He was solid."

"He was a liability."

"But things worked out in our favor."

"You can't count on that," she warned him. "You're a made man, but never think that means you're safe, or that you can let down your guard. Someone is always looking to move up, Orvil, and the surest way to do that is by taking you down."

"Well, if I could brag about shooting Black it would just make me a target," Orvil said.

Iona realized he was right, and it was a smart thing to understand. She sometimes underestimated him, but that was part of the game. She was the boss, and as such had to be above everyone in every way.

"So, what now?"

"Now you go to that new port and wait for our reinforcements," she said.

"Me?"

"That's right. This is your world," she told him.

"What about you, boss?"

"I have another project I'm working on," she said. "What do you know about the penal colony on Lucerine in the Maxillious system?"

"I know I never want to go there," he said.

"It's not as bad as some," Iona said, scanning information on her data slate.

"Bad enough," Orvil said.

"They produce polished stone for all sorts of things," she said. "The marble quarry is especially productive."

"The people there come out crippled and beat down, *if* they come out at all."

"There are some violent factions," she noted. "A variety of prison gangs operate on Maxillious."

"Why does it matter?"

"It matters because I don't think Morgan Black can do the job he was hired to do," she said.

"You don't think the most widely feared assassin in the galaxy is up to the job?"

"Not this job," she said. "You saw it yourself. He got too close to the mark. There are feelings there now. It would be like trying to assassinate your brother, or your best friend."

"You pay me enough money and I'll kill both my brothers," Orvil said. "And one's a priest."

"I need someone who will stop at nothing to do the job," Iona said. "Someone who can stop Hurts in his tracks."

"Like who?"

Iona tapped a tab on her slate and then turned it around. Orvil leaned close, looking at a very tough looking man with stubbly gray hair, a scar on one cheek, weathered skin, and hatred in his eyes.

"Who the hell is that?" Orvil asked.

"Leon Hurts," Iona said with a wicked smile. "I get him off Maxillious, and he'll do the job."

"Hurts? He's related to the mark?"

"It's his father."

"What would make you think even a lifer like that would kill his own son?"

"Because Travis is the person who put his father in jail."

# 38

Their last stop was Datzun Superior. There was no reward for Adam Turney on that world, but Travis had already collected eight hundred and seventy-five thousand credits in rewards. He had spent almost seventy thousand resupplying the ship, and getting more equipment such as his new Ranger rifle and the medical scanner. He planned to give Ava a full hundred thousand credits. With that she could put a down payment on a home for her and the baby, and still have enough to figure out what she wanted to do with her life. They had talked very little about the future, just enjoying their time together as they flew across the galaxy turning in the prisoners and collecting the reward money.

Travis had already paid off what he owed to the bank for the *Purgatory*. The note had been for six hundred and ninety-seven thousand credits. The fact that he was able to pay it all off and still have eight thousand credits in his account was mind-boggling to Travis. His big gamble had paid off huge. He needed to get back to work soon, but with his ship paid for and fully stocked, he could go anywhere and live for a while just on the food and supplies he had on board.

Ava hadn't gone with him to deliver Adam Turney to the authorities who wanted him for questioning in the disappearance of a young woman nearly a year earlier. By the time he got back to the ship, the news of a break in the case was being broadcast on the local networks.

"He confessed," Ava said as Travis came back on board.

"Already?"

"I suppose so. It made the news."

"The family of the girl will be relieved."

"There's no happiness in death, is there?"

"I don't guess so," Travis said. "But closure is better than nothing. If Turney really did it, and can take them to her body, that will count for something."

"So, what now?" Ava said.

The pilot seats in the cockpit of the ship could turn to face each other. They were docked at the orbital station above Datzun Superior. Through the window they could see ships coming and going. Most were commercial freighters full of goods from other worlds. They would be offloaded with imports, and reloaded with exports. Trans-system shipping was big business. There were some spaceliners too, and Travis was happy that he would never have to book passage on one again. No more long flights stuck in a tiny seat and surrounded by strangers.

"There's a pair of desperados rumored to be on Las Brazzas. It's rough country, and the authorities can't track them down."

"Why not?" Ava asked.

"Probably because the local guys are using drones and hovercraft."

"Why is that a problem?"

Travis shook his head. "They're too loud. The bad guys hear them coming and hide."

"What's your plan, just hike in and find them?"

"Not enough boot leather for that," Travis said. "I'll take horses."

"Won't they hear horses too?"

"They might, but they won't suspect a lone rider to be coming to collect them," Travis said. "It's not the first time I've gone into rough country to get the bad guys."

"How much is the reward?"

"Eighty thousand credits for the pair of them," he said.

"That's all?"

"It isn't about the money," he told her.

"You would risk your life for just eighty thousand credits?"

Travis didn't believe in safety. It was really just an illusion. There were varying degrees of danger, but a man could be run down in a busy city, or mugged in a dark alley just as easily as he could on a fringe world like Las Brazzas.

"It's what I do," he said.

"And what if I asked you to do something else," she said.

"You won't," he told her.

"It would be so much easier."

"Not in the long run," he said.

"You don't want to be with me?"

Travis had fallen hopelessly in love with Ava Lynn Baxter. He hadn't intended to, even after their kiss. The logistics were just too messy. It seemed like an impossible situation.

"More than anything," he said.

"Then let's find a place," she said.

"This is my place," he told her. "This is my dream, Ava. I've worked hard for it. I had to scrimp and save for years to earn enough for the down payment. Now it's mine, free and clear. I can't just walk away now."

"And I can't raise my baby on this ship," she said. "It's just not practical."

"Tell me what you want to do," he said.

"I want to stay," she said. "You have no idea how much I love the freedom of being on this ship. It's more of a home to me than I've ever had before. And when I'm flying it …"

He understood the look of rapture that came into her face when she flew. It was exciting and fun to him, but Ava absolutely lit up when she was in control of the *Purgatory*. There were times when he thought she liked it more than she liked him.

"But the baby," he said.

"He's not due for two more months," she said.

"Who knows where we'll be in two months," Travis pointed out.

"Exactly," she said. "I … we need more time to figure this out."

"Well, I don't exactly hate having you around."

"You better not, Travis. I'll stop cooking if you're going be like that."

Ava had proven to be a whiz in the galley. The ship had limited space, and tiny appliances, but she had found ways to make amazing meals with the fresh foods they picked up in the various ports where they delivered their prisoners.

"Sorry, I went too far," he said, in mock seriousness.

"That's more like it," she said. "Now help me up so I can kiss you."

He got to his feet and pulled her up out of the pilot's seat. She could get up herself, but the baby was getting bigger and she was struggling a bit with heaving herself out of the deep pilot's seat. When they kissed it was familiar, but exciting. Travis couldn't help but worry about the baby. It was constantly on his mind. Even something simple as hugging her was starting to get awkward with her baby belly.

"If you're going to stick around," Travis said. "We could get you a more comfortable chair for the living quarters."

"I wouldn't mind it," she said.

They had already purchased her new maternity clothing, and she was taking prenatal vitamins. The baby's heartbeat was strong. And the information Travis had read said that most first time mothers carried their babies beyond the due date. But nothing was guaranteed. Travis wondered how Ava would survive if something happened to the child. There were times when her grief, supercharged by the pregnancy hormones, caused her to cry for hours. She tried to hide it from him, but like most law enforcement officials Travis was very observant. She would slip into the bathroom and claim to be cleaning, but he could hear her sobbing. He didn't know if loving him made the grief worse. It was a topic he was loath to broach. The truth was, he hadn't wanted to do anything that would make their relationship awkward. He didn't want her to leave, but that was selfishness, he told himself. He needed to put her needs, and the needs of the baby, above his own desires.

Still, a few more weeks together, even if he was working, sounded right to him. The future was a blank page, and their story was yet to be written. He didn't want it to end before it had really gotten started.

"There's a furniture store here," Travis said. "One that specializes in ship furniture."

"Well, what are we waiting for?" she said with a smile. "Let's shop."

They secured the *Purgatory* and left the ship hand in hand. The orbital station above Datzun Supreme was a busy place. Most of it was warehousing for goods coming and going from the planet below. It wasn't a major commerce or business planet, but it wasn't a colony world any longer. There were restaurants, lounges and a variety of stores in the station. Kiosks selling everything from tee-shirts to gourmet coffee lined the walkways. People were coming and going in all directions. Travis led the way through the throng to the furniture store, where Ava picked out a recliner that rocked and swiveled. It was smaller than the lounger already on the ship. They ordered it to be delivered, and bought more pillows and a second set of bed sheets at a kiosk on the way back. They never noticed the tall man in a pilot's jumpsuit tracking their every move. There were plenty of people in flight clothing, from the pilots working the spaceliners to the console jockeys flying the shuttles back and forth to the planet's surface. Some wore the standard dark grey jumpsuits that were similar to what military pilots wore. Others wore fancy uniforms. Everywhere one looked there was someone in some type of official dress. Travis didn't see the tall man, the one watching them, and reporting back to his employer that he had found Travis Hurts in Datzun Supreme. And he could track their ship if he just got close enough.

Danger, it seemed, really was everywhere.

# Epilogue

"I just got word," Dice said. "He's leaving Datzun Supreme, headed toward the fringe systems."

"Probably on another hunt," Morgan Black said, his face a dark hologram with his hat and mask in place.

"So, what are you going to do? I thought this would be handled by now."

"As did I," Morgan said.

"My sources tell me you botched the job."

"I was caught unawares just seconds from completing the assignment," Morgan explained.

"Yeah, from what I hear, you're lucky to be walking and talking, my friend."

"Luck has nothing to do with it," Morgan said. "Destiny is immutable."

"Yeah, well, I ain't religious," Dice said. "And I'm paying you a lot of money."

"I am aware," Morgan said. "But your underling has other plans."

"Freeze ain't the issue."

"She is on my list," Morgan said.

"That a fact?"

"Her people interfered with my job. I'm afraid I cannot let that pass."

"Interfered how?"

"She tried to ambush the subject while I was at work on his vessel."

"You're shining me on here," Dice snapped.

"I would never," Morgan said. "She had her people take a shot at the subject. When that failed, they carried out an ambush. I was caught in the crossfire."

"If that's true, how is it you're still drawing breath? I don't take accusations against my affiliates lightly."

"Nor should you," Morgan said. "I was wounded, but wearing clothing with laser absorbing fibers. That saved my life."

"And you have proof of this attack?"

"Other than the scars on my own body," Morgan said. "I do not. You must take my word for it. Iona Freeze must be held responsible."

"You take her out and we could have a problem," the organized crime leader said.

"I will take out the bounty hunter, as previously agreed. But I must insist that you remove your protection from Iona Freeze."

"So you can kill her? That's a big ask."

"One way or the other it has to happen," Morgan said. "I would rather not go to war with your people, but if that is the only way ..."

"All right, look, take care of the problem you were hired for in the first place. I'll see about Freeze. Something might be arranged."

"Your consideration is all I ask," Morgan said.

His image flickered, then disappeared. Dice turned to his associates. "Well?"

"His story lines up with what the Volinski Syndicate is claiming they have proof of," Sid Ott said.

"But they won't show us what it is?" Dice asked.

"Not unless we pay them. They're asking a lot."

"So what?" Lucius Griggs proclaimed. "Screw 'em. We don't get jammed up by that weak crew. They're just trying to hold off the reaper after Hurts wiped out their crew on P2."

"We don't meet their price," Sid explained, they'll publish the video."

"And that's a problem because?" Lucius asked.

"Because," Harv Butler said, "then everyone will know we're trying to kill the bounty hunter."

"We don't need that kind of heat," Sid added.

"So, we pay the Volinski Syndicate," Dice said. "We'll take it from Iona. It's her mess, she can clean it up."

"And if she won't pay?" Sid asked.

"Then maybe Morgan Black gets his wish," Dice said. "Iona Freeze is starting to be more trouble than she's worth."

# Author's Note

Thank you so much for reading *Infinite Threat*. I can't remember the last time I had so much fun writing a book. There's something pretty incredible about the Travis Hurts galaxy. It feels like maybe my best book yet, and as I write this note, I'm two-thirds finished with the next book. I've got big plans for the series. I really hope you'll leave an honest rating/review on Amazon and/or Goodreads. And you can keep reading for a tiny (unedited) sample of the next book in the Travis Hurts series.

# Travis Hurts #2 Sample
## Prologue

In the space between the buildings there was almost no light at all. It didn't bother Sanada Soto, he was used to the dark. In fact, he often trained in total darkness in order to develop his other senses. The alley was filthy too, littered with garbage, and in the stillness of the night Sanada could hear the rustling of vermin as they scampered through the refuse. It was simply part of hunting animals in human skins. They preferred the darkness, the better to hide their foul deeds. And they traveled the paths that most people avoided, but not Sanada Soto. He was an executioner, a death dealer whose convictions ran deep. He would need a ceremonial bath to wash away the smell of the alley, but that was customary after a kill anyway. And Sanada felt it only proper that those who trod the foulest paths be left in them.

His quarry was close. Sanada was a student of human behavior, and if mankind had a common flaw, it was that of habit. Water always sought to be level, warm air always rises, and humans naturally fall into routines and habits. Sanada had them himself, although in his quest for self awareness he sought to break his habits whenever possible.

Edgar Wayne Kearny was a man of habit. Like an owl he only appeared at night, first scoring Dreamers from a dealer on the corner of Maple and Elm streets. Then using his illegal narcotics to woo Katy Sharp into letting him into her apartment. Sanada Soto didn't think Katy was living up to her family name. She was, like so many people, without discipline. What Edgar and Katy did, other than the drugs, was anyone's guess, and Sanada preferred not to entertain such lewd conjecture. But in the wee hours of the morning, before the earliest risers started their day, when most people were sound asleep, Edgar would cut through the alley on his way back to the hovel he called a home. And so, that was where Sanada Soto waited for him.

He did not have to wait long.

Edgar Wayne Kearny appeared at the far end of the alley. He carried a tiny, red LED so that his heavily dilated eyes could see where he was going. His footsteps were uneven as he staggered toward home. Sanada watched with fascination. The man was wanted for the murder of a wealthy man who had been the victim of a home invasion. And that was just the crime that the authorities could tie Edgar to, although he was a suspect in several more. The price on the man's head was fifty thousand credits, but Sanada didn't believe in the justice system, nor would he soil his reputation by taking reward money. His way was more direct.

"What the—" Edgar muttered when his dim, red glow reached Sanada. "Are you real, man?"

Sanada didn't answer. He was in the traditional Hakama, which he wore over his Kyahan, with a custom Horo, or traditional cloak. Unlike his ancestors, Sanada hid his Kodachi in the voluminous folds of his horo. It was only thirty-three inches long from tip to the butt of his the silk wrapped handle. The curved sword was hand forged by Sanada himself, from alternating layers of steel which he forged welded together, cutting and re-welding many times to create a blade that consisted of over a thousand layers. Once hardened, Sanada had used acid to reveal the pattern of the different types of metal. He had then sharpened it by hand over a period of several weeks in the traditional manner. The forging of his weapon had been an act of discipline and an homage to his ancestors. As would it's wetting of blood, and it's taking of life.

Edgar nervously looked over his shoulder. They weren't in the middle of the alley. There was less of it in front of the felon, than what lay behind. Sanada was not the type of person who left things to chance, and he knew that going back would not be an attractive option to Edgar.

"I'm just looking to pass," the wanted man said.

"Your journey has reached its end," Sanada said.

"Look man, if you want something, I ain't the kind that gives it up," Edgar said, pulling a switchblade from his pocket and flicking it open with a flourish.

In response, Sanada drew his Kodachi, the razor sharp blade hissing quietly as he slowly drew it from it's wooden sheath.

"That's how you want it play it, huh?" Edgar said.

Sanada might have honored the fact that Edgar had no fear, but there was nothing honorable about the man. His brain was still addled from the drugs he took. Sanada could smell the cheap wine Edgar had been drinking too, and the husky scent of body odor. Edgar drew a small laser pistol, but before he could bring the weapon to bear, Sanada swung his short sword in a practiced slash. The blade sliced the outer part of Edgar's fore-arm, easily parting the muscle and tendons that gave his hand strength. The gun fell from his hand, as his fingers suddenly lost their grip.

Edgar hissed in pain, grabbing the cut. Sanada Soto knew

what came next. It wasn't the shout for help that a normal person my cry for. But it was the panicked dash for safety back the way he had come. In a graceful overhand slash Soto whipped the razor edge of his Kodachi across Edgar's neck as he sought to turn and run. The blade sank deep, severing Edgar's jugular vein and windpipe before scraping across his upper vertebrae.

The felon dropped to his knees as blood spurted from the side of his neck. Sanada Soto stepped back to avoid the spatter. Edgar Wayne Kearny made gurgling gasp for air, as his lungs filled with blood and he toppled to the ground. There was no need to make a killing stroke, the damage was done. Edgar would never rise from the filth of the dark alley. Soon the vermin would begin to feast on him. The body would be found eventually, and disposed of. Somewhere a notation would be made in Edgar's criminal record file, and then he would be forgotten.

Soto pulled a silk handkerchief from an inner pocket of Horo. A short hard flick of the blade sent most of Edgar's blood flying off. Soto used the handkerchief to clean the rest away, and finally dropped the small square of silk into the rest of the litter in the alley. He doubted the authorities would spend much time searching for clues in the refuse around Edgar's body. No forensics team would study the blood spatter. The almost surgical cuts would soon be gnawed to tatters by the vermin drawn to the scent of his blood. Perhaps the bloody silk square would be found. It was most certainly out of place among the refuse of the alley, but Soto didn't expect much effort from the authorities in solving the crime, not sense the victim was a wanted fugitive.

Turning Sanada Soto left the scene of the execution. In his mind, the galaxy was a little bit brighter without the darkness of Edgar Wayne Kearney.

# Travis Hurts #2 Chapter 1

"Hey friend," the tall stranger said.

"Help you?" the delivery man asked.

They were weaving their way through the space port in orbit above Datzun Superior. It was a busy place, full of shops and kiosks. The lower levels were massive warehouses full of goods waiting to be taken down to the surface of the planet, or sent out to other systems. There were shuttles for passengers, and space-liners in the port. There were also private ships, such as the *Purgatory*, which was where the deliver man was taken a new rocking recliner.

"You're delivering to the *Purgatory* in slip thirty-seven?" the tall man asked.

"Maybe," the delivery man replied.

The tall man was in a pilot's jumpsuit. The front was unzipped to about the middle of his chest. He reached in and pulled out a wad of hard currency. It was paper money, large denomination bills in a thick fold. The delivery man was pushing a hover-sled with the piece of furniture on top.

"How much would it take for you to look the other way for a

moment?" the tall man asked, discretely pulling several hundred credit notes from the fold in his hand.

"Depends," the delivery man said. "I won't get involved in something dangerous."

"Oh, no, nothing like that," the tall man said. "My employer simply wants to keep track of the ship, that's all."

He reached into his jump suit and produced a small tracking fob. It was round, with an adhesive tab on the back.

"Five hundred," the delivery man said.

"You drive a hard bargain," the tall man replied.

He handed over the money, which the delivery man stuffed into a pocket while the tall man pulled off the protective tab from the back of the tracking device. He reached under the edge of the rocking recliner and stuck the fob to the inside wooden frame.

"That all?" the delivery man asked.

"That's it," the tall man replied.

"Pleasure doing business with you."

"The pleasure is all mine," the tall man said.

He stopped at a coffee kiosk and ordered a drink, but continued to watch the delivery man who pushed his hover-sled into the long docking arm where the *Purgatory* was in the thirty-seventh docking slip. The tall man took his coffee, but didn't taste it. He ambled slowly toward the docking arm. There were several on each level of the space station, each one positioned in a way that it didn't crowd the others. Big freighters docked at the lower levels, where the long walkways were lined with revolving belts in the floor to move the heavy cargo. The space-liners were big ships too, but they docked on top of the space station, leaving the outer arms to smaller independent ships, and shuttles ferrying people back and forth to the planet below.

The tall man made his way through Gate E, and held the cup up to his lips without actually drinking the scalding beverage. It was simply a prop that was useful for hiding his face without arousing suspicion. Space ports, and orbiting platforms were high security areas. Cameras ran facial recognition and gait matching security algorithms on everyone they picked up in their video feed. The tall man knew how to beat the system. Not that he relished lingering on the space port. As soon as he was certain the tracking device was on the ship, he could report to his superior and get off the station. He wasn't yet in the system, at least to his knowledge. If he was, it would be as a known associate, or a person of interest. No one had ever accused him of a crime, although that was trade. Still, he knew sooner or later he wouldn't be able to stroll through a space station without getting arrested. And until then, he would take every precaution so that the authorities had trouble tracking his movements.

The deliveryman couldn't help but chuckle. He thought criminals were stupid. The tall man had given him a full day's pay just to stick a little device on the rocker recliner he was being paid to deliver to a ship. There were all kinds of people in the world, and the delivery man knew it was best to keep his nose clean. But with inflation, and taxes, he barely made enough to cover the bills back on Datzun Superior. Occasionally, people tipped him for making a delivery. That was his only disposable income, and it was not guaranteed. The five hundred would cover his tab at Quincy's Bar, and still leave some cash in his pocket for a rainy day. Not that weather was a consideration in space, but he couldn't make tips if there was no furniture to deliver. It was best to have a little fun money set aside for those inevitable dry spells.

He reached slip thirty-seven. The *Purgatory* was attached to the side of the docking arm. He pressed a button to alert the ship's occupants. The airlock immediately swished open, and a rather plan looking man in a long coat greeted him.

"You're here fast," the man in the coat said.

"We aim to please," the delivery man replied. "Permission to come aboard?"

"Granted," the man in the coat said with a chuckle. "Right this way."

The delivery man was surprised as he pushed the hover-sled into the cargo section of the ship. There were six prison cells made of thick, steel bars. They were all empty, the cargo section meticulously clean, but he could feel the hair on the back of his neck stand up at the sight of the holding cells.

"I'm a Fugitive Recover Specialist," the man in the coat said.

"You're law enforcement?"

"Technically yes, but I'm sort of an independent contractor," the man in the coat said, extending a hand.

The delivery man shook the FRS's hand, and continued following him through the engineering section and then into the small living quarters of the ship. It was just as clean and neat as everything else. They were greeted by a woman, and the delivery man noticed she was pregnant.

"Oh, thank you for delivering that so fast," the woman said. "It's going to be so nice to get off my feet."

"Sure," the delivery man said, feeling a sudden wave of intense guilt. "Where would you like it."

The man in the coat helped the delivery man lift the chair off the sled and set it down. There was some plastic over the foot of the recliner. The delivery man removed it, and slid his hand under the edge. The tracking device wasn't hard to find if you knew what to look for. He popped it off and casually stuck the tiny disk in the middle of the wad of plastic he had pulled free.

"Go ahead and try it out before I go," the delivery man said.

"You don't have to tell me twice," the pregnant woman said.

She settled onto the chair with a sigh. The reclining mechanism was electric. He pressed a button on a tiny remote and the leg support extended while the back reclined.

"Oh, this is wonderful," she said.

"It's got heat, vibration, adjustable lumbar support," the delivery man said. "It's top of line."

"Travis, I'll be here for the foreseeable future," the woman said.

The man in the coat laughed. "No worries, I'll see our guest out."

"Thank you," she said.

The delivery man pushed his hover-sled, now empty except for the wad of plastic that contained the tracking device back through the engineering section of the ship and into the cargo bay.

"I appreciate the speedy service," the law man said, pulling a small gold coin from his pocket.

"Oh, I can't take that," the delivery man said.

"You can't take tips?"

"No sir, it's store policy," the delivery man lied.

"Well, you have my thanks," the man in the coat said.

"Anytime," the delivery man said, pushing his hover-sled back through the airlock.

The door closed behind him, and the delivery man hurried back down the docking arm. He had every intention of simply throwing the plastic away with the tracking device still inside, but then he passed the tall man who had paid him to deliver it. The man didn't make eye contact, but he surely was there to insure the device was taken onto the right ship.

Fortunately, the furniture delivery man wasn't the only person taking cargo to the ships in docking arm E. Ernie Watson was making a victuals delivery. He and the furniture man were friends.

"Hey Ernie. Working hard?"

"Not if I can help it, Rick. You know how it is."

Ernie slowed down and Rick stepped close to the load of

canned goods being delivered. They were in flat boxes with no top. Rick was no slight of hand artist, and his heart was elevated as he tried to casually slip the tracking device inside a box of canned vegetables.

"How's tips?" Rick asked.

"Light," Ernie said. "Things are tough all over. You?"

"Same," Rick said. "Buy you a cold one at Quincy's tonight?"

"If you're buying I'm drinking," Ernie said.

"See you there," Rick said, slapping his friend on the arm.

Ernie continued down the corridor, as Rick made his way onto the station proper. Just before passing through the gate he looked back. Ernie was loading going into an airlock at slip twenty-eight. Rick hoped it was close enough to the ship the little device was supposed to be on. He didn't need trouble, but he didn't like the idea of criminals tracking a lawman. Not to mention his partner was having a baby. Removing the tracking device was risky. Rick didn't know how it worked. It might have deactivated when he pulled it off, but he would sleep better knowing the lawman didn't have bad guys on his tail.

Leaving gate E, Rick joined the flow of people moving through the station and did his best to forget the incident ever happened.

# Also by Toby Neighbors

www.ingramcontent.com/pod-product-compliance
Lightning Source LLC
Chambersburg PA
CBHW052025240626
47153CB00006B/1954